DEMON BONDS

THE MAKING OF A DEMON

PSY DEMONS
BOOK ONE

MARGARITA MATOS

* * *

I dedicate this book to my girls, Isabella and Annabella, who gave up the dubious pleasure of my company while I wrote and to my husband Michael, who makes sure I know what love feels like each and every day.

AUTHOR'S NOTE

Dear Reader,

Thank you for picking up Demon Bonds. This story holds a special place in my heart, and I'm so glad it found its way to you.

Before you dive in, I want to make sure you can read with care for yourself. This book contains content that may be difficult for some readers, including:

- Torture (including scenes of physical and psychological suffering)
- Violation / non-consensual situations

These themes are handled with intention and are woven into the growth of my characters — but please honor what you know about yourself as a reader.

If you choose to continue, I hope Ginny's strength moves you as much as it moved me to write her.

ONE

On the morning of my twentieth birthday I lay in bed, wallowing in useless self-pity until my brother called my name from the other side of the bedroom door. For him, I pulled myself out of bed with a wince and reached for one of the three gray dresses.

The baggy dress accented the sharp angles of my body and the gray brought out the yellow and green bruises on my arms and legs. I smoothed my matted hair back and forced a smile into my voice as I yelled loud enough for even a human to hear. "Okay, you can come in."

The dead bolt scraped as Henry unlocked my bedroom door. His mussed curly hair and that smile were worth getting up for. "Happy Birthday, Ginny. Did you make a wish yet?"

I shrugged. "You know I gave up on wishes a long time ago. Are you ready to go?"

Henry's aura glowed bright with his emotions, brighter than any human I've ever met, and that scared me. My stomach knotted at the thought of what our guardians, Rick and Jessica, would do if they figured out Henry was about to get his demon power.

"I think it's messed up I get two hours of freedom on your birthday. I'm sorry," Henry muttered, his smile faltering as he glanced at his feet.

"I don't mind. I have you. If you smile for me again, that will be enough." I'd rather he get out than me.

Henry looked back up and his smile became more genuine, creating familiar warmth in my chest. It flowed from his aura to give me hope for a future where I might see it one more time. The Blackwells knew Henry was the only thing keeping me going. They understood just how to manage me. The bastards.

"We'll get you a chocolate cupcake." Henry declared. "And maybe a book. How'd you like that?" he asked, his voice ending on a wistful, almost pleading note.

I hugged him for a few precious seconds, noting he'd lost weight this past week. I whispered so that the humans listening on the other side of the door couldn't hear. "Please, don't ever come back."

Henry shook his head and stepped back. His aura shone bright blue with a determination that matched his gaze. "I won't leave you alone for long. In two hours, I'll be back, we'll eat and we'll laugh, and everything will be okay just for today."

He spoke a comforting lie I wanted to believe, but couldn't. I whispered, "There's something inside me that scares the hell out of me. I keep thinking that maybe there's some truth to what Jessica says. Maybe I need the drugs to control whatever is happening to me."

I didn't tell him I could read auras now, that I could see his emotions as clearly as if they were my own. I didn't tell him people's emotions infected me like a disease, that I struggled with the desire to lash out at everyone around me, especially the Blackwells. I didn't want him to know how bad things had gotten. I didn't want him to know his freedom was a ruse to get him out of the house so no one would complain when Rick and Jessica experimented on me. They weren't even sure I'd survive the day and I wasn't sure if I cared.

Henry set his jaw and hugged me one last time, squeezing me with strength he shouldn't have. More evidence he wasn't human. I hugged him back, soaking in his warmth and blinking away tears so he wouldn't see just how shaken and scared I felt. "Take care of yourself."

Henry huffed. "No matter what Rick and Jessica claim, you're not evil and you don't need them. I'll be back because without you, I might as well be dead." He stepped away from me and took a deep breath. "Swear to me you won't let them hurt you anymore. Last week, I thought it was over. I thought…."

I didn't make him beg. Even though I wish he'd leave, he wouldn't because he loved me as much as I loved him.

I kissed his forehead. "I swear it." God, please don't let this be a lie. I have no idea how I'm going to keep that promise. I released my brother and let him go for two hours of freedom, knowing he would worry about me every minute of it.

When Henry closed the door again and I heard the click of the deadbolt, the power living inside me pressed for a way out. I swallowed the urge to lash out, mostly because there wasn't anything in this room to lash out against, not yet.

I looked around my prison. Precious little furniture occupied the tiny space, not enough to set a fire that could burn the whole damned house—uncovered cement floors, a box spring with threadbare linens, three outfits in the closet, a Bible to keep me entertained, a stereo that was my only solace, bars on the window to keep me from escaping, and a curtain to keep out nosy neighbors who might see something that would cause them to call the police.

Last week, they injected me with a drug that burned through my system creating so much pain I screamed until my voice broke, my throat grew hoarse, and my consciousness blurred.

Henry had barged through the door, ready to defend me. I can only remember bits and pieces, but he and Rick fought. Whatever Henry threatened Rick with, it was enough to get him to back off for a whole week.

Today, the Blackwells let Henry go out with one of the guards from the lab so he wouldn't be here for whatever they planned, and I had just promised I wouldn't let them hurt me. As I waited for my fate to arrive, I jammed a bobby pin into the keyhole for the deadbolt on my door, then started to write in the notebook I kept stashed beneath my bed.

It's my twentieth birthday and I have so many wishes. I wish Henry would listen to me and never come back. I wish my memories could burn away, that I could erase every last thing that was done to me, that I could erase what I am. But most of all, I wish for a way to keep my brother, Henry, safe.

I hesitated before committing the rest of my thoughts to paper.

He's not human. He's stronger than I remember, and his aura shines bright with his power. Yet, when I look at him I can still see the little boy who used to run into my room during thunderstorms. Except now, I'm more afraid than he is. I'm afraid of what the Blackwells will do if they find out his power, whatever it is, is about to manifest. I want a better life for him than I've had. If I'm going to give it to him, if I'm going to protect him, I'll have to be stronger than I've ever been. So my birthday wish is more like a prayer to whoever is listening to the prayers of demons like me. I pray for the wisdom and the strength to give my brother a good life. In exchange, I'll give anything, up to and including my soul.

I wrote because it helped me deal with all the crap in my life, but I'd be damned if I let my writing betray my brother to the Blackwells. So, I took a match out from my secret stash and burnt the page in my own cathartic ritual, ignoring the voices of Rick and Jessica in their bedroom. They were discussing what drug to use on me today and I couldn't care less, because I no longer had any intention of letting them give me those drugs.

Tiny flames licked at my fingers as the paper burned, the pain serving as a beacon through the numbness that threatened to swallow me. Smoke spread through my small room, overlaying the stink of sweat and terror that always lingered. I held onto the corner of the diary page, letting my fingers blister while the fire consumed the record of my fears, my pain, my hopes that hurt more than a punch to the neck or a kick to the gut, until all that remained was the edge of paper pressed between my fingers and ashes spread across the cold bedroom floor. I could take a lot of pain. I'd grown used to it, and learned to use it to call forth the power that lived inside me, the dark ball of anger that wanted to lash out, to consume, to destroy.

Rick and Jessica made a mistake. Henry wasn't here, so I didn't have to worry about him. It didn't matter if the power inside me escaped, consumed everyone in this house, because he couldn't get hurt.

I waited wedged in the corner of my room, listening for any sign of my guardians. Their discussion about my pending fate ended with the clink of glass containers rubbing against each other, and the soft click of a case or a chest of some sort. Rick's heavy footsteps echoed down the hallway like drumbeats. By comparison, the clacking of Jessica's heels against the wood seemed almost dainty. If I didn't fight, in another minute or two, I might be burning from the inside out with whatever drug Rick and Jessica decided to use today.

They were used to doing with me as they pleased so long as they kept Henry clothed, fed, and unmolested. Now, I had more than my promise to Henry to worry about. If I didn't fight today, they'd do to him what they'd done to me. I prayed that Rick and Jessica had lied when they claimed I couldn't live without them, their drugs, their beatings, and their treatments.

The deadbolt groaned, sticking. The bobby pin I'd jammed into the keyhole made it difficult for them to turn the lock, giving me a minute or two of reprieve.

Either Rick or Jessica knocked. As if I would help them get in here to drug and hurt me. Rick yelled, "Open the fucking door or you'll regret it, you piece of demon shit."

If the last twenty years had taught me anything, it was that they were going to hurt me no matter what I did. I stalled, giving the power inside me more time to gather. I stalled, but they'd break through eventually.

I flexed my blistered hand. Once, a long time ago, I wished for them to understand the pain they'd caused, to see me as another living being. I thought that if they could understand, they wouldn't hurt me anymore. I thought they hurt me because they didn't get that I felt pain just as much as they did. Now, I just wanted them gone. Their reasons for doing what they did no longer mattered. This nightmare would end today.

The door shook as Rick kicked it over and over. My chest hurt with the effort to keep from scurrying into the closet. It would delay them further, but such cowardice saved my body at the expense of my soul. Today, I needed to be stronger than that. The wood shook until Rick broke through.

Rick smelled of alcohol and his aura glowed with a color approaching the russet of his hair. He was angry. His big beefy hands flexed in anticipation. Jessica stood beside him, her face contorted in a mask of concern. Still, not a single blond curl was out of place. Her makeup had been exquisitely applied to highlight gray eyes, as cold as the slate in the bitch's heart. No surprise there. Jessica loved to hurt anyone she considered beneath her, and I was as far beneath her as any humanoid could get.

God, I was so sick of being afraid, of huddling in corners, of being shuttled to labs, of being used for research, for the supposed benefit of all humans. What the fuck have humans done for me that I should suffer for them? I'm not less than them, and they sure as hell aren't special. I've never done anything to hurt anyone. God, forgive me for what happens here today. I really don't think I have a choice.

The molten rivers of anger that always lived beneath my fear and pain stirred and swelled. Today I was not going to just take it. Today I would fight. I closed my fists once again as Rick approached me. He placed one rough hand on my arm and twisted. Instead of bending forward to relieve the pressure, I resisted, and ignored the tendrils of pain spreading out from my elbow. I punched back with my other hand.

My strike veered harmlessly off Rick's shoulder. His fist hammered my lower back, the pain eating at my resolve. But I did not bend forward. I was not going to give up. In front of me, Jessica yelled, "Hurry up. I'm ready." She tapped a syringe filled with a reddish liquid.

I needed to break away from Rick. That drug would drain me of what strength I'd gained over the past week. It would break me or incapacitate me, maybe even kill me. Rick would watch every moment of my agony as though I was the star of his favorite TV show, a look of sick fascination on his face the whole time.

Another punch landed in my stomach. I swallowed down the vomit that rose to my throat. My vision faded around the edges, but I fought to stay conscious. I'd learned from countless beatings, burns, and taunts. One more day of pain for a lifetime of freedom. Even if I am a demon, I deserve to live.

All the anger and hurt and resentment I'd swallowed for so many years flared, fanned by the pain I'd suffered. Jessica advanced with the syringe, holding the promise of pain and a weakness that drained me of my power and strength. Despite my rising fear or perhaps because of it, power burst free of me, spilled out like smoke punching through my chest, doubling me over in a way that Rick hadn't been able to force.

But the pain was over in seconds, leaving a cloud of vileness that surrounded my tormentors, strangled them and choked them. Rick stepped back, releasing his hold on my elbow, waving his arms around trying to dispel the fog. Jessica's face turned bluish as she gasped for breath. She tried to scream, but couldn't draw enough breath. All that came out was a squeak. Rick clawed at his throat leaving deep scratches on his skin.

Like roaches when you turn on the lights, they scurried from the room, but my creation would not let them escape. It coalesced, became thicker and tightened its hold on their throats, coated their mouth and nose and lungs. The whites of their eyes turned red, and their skin, a mottled purple. Jessica struggled to draw breath, soft squeals of fear escaping her lips. Rick beat at empty air, his blows harmless for once. The light from their auras pulsed with pain one last time before fading forever.

I couldn't pull the darkness back. My power avenged me, a creation that would not stop until its mission had been fulfilled. I should have helped Rick and Jessica, called an ambulance, anything. A good person would have called for help or given them CPR. A human would have, but I wasn't human. I would have known that even if I hadn't heard their taunts proclaiming me a demon. God forgive me, but a secret part of me rejoiced when their hearts stopped beating.

They were dead, and no amount of guilt or remorse was going to bring them back. I would suffer for my sin, but they would never be able to hurt me or Henry again.

* * *

The tiny speakers of the stereo beside me moved rhythmically while the artist screamed, "Shout, shout, shout at the devil." The loud sound hurt my ears I hoped enough to do some permanent damage. I needed a little pain, a little atonement, and a thick spine to get off this bed and out my godforsaken door.

Numbness threatened to drown me but I fought it back. Now wasn't a time to break down. It was a time to plan for Henry's future. First, where would I go? I'd never met my real parents or anyone who gave a damn about me besides my brother. Did we disappear? Did we call the cops? Could we trust them?

I turned up the music, wincing at the shooting pain in my eardrums, but needing to drown out what I couldn't hear: the silence of the dead. Images played across my mind in a continuous loop, showing me the power of the creature lurking inside me.

Outside the broken bedroom door, their bodies cooled. No blood or bruise betrayed their death. They looked exactly as they had in life, except they didn't breathe and their expressions were frozen in the fear they'd experienced in their last moments. I couldn't bear to step over their bodies, to taste once again the intermingled horror and pleasure of what I'd done. So I sat on my bed and tried to forget.

If I were normal, I could walk out the front door, hop on a bus, and disappear into the masses of a big city. Even if the cops figured out what had happened, I could be happy, just me and Henry for a while…until someone hurt me, and I lost control again. Damn it, I had to deal with what I'd just done, or it would eat me alive and break me in a way the torture hadn't managed to do.

The clang of metal rang over the music. Henry's home. I looked out the window and saw a car parked on the curb, probably belonging to the guardian that had gone out with Henry. I heard the front door being opened and the alarm code being punched in. I struggled to keep quiet while the guard called out to Rick and Jessica. He didn't wait for a response, thank God.

Instead, he re-engaged the alarm, shut the door and drove away in his car, leaving Henry inside the house.

I wouldn't leave my brother behind, but I had no idea how to take care of him or how to keep him safe. I made that promise not knowing what was inside me, but now I know. What will I do the next time I lose control? What can I do if this thing inside me comes out and attacks him? I could lose control at any moment. I pictured my brother choking, his face turning purple, and I heaved, had to fight to keep the bile in my stomach from rising.

Panicked, I pulled at the bars on my window. Despite my growing strength, the damned things wouldn't budge. Downstairs, something thumped, and Henry cursed.

My heart beat a countdown. It was too late to leave and I had no idea what would happen to Henry if I left. Henry lost his parents of sorts today and he needed me. He needed me to find him a home and make sure he had food to eat, a roof over his head. But how am I going to keep him safe from me? I grabbed onto the windowsill so hard, the wood splintered. Maybe if I had more time, I could break the casing. Then the words Henry had spoken came back to me. Without you, I'd be dead. I couldn't leave him. I had to fight to stay, to keep my fear controlled. With the creak of each stair, I had a harder time drawing air into my lungs.

Concentrate.

Breathe.

I love Henry. I can't hurt him. He's everything, the only person who loves me, the only person I love. I prayed to God, Devil, Powers that be. I would do anything—give anything—if they could just help me keep Henry safe. The power that lived within me stretched and reached for a fountain of energy I sensed far away. When it connected, a stream of strength flowed to me, leashed the power inside me. A measure of peace spread across my limbs and I felt as though my prayers had been answered.

I focused on my breath and counted. Henry yelped and screamed, "Ginny, where are you?"

Panic stood out amongst the emotions surrounding Henry. I swallowed the lump in my throat. "Please don't come in here."

He ignored me and climbed through the broken door, over the bodies I'd been avoiding all afternoon. I braced for his rejection, but it never came. He rushed to me and hugged me. Relief replaced his fear, and his relief soothed me. He wouldn't miss our guardians or their daily treatments any more than I would. I hugged him tighter to me. "I'm sorry. I'm so sorry."

Henry kept holding me. I waited, silently apologized, and prayed nothing would happen to him. Henry stepped back and scanned me top to bottom. "Are you okay?"

When I nodded, he said, "Don't worry about them. We're going to get out of here. They can't hurt us anymore."

I swallowed the sob threatening to spill out of me.

Henry squeezed my hand. "Come on."

I didn't let go of his hand as we stepped past the bodies. I closed my eyes and held my breath, but I made it to the hallway and into the Blackwell's bedroom. Before I even stepped through the threshold, Jessica's perfume overwhelmed me, a cloying chemical scent designed to boost pheromones or some such nonsense. I told Henry, "Stay in the hallway for a moment, please."

The smell nauseated me, but I forced myself to keep walking, to push the woman's clothes aside. I stopped to put on some jeans and a T-shirt from the closet. I hated the scent that lingered on the clothes, but I hated my drab gray dresses even more. I suppressed a giggle that I would worry about clothes at a time like this. After I finished dressing, I called Henry into the room.

At the bottom of the closet, I found two more cases of syringes, a case of clear red liquid, and another case containing various drugs labeled with long scientific names I couldn't decipher. Henry retrieved the syringe and vial Jessica had dropped in my bedroom. If anyone found these, they'd wonder what they were for and they might ask questions as to what Henry and I might be.

I hid the two cases and the syringe in the attic where the amount of junk would deter anyone from searching too closely. Running back downstairs, I went to the master bedroom. The only phone in the house was there.

I stared at the phone.

If I leave now, I'll be free, but how long until someone gets hurt? I need help. Maybe the humans won't be so bad. But even if they are, I can fight them now. The thought of using my power sent shivers of dread through me, but I'd do it for Henry if I had to. The humans would help me take care of Henry as long as they didn't suspect I was a murderer. I don't think anyone would be able to overlook such a thing, but damn it, I needed help. I had no clue how to live in the human world. I reached for the phone and Henry put his hand over mine to stop me from picking up the receiver. "What are you doing?"

"I'm calling the cops. Rick and Jessica are dead. If we run, they'll think we've killed them."

Henry looked at me. "So what? We should just go disappear. You are not human and I'm scared of what the cops will do if they find out. The cops won't know who we are. We never went to school, and we don't have records. We might as well not exist."

I wanted to go, but what if I couldn't control myself? What if I had to leave in a hurry and leave Henry with no name, no papers, no one he could call on to help support him? Worse, what if he got blamed for my crimes? I was more afraid of that than I was of going to jail. Steeling myself, I said, "We have to do this. Just trust me."

Henry didn't like it, but nodding, he stepped back. He waited with his lips pursed shut while he shifted from one foot to another.

The moment I dialed 9-1-1, our fates were sealed. The operator picked up after a single ring. "Hillsborough Police."

I said, "My guardians." I waited a few seconds for effect. I didn't have to work very hard to sound scared. "They're dead."

The dispatcher asked, "Are you in danger?"

"No."

"What's your location?"

"I'm at 132 Sanford Lane."

"I'm sending someone to help you. Can you tell me what happened?"

"I don't know. They were angry and drinking and doing drugs. They just died outside my bedroom." I had no need to fake my voice breaking down. I held onto the phone so hard my hands shook.

Henry pried the phone from my grip, wiping some of the sweat off it with his T-shirt. "I think my sister is going into shock. Can you just send someone, please?"

The operator said, "Of course."

Henry hung up and didn't give the operator a chance to say anything more. We ignored when the phone rang again.

We walked down the stairs to the first floor and sat on the pristine white furniture in the living room to wait in silence, our hands clasped together.

CHAPTER
TWO

The police took an eternity to arrive. I sat with Henry while he fiddled with a loose thread on his shirt. After he'd ripped it out and rolled it in a ball, he looked up at me. "What happened?"

I swallowed and straightened my shoulders. Whatever he thought of me, I deserved. "I killed them. I told you my power was out of control. They were coming after me, and I let go."

He nodded calmly. "Good. You should have done that years ago."

I exhaled, tears flowing down my cheeks. "I'm sorry."

He pursed his lips and held my shoulders. "I'm not. They hurt you, and it's not wrong to hurt them in turn."

I did quite a bit more than that, but I didn't have the fortitude to keep arguing. I hugged him and held him, soaked up his comfort.

When the police finally got there, I opened the door to a tall man with kind gray eyes and a woman with red hair and a healthy dose of skepticism. The alarm sounded but there wasn't anything I could do about that. The policeman asked me to shut it off but I shrugged and told him I didn't know the code.

He inspected the alarm, read some numbers off the keypad and made a phone call. Within about a minute, the alarm shut off. Outside, an ambulance parked in the driveway behind Jessica's red convertible, beside a police car. A short, black man with gray hair and a white lab coat carried a large leather case from the ambulance to the house. I moved in front of Henry, squaring my shoulders, angling myself to block him from the old man's view.

The old man smiled, extending his hand. I looked at his empty hand and extended my own, finding his grip warm and strong. He had no aggression, no apathy. Quite the opposite; I sensed pity, and it helped dissolve the lump of tension in my throat. Henry and I might get through this ordeal.

The doctor had me sit back on the sofa while he checked my eyes, my reflexes, and my blood pressure. He gave me water and a sedative that I secretly tossed away. The male officer, Officer Jeffries, asked me some questions across the coffee table while the doctor examined Henry beside me. So far, so good.

"What's your name?"

"Ginny."

"Your last name?"

I hesitated. If I took the Blackwell's name I might sound normal, but the thought of connecting myself to them in such a way made me shiver with revulsion. "It should be Blackwell, I guess."

Startled, the officer stared at me. "You must have a last name. You're a grown woman. What name did you use on your school and college forms?"

I laughed. I'd never gone to school. I'd learned to read and write by studying the Bible and some old books left lying around the house. Some of the lab technicians had shown me books and encyclopedias to measure how fast I learned. Some had even let us watch TV over Jessica's intense objections. She never intended me to learn or to go to college.

"I had no need for a last name. I never went to school. I grew up in this house and I never left. Henry was allowed to leave sometimes, but only if I stayed."

The officer cast his eyes down, clearly uncomfortable and a little angry. "Did they hurt you?"

I shrugged and avoided the question. "Don't you want to know what happened?"

The officer wasn't comfortable, but to his credit he didn't let me change the subject. "I do, but at the moment I need to get more information about your background."

I pursed my lips and crossed my arms.

The officer studied me, his gray eyes the same shade as Jessica's, but much kinder. "Fine. We can revisit this later. What happened?"

I repeated the story I told the 9-1-1 operator. I made sure to let my voice break down at intervals and to cry when I had no further details I wanted to share. "They kicked down my door, and then —" I covered my face with my hands and sobbed.

Officer Jeffries fumbled for tissue to pass to me, but he pressed me for more information, gently. "And then what?"

I closed my eyes, trying not to remember, but all I found was a crystal clear image of Rick and Jessica as they were choked to death by my creation. "They flapped their hands and their eyes bugged out and they acted crazy. They just seemed to be scared of something I couldn't see, and then they died."

Officer Jeffries cleared his throat. "Do you think they used drugs?"

I looked up at him, trying to keep my face calm, hoping I hid my alarm from the man's intelligent gaze. "I don't know. What makes you think that?"

He smiled. "You told the 9-1-1 operator."

Oh.

The female officer came back downstairs. She took Officer Jeffries aside and talked in hushed tones I could hear without any trouble, thanks to my demon biology. "The girl's bedroom door is busted in. There is a deadbolt on it and bars on the window like she liked to sneak out often. There's two dead bodies up there like nothing me or the doctor have ever seen. It looks like the guy busted in the door, then tried to run away. We're going to send for some drug panels, but it's like they dropped dead right outside her bedroom. I can't figure it out."

Officer Jeffries stared at his partner. "You think she did something to them?"

The redhead shrugged. "Pretty little thing like her, maybe they kept her locked up. Maybe they did other stuff. But whatever they did, she's alive and they're not. We're going to send for a drug panel. I say if there's anything weird about it, we arrest her. That girl freaks me out."

Officer Jeffries pointed at me with a frown. "That girl weighs a hundred pounds at most. She didn't bust the door on her own. Those people up there were up to no good, and we need a little thing like evidence before we arrest anybody. Don't forget that." He turned back toward me and sat down next to me.

Looking me in the eyes, he said, "Are you sure there isn't something you'd like to tell me about the Blackwells?" He meant well, but I wasn't confiding in anyone, so I shook my head. He took a deep breath and let it out. "If you want to play it like that, just know I'll help any way I can. Come on, let's take you to the station while we sort this mess out."

Whatever their reasons, both officers avoided touching me. They put Henry and me in the back of their car like criminals. Fitting. We held each other's hands while I concentrated on breathing and keeping the fear and anger inside me far away from anyone who might get hurt.

I drew from that well of strength I had found earlier, drawing calming power from it, until all the noises faded into the background. The power had texture to it like a dark, moonless night that offered comfort and hid all your sins. My consciousness used the energy offered to sink into cold dark nothingness, the void spreading across my mind like a blanket, shielding me from the part of me that had committed murder today.

Henry shook me out of the trancelike state when the car stopped. The officers led us into the police station. We followed Officer Jeffries past the hall where a handful of officers went about their daily work, whatever that was. Hillsborough Police precinct had a lot of space, but not a lot of people, yet the emotions of the twelve current occupants of the building assaulted me like a dozen yapping dogs in the dead of night, and they grew more annoying with each passing moment. Within ten minutes, I had a screaming headache and nausea. I had trouble walking in a straight line, forcing Officer Jeffries to hold my arm to guide me toward a room in the back with double-sided glass as a wall. A table and four chairs completed the institutional look of the room.

"Stay here. Someone will come in a few minutes to talk to you." He put his hand out in a reassuring gesture. "Don't worry. You haven't done anything wrong. It's just process."

I'm not as worried about what I've done as I am of what I could still do.

The officer's emotions and Henry's anxiety beat at me. I closed my eyes and tried to find a place of peace within myself, a sanctuary I could use to separate myself from the emotions around me. Unfortunately, the more the emotions battered me, the more sensitive I became. Half an hour after Henry and I had been left alone in the windowless room, I sensed an angry individual brought into the growing radius of my power. I heard the ding of an elevator, followed by the bang of metal and slurred curses describing what the man would do to the officer's mother.

The prisoner's anger fed me and tainted my own emotions. Already weak from the officers' steady yapping at my senses, I struggled to breathe through the mass of anger as energy coalesced in my chest. I wished with all my will that his emotions would just shut off, that he would pass out or something. Anything to stop the beating on my tenuous control.

Henry's hand slipped into mine. "Are you okay?"

I shook my head and pulled my hand from his grip, wrapping my arms around myself. I didn't even trust myself to open my mouth in case that would provide an outlet for the fog of energy building inside me. The man upstairs finally shut up and my wish must have been granted because I felt his emotions weaken as though he fell asleep. His anger faded.

Unfortunately, the officer near him experienced a wave of anxiety. I struggled not to throw up as I realized what the ambulance approaching meant. I shot up from my chair and paced to the side of the room farthest away from Henry.

Please don't let me have killed again. Don't let me be what Rick and Jessica accused me of being. If there is anyone out there, anyone listening, help me. Help that man upstairs.

I moved to the door and put my ear against it, listening for the chattering of the ambulance workers. They thought alcohol poisoning, but I knew better. I had hurt another person, one who'd never hurt me.

I sensed around for the man's aura, thin, but there. I didn't kill him. I slumped to the floor, no longer able to hold back the tears of exhaustion and relief. The ambulance sped away from the precinct, carrying the man and his poisonous anger away. The officer's emotions didn't seem so bad anymore. They were still annoying, but I could handle them. I have to.

I paced again while Henry studied me. A few minutes later, an attractive blond woman with brown eyes came into the room. Genuine empathy filled her aura, which soothed me a bit. The woman sat at the table and gestured for us to sit in front of her. As we sat, she took out a notebook, and said, "Hello. My name is Cara and I'm with Child Protective Services. Can you tell me your names and ages?"

"I'm Ginny, and this is Henry. I'm twenty and he's sixteen."

She smiled. "How long have you been with your guardians?"

"As long as I can remember."

Cara raised her eyebrows. "Do you remember when Henry joined you? Do you know if he's your biological brother?"

I tried to remember, but every memory I had contained Henry in it. I shook my head, ignoring the pain that flared at the movement.

Cara smiled in an effort to reassure me. "How about next of kin? Is there any family that can take care of you until we sort out who your new guardian will be?"

I thought about it, then asked hopefully, "Do you think we could go into foster care?" Foster care would at least put a roof over Henry's head and food in his stomach. It would be a relief to have someone who would take care of him in case I lost control of my power and had to do something drastic like disappear or end my own life.

Maybe I sounded a little too hopeful because Cara looked at me quizzically. "I don't know yet. You're over eighteen, but I'll do my best to make sure you and Henry remain close. What can you tell me about your home life?"

I said, "It was normal."

Henry said at the same time, "It sucked."

Cara looked between us, then addressed Henry. "How did it suck?"

I put a hand on Henry and squeezed. If these people started testing us for drugs, they might figure out I wasn't human. If they found out I was a demon, they might lock me and Henry up in a

24

laboratory. I couldn't let that happen. "They just beat us and stuff."

Cara sucked in a breath. "Do you have any bruises? Do you need someone to take a look at you?"

Both Henry and I rushed to say, "We're fine," in unison.

Cara didn't say anything; she just waited for us to relent. Finally, I said, "It's not much. Just a little bit." I rolled up my sleeve to show her the bruise on my forearm where Rick had held my arm in a twisted position. I healed pretty quickly so it had already faded to yellow. "See."

Cara looked at the bruise carefully. Her touch was sure and comforting. "I'm sorry you had to go through that." Then she muttered under her breath low enough a human wouldn't be able to hear, "I'm glad they're dead." I liked her just for that. Henry must have heard her, too, because he put his head down so she wouldn't see his smile. I would talk to him about that later.

Cara asked a few more questions, trying to find family or next of kin, but there was no one. Finally, she promised she'd do everything she could for us.

Cara came back a few minutes later to drop off Subway foot-long sandwiches, chips, and soda. Her aura had a tinge of guilt, but I didn't think she had anything to be guilty about, so I did my best to put her at ease. "Thank you for everything. It feels good to just have someone who cares even a little bit."

Cara smiled tightly. "I don't have any place for you to stay at the moment, and no judge I can call. You'll have to stay here until morning, I'm afraid. It's only a few hours and I'll make sure someone comes by to pick you up first thing."

I thanked Cara while Henry started in on his sandwich. Cara backed out of the room, leaving us alone. I was incredibly grateful. I waited for Henry to eat his sandwich in eight huge bites, then offered half of mine to him. He turned it down, inhaling his chips and soda. I ate after he was done with his food, but saved most of my soda. I had no idea when we would see another living being and didn't want to spend the night thirsty.

It was a good call because the police officers seemed to forget about us after that. We didn't want to talk about what happened in case someone was listening, and we didn't want to talk about anything else either, so we waited in silence. When I got tired of pacing, I sat on a row of three plastic mismatched chairs. The power within me seemed to have settled, so I didn't worry it would threaten Henry. So far it hadn't done so and I hoped it never would. Henry put his head in my lap and fell asleep cradled against me.

I spent the rest of the night fantasizing about being taken to an orphanage with Henry. A place where we'd be fed three times a day and no one would ever hurt us again. If anyone tried to separate me from my brother, I'd run away with him and find a small town with few people, maybe someplace in the mountains or even close to a beach. I'd never seen the ocean. Comforted by the fantasy, I nodded off and dreamed of a beach where I didn't need to fear anyone or anything.

When I awoke, I couldn't tell if the sun was up or not because there were no windows in the cramped room. Officer Jeffries shook my shoulder. His partner stood behind him with her arms crossed and a don't-mess-with-me attitude.

I smiled, which only seemed to make the redhead officer more suspicious, judging by her frown and the tinge of annoyance in her aura. "Good morning, officers." I smiled wider.

Officer Jeffries smiled back at me. He really was a nice man. "There's someone we need to introduce you to."

"Is it the case worker?" Please let us be going to foster care, not jail.

Officer Jeffries shook his head. "Your guardians made arrangements in the event of their deaths. Someone has come forward to take responsibility for you. He has the right paperwork and he was pretty insistent we release you right away. We could wait for a judge, but since we don't have any facilities to house you and your brother together…" He cleared his throat. "Anyway, your new guardian, Jerry, is here. We'll get in contact with you if anything changes or we need to ask you more questions." Officer Jeffries tone did not tell me anything about Jerry or what he thought of him. That in itself was a clue. At least, I wasn't going to jail for the murder of Rick and Jessica.

I shook Henry awake and held his hand tight within mine as we followed the officers toward an office tucked in the corner of the precinct. As we walked to meet this Jerry character, I wondered whether I'd made a mistake. I knew that not everyone who associated with Rick and Jessica had been bad people. Some of the lab technicians had been just like the Blackwells, but some had let us watch TV while they observed us and let us eat all kinds of stuff, even chocolate. They made up some of my fondest memories of growing up.

Then there was Henry to consider. I still wasn't sure I could keep him safe without help and I couldn't stand the idea of being separated from him. God, please help me figure this out. Should I go along with this or run?

Officer Jeffries introduced Henry and me to a man wearing a perfectly fitted black suit and an air of authority. Two lawyers with suitcases, polished shoes and suits flanked him. Even the redhead seemed to stand a bit straighter in his presence.

Jerry waited for the officers to finish his introductions and extended his hand to Henry first and then me. I scanned him. He was good-looking in his trim gray suit. Tall, with a swimmer's body, spiked blond hair, and kind of dorky glasses. He was too young to be a guardian, barely an adult, and he didn't look at me with anger or fear. While he smiled, I tried to sense his emotions and got nothing but a blank slate. I tried again when he shook my hand and nothing.

I skipped the smiles and hellos to ask, "Who are you?"

Officer Jeffries placed a hand on my shoulder. "We told you, Ginny, he's Henry's new guardian."

Jerry cleared his throat. "I'm your new guardian and I'm here to take care of you both. I take that responsibility seriously. You will come to my home to live with me. I hope that in time you come to trust me."

I spoke before I thought about it. "I don't give out my trust so easily." I really shouldn't upset him. As Cara said, I was twenty, and technically, he didn't have to take me with him. I needed to stay with Henry and figure out what Jerry was about.

Jerry smiled. He looked at me like I had something he wanted. Maybe things would be better with him. Maybe he could help me build a good life for me and Henry, where we wouldn't have to fear being experimented on, where we could go to a real school instead of a mocked up version put together by lab technicians so they could communicate with us better. It was worth a shot, and if he turned out to be like Rick and Jessica after all, I knew I was strong enough to stand up to him now, even if the thought of hurting another person turned my stomach.

I showed my teeth in what I hoped resembled a smile. At the very least, he would provide a home for me and Henry.

Jerry thanked the officers for their help and turned to leave. I grabbed Henry's hand and led him out of the room. Henry whispered, "Are you sure you want this? This is our chance to run away."

I ignored him and kept walking. No one argued with Jerry's right to take Henry and me away. Had they tried, the two mean-looking lawyers behind him would have probably handled it.

Even when I concentrated, I couldn't sense any tendrils of emotion around Jerry. That was a comfort. I had never met anyone like him, and maybe it was meant to be that I would live with the one person in the world who I couldn't sense. Maybe it was a sign of better things to come.

I smiled in my best approximation of appreciation and vowed to keep what lived inside me tucked away. Henry grimaced beside me and reached out for my hand. My face didn't feel so stiff. I could adapt. I could do better.

THREE

J erry didn't ask me or Henry if we wanted to stop by the old house. We didn't, but it would have been nice if he'd asked. Instead, he flew us via private plane somewhere north and cold. Like Rick and Jessica, Jerry didn't seem to care about our opinion. Unlike them, he did seem to care a little bit for our comfort. He handed me some pain killers as I struggled to deal with the sound and pressure changes. My demon senses made flying a painful ordeal. I refused the pills, but still considered the fact that Jerry offered them a good sign. After the flight, Jerry handed us heavy coats and guided us to a limo.

"You seem to live well," I said.

Jerry smiled, justifiably proud of his riches. "I'm glad you like it. Work with me, Ginny, and I'll share this and more with you."

I stepped into the limo. The driver closed the door behind me, shutting Jerry, Henry, and me in the back compartment. The inside smelled like leather, whiskey, cigars, and expensive cologne. The space quickly became too warm for the coat I was wearing, so I opened it and fanned myself. I turned to Jerry. "What do you mean work with you?"

Jerry looked at Henry and handed him a glass of water; me, a glass filled with fragrant amber alcohol. "Whiskey," he told me. At noon. I held it in my hand, but didn't drink.

Jerry sipped at his glass. He didn't seem like a drunk, just someone who drank to relax. "We can discuss that later. Why don't you relax for now?" He turned his attention to the passing winter foliage outside, his fingers drumming against his leg. The airport had been small and there were no hints of civilization nearby. Jerry seemed to live in the middle of nowhere. He was strong and fit for a human, but I could still overpower him if the need arose and the far away location of his home meant I could get lost in the woods for days if I needed to.

So far, Jerry hadn't done anything to make me feel lesser than him. If he knew I was a demon, he didn't show it, and he'd been polite, even attentive, at times.

We drove for at least an hour through roads covered in trees. After a while, it all started to look the same until the limo drove through black metallic gates, followed by about five minutes worth of private road surrounded by more trees. Henry moved closer to the window and whistled at the house that finally appeared beyond the trees. "Nice."

Jerry's home sat nestled in the middle of a large clearing, surrounded by firs and other pine trees. His garden looked well-kept even in winter, shaped like a maze with fountains emptied of water for the winter spread throughout. The statues on the fountains featured angels playing various instruments. "Your home is beautiful, Jerry."

Jerry smiled, placing a hand on my back to lead me from the limo up the stairs to the entrance. "I'm glad you like it. I'd like you to be happy here."

I looked at him, studying his expression and finding no sign that he'd lied. "I'd like to be happy here, too." Jerry smiled in return while Henry huffed behind me. He obviously didn't trust Jerry's kindness. I didn't know what to think at this point.

A skinny butler that seemed to have a stick up his you-know-what opened large carved wooden double doors. He took our coats and greeted Jerry with a smile and a "Good day, sir." Henry and I didn't seem to warrant a welcome, not that I cared. I was too busy gawking at our new surroundings.

The inside of the house Jerry offered to share with Henry and me had a foyer for receiving guests, featuring a crane mosaic cut into the stone. The place smelled clean, and had sparse but expensive furniture. Light spilled over a huge space with ceilings at least thirty feet in height and windows taller than me that could open in summer to let the outside air in, but were now covered in heavy curtains in rich fabrics. Jerry apparently didn't worry about keeping neighbors away, probably because the home was so far from any other human beings I could hardly hear the cars down the road even with my enhanced hearing. The house reminded me of the castle in *Beauty and the Beast.*

Jerry pointed to a gated hallway to the left of the double stairs in the center of the large space. "That's my private wing. I conduct business out of there, and I expect you to stay away and respect my privacy."

I nodded, figuring I'd snoop around later when I had the opportunity. Although I wanted to honor Jerry's wishes for privacy, I couldn't afford not to learn everything I could about him.

Next, Jerry showed us the magazine layout-style living room, den, kitchen, two dining rooms, pool, and then took us to Henry's new bedroom, a masterpiece by sixteen-year-old boy standards. Henry took one look at the video game consoles laid out in front of a huge TV and yelled "Sweet" as he rushed to take a closer look. He didn't even notice when Jerry stepped beside me and leaned down as though to tell me a secret, his lips inches from my ear, then said, "Let me show you your room. I think you'll like it."

I jumped, more than a little unnerved. I really needed to keep myself in check. Jerry whispered to me. He hadn't raised his fist or pinched me with a syringe filled with unknown fluids. My response was way out of proportion.

I followed him through the halls, dragging my feet only a little. When we reached my new bedroom, Jerry put his hand on my back. I stepped forward so that his hand dropped off me. He didn't try to put his hand on me again, choosing to lean against the doorframe in a relaxed pose instead. I took a breath to try to calm my heart rate. I was about to live under the same roof as Jerry. I couldn't afford to get jumpy every time he touched me. He'd been incredibly nice thus far.

Jerry had decorated my room in various shades of white. A little clinical, but feminine at the same time. I couldn't resist running my fingers over the textured walls and the super-soft bedding printed with flowers of cream on white. Delicate and beautiful. Jerry closed the door behind him, locking us in. I took another calming breath and smoothed my hands on my jeans.

"Let's lay our cards on the table, shall we? I know you're not human."

I dry-swallowed the lump forming in my throat. I couldn't confirm or deny what Jerry had just said so I kept my mouth shut and waited, but Jerry seemed to be better at that game than me. He leaned against the locked door, muscular arms crossed, accusatory green gaze focused on me.

Seconds passed, then minutes while I scrambled to come up with a response that wouldn't give me away. "What have you been smoking?"

"Nothing like what you've been injected with, I assure you. My sources tell me you're some kind of demon. You assimilate facts quickly yet until a few months ago, you weren't very good at picking social queues. You got better at understanding people right around the time your blood started to change. I can only assume your demon power is psychic in nature, something that helped you understand people and society better. What I don't know is what power you possess, so just tell me."

"If you knew they were experimenting on us, why the fuck didn't you do something about it? What kind of person are you?" I almost apologized for the curse by habit but he didn't deserve it. My whole life had been one big experiment, even the supposed kindness of some technicians in talking to me and letting me watch movies.

Jerry had the grace to look a little ashamed. "It's not that easy. Believe me, I've been trying to take over your guardianship for a while."

Maybe he was like me and that's why I couldn't read his emotions. I so wanted to believe he was like me, that I did something really stupid. "I can read emotions."

"I knew it." His self-satisfied smirk didn't comfort me. At least I didn't tell him I could kill with my power. That probably would have gotten me thrown out and separated from Henry or worse.

Still, just in case he attacked me, I looked around for something I could use as a weapon that didn't involve letting my power off its leash. I didn't want to do that unless I had no other options. The bedside lamp looked promising. I inched closer to it and asked, "What are you going to do about it?"

Jerry shrugged. "Your guardians and I belong to an organization dedicated to…monitoring those like you. They were zealots, but I'm not. Rick and Jessica's records indicate you were under some rather painful treatments. I don't believe in torture, so you'll be safe from that as long as you follow my rules. If you don't, I'll wash my hands of you and you'll be at the mercy of other, less accommodating, guardians."

I sat down on the bed, studying the pattern on the marble of my new bedroom that Jerry had prepared for me. The decor seemed cold and not what I would have chosen for myself, but he'd still put more effort into my room than anyone had ever made on my behalf. He'd provided video games to keep Henry entertained. "I'm twenty. You look like you're maybe twenty-five. You have no authority over me, legal or otherwise."

He shrugged. "I don't need legal claim to get your compliance. I can send your brother wherever I wish for the next two years. We both know you won't leave him, and that gives me an advantage."

Without looking at him, I asked, "And what are your rules?"

"Simple. No running away. Don't harm anyone, obey me without question, or else I won't be able to keep you and your brother safe."

I still got no emotions whatsoever from Jerry, making it really hard to tell if he spoke the truth. I studied his face, searching for clues to tell me if I could trust him. "What do you get out of this?"

Jerry's self-assured smile didn't waver. "Let's just say I like you, and leave it at that."

"What are you?"

"Human."

"Why can't I read your emotions?"

"Luck."

"I don't believe that."

He laughed, a full-throated laugh that reached his eyes and made him seem young, carefree. An unwanted tightness bloomed in my gut, making my whole body tingle with want. I squashed it down. I'd judge him by his actions, not my own hopes.

"Smart and beautiful. I knew I liked you. Settle in, enjoy my hospitality. There's food in the kitchen downstairs. You're free to go anywhere on the estate grounds except my work wing. We'll go shopping this evening to get you toiletries, clothes, and such." He turned away, opened the door, and stopped before closing it behind him. "It was nice finally meeting you, Ginny. I'm an easy guy to get along with. I think you'll enjoy my company in time."

I didn't know whether that was a threat or a promise. The thrill running down my spine and the tightening of my gut at the thought of a promise made him dangerous indeed. I needed more information, and I needed it now.

I listened to Jerry's footsteps as he got farther away. When I thought he was far enough not to hear me, I followed him.

Jerry went from my room directly to the wing he'd forbidden me to go into. There was a big metal gate barring the entrance. He made sure to close it behind him. I hid just outside the gate, behind an arch, while I listened to him go into a room, probably an office of some sort judging from the sound of shuffling papers. He dialed a long string of numbers, much longer than ten digits. A weird tone rang three times before a man with a Spanish accent answered.

The stranger asked, "Have you secured them?"

"I have."

I leaned closer to the bars in the metal gate, trying to see down the beige carpeted hallway, through the wooden door to Jerry's office. The raspy voice on the other side of the receiver asked, "Do you think they will give us any trouble?"

"No. The girl is pretty, young, and impressionable. I can handle them."

My hand fisted. I may be young and impressionable, but I was also a strong demon who had killed. The man on the other side of the phone said, "You think a demon is pretty. I'll be the judge of how well you *handle* her."

"Alonzo, I don't think that will be necessary." Jerry's voice held a note of warning.

"Make sure everything is in order for my arrival tomorrow."

The man hung up. Jerry cursed. The phone crashed against a hard surface and Jerry stormed out of the wing. As soon as he passed the gate, I stepped out of the shadows where I had been hiding and faced him. "So, what was that about?"

Jerry looked surprised at first, then narrowed his eyes at me. "Were you eavesdropping?"

I straightened my posture and faced him. "Of course I was. You were discussing my future with someone on the phone and you're upset. Tell me why."

"I don't recall our deal saying anything about me telling you my private conversations."

I folded my arms. "I don't recall agreeing to any of your terms. I imagine it would be pretty hard to keep me and Henry here if we resisted."

Jerry scowled and advanced on me, forcing me to back up until I couldn't go any farther, caught between the gate and a scary version of Jerry leaning over me. "If you make good on that threat, I promise, you will regret it."

Jerry turned and stormed off, leaving me stunned. As soon as I recovered, I realized he'd forgotten to lock the gate to the forbidden wing.

Time to do some snooping.

The beige carpet sank under my feet, muffling my footsteps. I hurried down the hallway and opened the first wooden door I came upon, surprised at its heaviness. The door locked from the outside. The room featured a white hospital-type bed, a small wooden bedside table, and a bureau. My heart sped at the restraints hanging from the side of the bed.

I listened for Jerry's footsteps, but the forbidden wing remained as quiet as death. I closed the door and opened two more identical rooms. The third room contained three display cases lining the walls and a few drawers beneath them. The display case on my right, closest to the door contained an arrangement of old-looking swords that looked like extended crosses, medieval-types, I think. The second contained long wicked-looking curved knives and the third contained what looked like pictures of various medieval torture devices and a few samples. I checked the drawers from the right and then going around the room counter-clockwise. All were closed except for one in the bottom corner of the case on the left. I opened the sole drawer not locked. It contained small easy-to-hide blades, one in particular called my attention. It looked like a silver hair decoration with two ice blue jewels on top, but it was a knife with a matching hilt. I wondered what it would be like to possess something so beautiful and deadly. I reached for the knife thinking I needed protection, but then thought better of it. Jerry would notice if that was missing. Instead, I moved to a plain black folded knife small enough to fit in the left pocket of my jeans.

I closed the door behind me and headed to the next room on the corner of the wing, which turned out to be Jerry's office. He kept a neat office, except for the surface of his oversized mahogany desk. The whole place smelled like tobacco and expensive cologne. Books on anatomy, biology, psychology, and other sciences covered one wall. Certificates and windows decorated the other walls. There was a large fireplace with a crucifix above the mantel and several figurines on display. Papers piled on top of Jerry's desk, competing with two computer screens and a broken phone for space.

I scanned papers filled with medical terms I couldn't understand. One title on a paper caught my attention, *How Demon Blood Enhances Humans*. The summary marked the paper as the result of nearly twenty years of study into the properties of demon blood and its effect on humans. According to the paper, the blood in my veins could be used to speed up recovery after surgery, reverse the effects of aging.

No wonder Rick and Jessica took two pints of my blood every month. I wonder how they used it. Did they use it to save lives or to keep themselves young? If Jerry uses it to save lives, would I be willing to help him, would I volunteer to let him use me?

Although the thought of needles made me break out in cold sweats, I thought I might work with him, if I could trust him. I would have dug deeper, but I heard heavy footsteps from far away.

I put the papers back as close as I could get them to the way I found them. I peered around the doorway, but couldn't see Jerry yet, so I rushed out of the room and ran toward the gate as his footsteps drew closer. He seemed to be coming from the right, so after I cleared the gate, I hid behind the dining room table on the left side of the wing. Jerry missed catching me by seconds.

I waited for several heartbeats, hoping he didn't come toward me. He went back to his office. I kept waiting to make sure he wouldn't come out again and find me snooping. When I was sure he wasn't coming back, I ran and didn't stop until I reached Henry's room and closed the door behind me. Henry paused and looked away from his video games when I entered. He took one look at me and rushed toward me, throwing his arms around me. "You don't look so good and your heart is beating pretty fast. What happened?"

I really needed to talk to him about his enhanced hearing, but now wasn't the time. We were in danger. "Jerry has some kind of deal with somebody. Whoever it is, he sounded scary, and he's coming to check on us himself."

Henry started moving toward the closet. "Too bad. I kind of liked it here. Where do you want to go next? New York, maybe?"

I thought about it. I was twenty, Henry was sixteen. Was I ready to take care of him in the human world, surrounded by people's emotions, or would I go crazy from the overload? Even if I thought I could handle it, was I willing to risk Henry's life that I was right? *Damn it.* I had to make this arrangement with Jerry work because the risk to my baby brother was pretty serious if I couldn't, and so far Jerry hadn't done anything to warrant taking that risk. "Henry, hold on. Jerry promised he would keep us safe if we followed his rules: don't run away, do as he says, and don't hurt anybody. It doesn't sound so hard."

Henry looked at me like he didn't believe what was coming out of my mouth. "And you believe him?"

I wasn't sure what to believe, but I nodded anyway.

"I know you're scared, Ginny, but we can make it."

I didn't want to talk about why I was scared. I didn't want to admit out loud I feared I might hurt him, see the light of adoration in my brother's eyes turn to fear...or death. "I don't want to leave. I want to stay. Maybe we can use this place as a starting point, a way to get an education, establish identities. Besides, I want you to have a place to live in case I lose control."

"What do you mean?"

I wanted to tell him, I wanted to say that emotions infected me, that people made me go nuts, that I might not be able to handle it in a city, but he didn't deserve to have that burden. It was mine to bear. "Nothing. I'm just scared."

Henry didn't look convinced, but he nodded. He put his arms around me, and then said, "I'll do whatever you say."

I hugged him back and hoped that I could live up to the trust my brother put in me.

CHAPTER

FOUR

I slept on blankets on the floor of Henry's room instead of my new pillow-top bed. Comforted by a full stomach, eucalyptus pillow spray, and warm fluffy bed sheets, I didn't awake until late morning when loud knocking jarred me out of my dreams.

"Ginny, are you in there? Look, I'm sorry about last night. I didn't mean to threaten you like that. It's just...." There was a thump against the door, so I assumed it was Jerry's forehead.

Henry and I waited long minutes without answering, gauging how likely he was to start hitting things and people. Henry looked me in the eye and mouthed, "He threatened you?"

I put my finger over my lips and shook my head, not really answering. Jerry spoke through the door. "I lost control. My world is complicated, things are unraveling, and I don't want to see you hurt. I just need you to work with me, or bad things can happen to both of us."

I let my head fall back against Henry's bed and took a deep breath. Letting it out, I asked, "Is that supposed to be an apology?"

Jerry's answering laugh helped release the knots of tension building across my shoulders. "Yes, it's an apology, I guess."

I wasn't sure how to respond, but he was waiting, so I walked across the carpeted floor, ignored Henry's disbelieving expression and opened the door. He wore a crisp new suit identical to the one he wore yesterday. He ran his hand through his already mussed hair when he saw me.

I took a deep breath, not liking the desire blooming in my gut. "Fine. I accept your apology."

He smiled, his dimples standing out. "Good. Find me if you have questions or want to talk. I'm busy for the next few days but for you, I'll make the time."

I put my hand out to stop him from leaving. "Alonzo's visit sounds like it affects me more than anyone else. What can I do to help?"

"I'm sorry, but the best thing you can do is behave and do as I say." He smiled regretfully and turned to leave. So much for making time.

"Wait!"

Jerry didn't turn around, but kept walking. "I'm your only ally. Don't push me." I knew then that there was nothing I could do to get him to reconsider, at least not yet. I decided to bide my time, pay attention, and figure out another way to have a say in our future. Talking to Jerry seemed like a waste of breath.

I waited for his footsteps to fade down the hallway before I closed the door and sat beside Henry's bed. Henry asked, "What the heck are you doing?"

I banged my head back a couple of times against the soft side of the bed, releasing a little puff of eucalyptus- and lavender scented air every time I did it. "I eavesdropped on Jerry last night when he went into the forbidden wing. He was talking to some guy named Alonzo. He sounded like a total jerk and he's coming to check on us. Jerry seemed jumpy about the whole thing, which scares the crap out of me."

Henry shot up a little too fast for a human and paced in circles around the room, at times jumping over the video game console in front of the wall-mounted TV I was going to have to address the changes going through him eventually, but now was not the time. He approached the windows and opened the curtains looking over the driveway. "Tell me again why we're not leaving. This could be our last chance."

I tried to reach for him to calm him down a bit, but he kept pacing away from me. "We need to stay. This is our chance to have a home and some support. If this guy Alonzo really wants to get a hold of us, he'll chase us down, and we won't have Jerry to help us."

Henry looked to me. "Do you really trust this guy, Jerry? You think he'll keep us safe, that he won't experiment on you."

I blew out a long breath. "I don't trust him completely, but I do think he has his own agenda and it doesn't involve handing us over to Alonzo. Let's stay put for now."

Henry paced, then sat with his back to the door, slid down, and let his shoulders slump. "I really hope you're right."

So did I.

* * *

Later that night, my back, shoulders and head hurt from the tension of going over potential scenarios all day while sitting on the floor of Henry's room. I lay down on the floor, shifted against the plush carpet beneath me, digging a video game case from beneath my behind. I sat up again, unable to find a comfortable position. Not even the eucalyptus of Henry's room or the warm comfort of his presence beside me could make me feel better.

Henry had argued with me most of the day, and I needed a break from the emotion he was throwing at me.

"Why don't you want to leave this place? What does Jerry have that could be worth risking our freedom?"

I blinked a few times to get the tiredness out of my eyes. I took a deep breath and tapped my fingers against my knee. *I don't want to see the expression on Henry's face when he hears this.* "You don't understand how broken I really am. Every time I'm around a lot of people, their emotions push at me. I hold off as long as I can, like a dam that bends under the pressure of holding back too much water, but no matter how hard I try, no matter how strong I think I've become, I always break and when I do, people get hurt."

Henry huffed. "You're just believing Rick and Jessica's crap. We were at a police station with at least a dozen humans and nothing happened."

I pressed my lips closed, took a few breaths, and looked Henry in the eye.

"What is it?"

I whispered so that he had to lean closer to hear what I had to say even with his demon hearing. His breath warmed the wet tracks on my cheeks. "That's not true. I sent a man to the hospital because he was angry." The words released something inside me. A wave of sadness and despair and anger flowed from me in sobs that shook my whole body.

Henry pulled me into his thin frame and put strong arms around me, gave me the comfort I should have been able to give him. He murmured comforting things in my ear about how I had taken care of him, held him, endured Rick and Jessica for him, a background song underlying my pain and soothing my soul. He held me, and I cried until exhaustion led to sleep.

Before I even opened my eyes, the wind caressed my face and moved tendrils of my hair. The air smelled like fresh earth, nothing like the eucalyptus of Henry's room. I shot up from a bed of flowers and grass to find myself in the imaginary sanctuary of my childhood—the secret garden.

As a child, I read the book at least a dozen times and dreamed of a place just like this to escape to. Ivy covered the walls and roses fell over trellises over the path where I stood. Lilies in white and red decorated paths throughout. In the center stood a huge tree shading a stone stool at its base.

On that stool sat the most gorgeous man I'd ever laid eyes on. Every detail of his features was conjured from my dreams, from his icy blue eyes, to his well-defined forearms and the jet-black thick hair that seemed perfectly mussed. But I knew this wasn't a dream, at least not in the traditional sense. I could feel and taste the emotions of the man before me. He sat against the tree, smiling at me, but he tasted bitter and sweet, angry and curious. There was an edge to his smile, a tension in his muscles that told me he could pounce on me in a millisecond and I wouldn't like the results.

"I'm Gabriel. What is your name?" His voice sent little shocks to my brain similar to what I got when I ate chocolate or drank a good cup of coffee. My body swayed like an invisible string pulling me toward Gabriel, yet he seemed unaffected. Despite the predatory smile on his face, his demon-bright aura flickered between curiosity and fury. It felt strange, familiar, like I'd sensed it before, and that scared me because I never met this man before today. This was not a man with whom I could afford to drop my guard.

I shook my head and didn't answer. Instead, I pinched the back of my hand, trying to wake myself up. When that didn't work, I ran around the garden, trying to find the secret door. Nothing. He waited and watched me, his aura growing angrier by the minute.

After I realized there was no way out, I faced him. My tongue stuck to the roof of my mouth.

He said with that soft voice I heard from psychopaths on TV, "That was an easy question. What is your name?"

I backed away a couple of steps before I caught myself and stopped. I opened my mouth to speak. It took a couple of tries before I whispered my name. "Ginny."

"Good. We are getting somewhere. Now, why did you steal energy from me?" At least he was getting to the point, no false pleasantries before he pounced on me.

I shook my head in denial. I found it a little easier to speak this time. "I didn't steal anything from you."

"I hate liars. Do not lie to me. You reached out to me yesterday. You pulled from my energy, you tried to bond with me. Why?" His body angled toward me, packing a crap-load of menace into the minute movement.

"I don't know what you're talking about." I resisted the urge to back away from him.

He narrowed his eyes. "How do you think I created this dream? You reached out to me, bonded your energy to mine, and I traced it back to you. In this dream, I hold absolute power and I will destroy you if you don't tell me the truth, damn the consequences. Now, tell me why, or at least, how."

I shook my head. "I've done nothing, I swear."

He stood, violent energy surrounding his aura as he stalked toward me, gray wings as large as me sprung from him and trailed behind him. Fire sprung from the walls. It burned the vines and roses on the outside of the garden. Flames slithered like angry snakes eating everything in sight, progressing toward the center, where I stood with this man towering over me. "In the past eighty years, no one has ever breached my defenses, yet a young demon, barely out of grade school, managed it yesterday and stole power from me. Before I deal with you, I need to know how you did it.

You have until those flames reach you to tell me everything that's happened in the last twenty-four hours, or I will let them eat you alive. Do we understand each other?"

I nodded and started recounting events of the past day. He listened, and his gaze settled on mine. As I spoke, he put his hand on my wrist and held it. There was nothing comforting or sexual about his touch. He touched me as though he were taking my pulse. I told him everything exactly as it happened except the part about killing my guardians. I lied about that, told him they had died of heart attacks.

He ground his teeth when I told the lie, but said nothing until I was done speaking. "You lied about your guardians' death. Tell me what really happened. Did you kill them?"

I wanted to deny it. The flames burned in a circle about three feet from me. A spark reached for me. It touched my bare foot. The pain was so sharp, for a moment my scream was trapped in my throat. It burned and hurt at the same time, speared from the spot where the spark hit my ankle. It burnt like a drop of acid, set on fire every nerve in the surrounding area.

Gabriel, still holding my hand, flinched as though he could feel what I felt. I couldn't think of a way out of this. I was tired of lying, and I was scared I was going to die. This creature standing before me, hurting me, might be enough of a monster to understand. "I killed them, okay. On my birthday, they experimented on me and they hurt me for the thousandth time. I was scared and alone, and I couldn't stop it. I created this thing made out of fear and I fed it to them, shoved it down their throats until they choked and their hearts stopped beating. Afterward, I was still scared, scared that I wouldn't be able to stop, that I would hurt Henry and...."

He released my arm and wrapped his arms around me. His wings disappeared. He tried to hold me to him, but I pushed him away. He didn't get to comfort me after burning me. I hoped he tripped on his own flames, but he didn't. The flames had stopped, leaving ashes behind and a patch of green where Gabriel and I stood under the tree.

"Was it the first time something like this happened?"

"It was the only time."

"Has anything else strange happened lately?"

"You mean besides super hearing and seeing people's emotions and almost killing an angry drunk in the police station?" I needed to turn down the sarcasm. This guy took moodiness to a whole new level and I didn't want him bringing the flames back.

He nodded. "How old are you, Ginny?"

"Twenty."

He turned from me, speaking in a foreign language. He had claimed he'd been around at least eighty years, but he looked no older than twenty-three, maybe twenty-five. I didn't know what he said, but I recognized cursing when I heard it. He turned back to me. His voice was more normal and he didn't seem angry anymore. "You're a psy demon. You just came into your demon power."

With every passing moment, I felt more comfortable with this handsome stranger. At least he wasn't about to murder me anymore. "What's a psy demon and why do you have wings?"

"Psy is a class of demon. There are psy or psychics, herculus, kinetics, and witches. I've never seen a psy who could manifest without touch, but it's possible. My wings are a demonic trait that appears with strong emotion. In a few years or a few months, you will have your own."

The thought of wings didn't exactly thrill me. How the heck would I be able to hide that? I put the thought aside to think about later. Right now, I needed to get the heck out of danger, worry about the future when I was safe in the present. "Well, not that I'm not thankful for the information, but if you're done scaring the crap out of me, could you put me back in my brother's room?

There's a big shot named Alonzo coming and I need to be there to protect him."

Gabriel towered over me again. The flames made a comeback, although they didn't advance. They seemed to be there as an extension of his anger. "Is that, by chance, Alonzo Nezmeth?"

"I think that's what Jerry called him, yes. Why?"

Gabriel grabbed my wrist again. I tried to pull away, but he wouldn't let me. "You need to get as far away from Jerry and Alonzo as you can get. Promise me."

I shook my head. "I am in the first semi-safe place I've been in since forever. I am not giving that up for you."

"I'll come get you. I'll keep you safe. I'll take care of Jerry and Alonzo for you."

I didn't want anything bad happening to Jerry. "Why? What will you do to Jerry?"

"I will eliminate Jerry." He said it like an obvious fact. "You bonded to me. It is an ancient process meant to initiate arranged marriages between royalty, often amongst warring factions that would otherwise never open up to one another. It will bring our dreams together, blend our power, and should one of us die, the other will be severely weakened for months or even years. The more we resist, the more physically attracted we become until we can't resist one another."

"How can we break it?"

"I don't know. Believe me, I don't relish the idea of not being able to trust what I feel. I will do everything I can to figure out how to break this."

"And who will keep me safe from you and your little flame trick?" I tried to pull my arm away again. Too many people had hurt me. Too many had taken advantage. "Jerry is the only one who hasn't hurt me."

"I haven't hurt you." He looked down. "Not really."

"Well, I'm the one that got licked by the flames from hell. I don't trust you any more than you seem to trust me. I'm not going anywhere with you."

Gabriel glared at me as though ready to throttle me. I pulled against his hold on my wrist. He didn't resist, his touch remained gentle but he followed me as I backed up until my back hit the tree. He put both arms on either side of me and leaned down. "You're too damn young to be able to do what you did. You're too pretty to be in the hands of Alonzo. He will use you, steal the light in your eyes and take every last drop of blood from you. I will not let that happen, so I'm going to ask you one more time, where are you?"

Gabriel's face was inches from mine. His icy blue eyes gleamed with an unearthly light. The pull to trust him was too strong, almost like a compulsion. I needed some distance and some time to think about it.

My eyes traced the contours of his nose, his high cheekbones, his strong jaw. I could feel his breath against my lips. Sparks of electricity worked their way up and down my body. My every cell reached out for him. I'd never been kissed. I'd never been touched in a good way, not like that, and I wanted to be. I could read desire in the tension of his body, the way his face angled toward me, the aura around him. I closed the distance between our lips.

When my lips met his, I opened them, and his tongue slipped into me. He tasted like coffee and sugar and sweetness and dreams. I wanted to spend the rest of eternity lost in that kiss. He pulled back and pressed his lips to mine a few more times in ever-shorter kisses. He bit my lip and licked away at it, and then he kissed my neck. The roughness of stubble on his cheek rubbed against me. His breath fanned against my ear. I arched my body into his shamelessly, seeking as much friction as possible. He whispered in my ear, "That's the last time I'll let you kiss me because as sweet as you are, you are too young for me."

I pushed him away and he let me.

"Don't tell me what I am."

"How's this, then? When your nascent powers were out of control and you were scared you'd hurt your brother, you reached out for another psychic demon. You reached out for me and you created a bond. Despite your youth, you are quite likely the strongest psychic demon in these parts, besides me. That bond you created makes it so that our psyches orbit around each other like two heavenly bodies. It creates this attraction, but it doesn't change the fact that to me, you're barely a child."

I looked him in the eye. "If you really believe that, what does that make you for kissing me back?"

He didn't respond.

"Let me go. You don't want me anyway. You're just another bully with painful fire tricks instead of fists."

"I can't let you go. You're my responsibility."

I rolled my eyes. "I've never been a responsibility. I'm more like a commodity and I don't trust you. Good-bye." I willed with all my strength to leave.

He regarded me, his mouth turned up in a semblance of a smile.

I tried again. This time I took the time to sink into that bottomless nothingness I found when I was exhausted and desolate and desperate.

Gabriel's voice broke through my thoughts. "That's better, but you need a shield of some sort."

"Why are you helping me?"

He shrugged. "I can't help it."

I stared into his eyes, so blue they seemed like glaciers. Maybe if I made a shield out of ice...I counted breaths and meditated, sank into the same peace I felt the day before when I needed to not hurt Henry.

Gabriel started cursing in that foreign tongue again. He yelled at me. "Stop, damn it, don't do it like that. You'll strengthen the bond."

I ignored him because I didn't feel any sort of bond to him. I kept going because it seemed to be working. I constructed a wall of ice around me, keeping him out. Gabriel's voice faded, to be replaced by nothing. After a few minutes, the ice faded and I passed into that place between dream and wakefulness. I forced my eyes open, glad to see I was in the real world with Henry asleep in the bed above me. My power hopped within me, filled with an erotic heat left over from my encounter with Gabriel. My skin tingled with an awareness that flared at even the small friction created by my movements against the plush carpet.

In the distance, I could hear Jerry talking to the staff, making arrangements for Alonzo's arrival. He instructed the cook to call the temp agency to hire an additional five waiters for dinner and to make a big breakfast for Henry and me because we needed to gain a bit of weight.

The gesture meant a lot because he said it as an afterthought with no subterfuge. He had no way of knowing I could hear him. It fueled my hopes for this new life. I could be comfortable here. Henry could be safe. We could eat a big breakfast and spend our mornings exploring the surrounding woods. Jerry had so far shown us only kindness. I rubbed my ankle where pink skin already covered the site where Gabriel's flames had burned me.

I'd stay with Jerry for now. Gabriel wasn't a choice. He was too strong, too passionate, too demon, too everything.

CHAPTER

FIVE

That afternoon, I waited in the informal dining room for Jerry to join me for a very late lunch. Despite repeated attempts, I'd failed to get Henry to stop playing *Grand Theft Auto,* so I would be eating with Jerry alone, if he ever showed up. I hoped he did show. If I wanted to make this work, I had to spend more time with Jerry figuring out what made him tic and making him care about Henry and me a bit more.

The cook, a man with red cheeks, redder hair, and a permanent smile placed a roast beef sandwich in front of me. My mouth watered at the mere thought of the meat and fresh-baked bread. "Thank you, Mr. Bartholomew. It smells like the most delicious meal imaginable."

The cook smiled, patting my hand on his way out of the dining room. *Jerry did say I needed to gain some weight. I don't think he'll mind if I start without him.* I grabbed the sandwich and took a bite that sent me to heaven and back, causing me to moan in appreciation.

I heard Jerry's approaching footsteps just as the cook disappeared behind the water feature separating the informal dining room from the professional kitchen. I heard Jerry in the kitchen just as I sensed Mr. Bartholomew's pleasure being replaced by wariness.

"Mr. Bartholomew, we have some very important matters to discuss. Please get your notebook."

I got up to spy into the kitchen, poking my head around the decorative wall, my fingers leaving an imprint on the cool glass encasing a dropping waterfall.

The cook dropped his head. "Mr. Stone, how can I help you?"

"Alert the temporary hires for the evening that they should never speak unless spoken to, and make sure the additional staff serves the food at precisely seven o'clock. The meal should have a soup, a salad, at minimum two forms of meat—neither pork— three sides, one of which is pasta, and two desserts. Have the appropriate selection of wines suited to the meal. The table should be laid out in the traditional European style, and each meal should be served and removed prior to the next course. Once the meal is over, bring out a tea service and a coffee service. We have no idea what mood Alonzo will be in. Any deviation from these instructions will result in immediate termination with no pay."

Alonzo sounded like a swell guy. The cook wiped sweat off his forehead with a clean towel as he struggled to write everything out. "Can you repeat that, sir?"

Jerry sighed. "I'll e-mail you a copy of the instructions."

"Thank you, sir." Poor guy's aura pulsed with anxiety as he fidgeted with his apron pockets and dropped his pencil.

I stepped out of my hiding spot to interrupt the conversation. The cook took a relieved breath for the first time since I'd been spying on him. Jerry dismissed him and the man stepped away into the walk-in freezer in back of the kitchen without ever turning around.

Jerry smiled at the sight of me, his shoulders relaxed a bit. "Hello there, sweetheart. I'm glad you're here. Come." He grabbed my hand and began leading me toward the forbidden wing. Today, Jerry smelled of cigars, cinnamon and cologne. His hand was warm and slightly sweaty in my own.

I held onto him tighter.

As we walked side by side, he said, "Is there something you wanted to discuss with me?"

"Um, yes, I wanted to know what I could do to, you know, help." I wanted to slap my forehead. I sounded like such a ditz sometimes.

His thumb rubbed over my wrist repeatedly. Who knew such a touch could be erotic? I tried to pull my hand back, but Jerry refused to let me go.

We were in the formal dining room now, which was big enough to seat twenty amongst antique mahogany engraved with gold leaf designs covering every surface. A matching water feature separated this dining room from the kitchens, just as in the informal dining room. Though the water feature in this room was much larger, extending up twenty feet and lit with a golden light that matched the gilding on the furniture and walls.

Jerry pulled the first chair on the left of the long table for me. He sat at the head of the table, beside me, his body angled toward me. "This is where you will sit this evening. Alonzo will sit to my right. You will be expected to be quiet at all times. Eat and respond to any questions posed to you. Not a single word should be spoken unless Alonzo or I ask you a question."

I reached for a glass of cold water, but there wasn't one. I left it in the other dining room along with my half-eaten sandwich. I took a deep breath and studied Jerry with his formal gray slacks, shiny black shoes, and a shirt in the same shade of green as his eyes. He had dressed his home and himself to please Alonzo. "Forgive me for saying so, but Alonzo doesn't sound like a nice man. In fact, he sounds kind of mean. Why let him come here at all, prepare formal food, and hire extra wait staff? Why does it matter?"

Jerry leaned back in the chair, his expression concerned, which did nothing to set me at ease. It reminded me of Jessica's concern and how fake that had been. "Believe me when I say I'm trying to do the best for you and your brother. My relationship with Alonzo is complicated. He is a friend, but also my superior. He can be over-zealous, but he is a pious man who has dedicated his life to serving humanity. As such, he's seen many things that have caused him to hold demons like you far beneath humans. Besides that, you are female, and thus twice damned. Worse even than that, he holds you responsible for the deaths of Jessica and Rick. I know you had little to do with that. I know they overindulged in drugs and that they abused you. My professional assessment is that there was an accident of some sort, the result of their own actions. But, Alonzo would like to make his own assessment. They were under his protection and he feels he needs to avenge them."

I dry-swallowed and nodded. I couldn't blame Alonzo for his beliefs, especially when he happened to be right about my involvement in my guardians' deaths. "What does he mean by avenge them?"

Jerry fidgeted with his cuff links. "I honestly don't know." Leaning forward, he held my hand in his again, his clear green eyes locked onto my own, full of compassion and only a hint of uncertainty. "It was an accident, wasn't it, Ginny?"

I blinked back tears welling in my eyes. My throat hurt with the effort to hold back my emotions making it difficult to speak.

Jerry pulled my right hand to his lips and kissed it. "It will be all right. You'll see. I believe God will show us the way."

I hoped God existed, but I wasn't convinced I believed in him or that such a being would bother with me even if he did exist. I didn't say any of that, but I shut my mouth and left Jerry to his beliefs.

Jerry stood without releasing my hand, then pulled me to

stand with him. He wiped the tears brimming from my eyes with his thumb, his hands caressing the sides of my face. "You're quite beautiful when you cry, you know."

I took several steps back, folded my arms around myself, and tried to smile for his benefit. I couldn't make my face fall into the smile naturally, so I dropped it. Jerry closed the distance between us and pulled my hands from under my arms, holding them in his own warm hands. The water dripped behind me, helping me to calm my racing heart a bit.

Jerry leaned toward me, leaving me pressed against the cool glass of the water feature. He closed the distance between us, stopped a breath away from kissing me. "I want to kiss you. Are you okay with that?"

I wasn't sure of what I wanted. I didn't feel the desperate ache I felt in Gabriel's presence, but that's probably because Jerry wasn't demon. That dark part of me didn't respond to him. A different part of me did, the part that wanted normal love and children and laughter and lightness. A mercenary part of me wanted to believe this man's loyalty could be swayed, that I was safe here and that I had found a home where I could build the life I wanted, with Jerry. That's what I really wanted in my heart of hearts, so I nodded and held my breath as he leaned down, his lips ever closer to my own.

He touched his lips to mine, then slipped his tongue inside my mouth. He'd been drinking whiskey and smoking cigars. I could taste it on him. He cupped my face as he kissed me. I held my breath and returned the kiss, wrapping my arms around his neck. He pulled back from me, kissed my forehead, and I unwrapped my arms from around him. "I like you, Ginny. I like you a lot. Come, I have a surprise for you."

I wanted to know what this surprise was, but my heart beat ever faster as we approached his bedroom. I stopped outside the door, unwilling to go in. He grabbed my hand and pulled me toward the room, but I resisted with ease thanks to strength granted by my demon genetics. I was stronger than any human when I wasn't weakened by drugs and hunger. "I would like to stay here. I'm not comfortable going into your bedroom."

He waved off my concern. "Relax, I'm not going to ravish you today. I just want to show you something."

I took a step and stopped in the doorway, going no farther. Jerry pursed his lips in annoyance, but didn't argue. Instead, he went to his large dark wooden closet, engraved with the sunburst pattern, echoed throughout the room. Royal blue drapes covering the French doors to the balcony overlooking the lawn had little gold sunbursts repeated through the edges. The plush carpet in dark brown had a golden sunburst woven into it.

I avoided looking at the bed, and instead focused on the long, black bag Jerry pulled out of the closet. He opened the bag to show me one of the most beautiful dresses I had ever seen. I forgot all my misgivings about being in his room and my worries for the evening. I ran my hands down the shining blue fabric that was softer and more beautiful than anything I'd ever worn in my entire life.

I whispered, "It's beautiful."

Jerry stood a little straighter and smiled a little brighter. "I'm glad you like it."

"When did you have time for this?"

"My assistant took pictures of various dresses in your size. I knew this was meant for you the minute I saw it. She had a courier service bring it over this morning. What do you think?"

"How did you know my size?"

He seemed embarrassed. "I sort of sneaked into Henry's room and looked at your clothes last night."

Considering he would have had to look at the clothes I wore to bed last night since I had nothing else to wear, his confession freaked me out a tiny bit, but he waited so expectantly I took pity on him and decided to overlook the invasion of privacy. It wasn't like I'd ever had any to begin with anyway. "It's the most lovely thing anyone has ever given me. Thank you."

Jerry cleared his throat. "Well, I'll take you back to your room. I have a ton of preparations to attend to before Alonzo's arrival." He handed me two shoe-sized boxes wrapped in cream crinkled paper with Castor & Pollux and a two headed horse printed on the box.

"What's this?"

"Just some shoes, cosmetics, and the like. Girl stuff, my assistant assures me."

I hugged him and kissed him on the cheek before rushing out of the room carrying my new bounty. I stopped outside my bedroom. *I need to show off a bit. Let's see what Henry thinks of my pretty new dress. I've never had anything so beautiful.*

I found Henry sitting on his bed, playing video games in exactly the same spot I'd left him. Several empty cans of Coke littered the floor beneath him. His room was similar to Jerry's now that I had seen both, only Henry's room was missing the sunburst motif, it was dominated by green instead of Jerry's blue, and it had a lot more electronics as well as pictures of sports stars on the walls, some signed. I appreciated that Jerry had given my brother such nice furnishings, comparable to what he had gotten for himself.

Behind Henry, tossed on top of tussled sheets, sat a black bag identical to mine. I cleared a spot to put my own things and picked up the cans lying on the floor, placing my body strategically between Henry and his video game. I didn't need to say anything else. He saved his game and turned toward the unzipped black bag with a heavy sigh. "Did you know he wants us to dress up for this Alonzo?"

"Yes, I am aware. He thinks it's important we look our best, and frankly, I think we need to work with Jerry, not against him."

Plastering a smile on my face, I added, "plus, I get to wear this. Look at the dress he got me." I showed him my dress. His expression turned my enthusiasm down a few notches.

"What's wrong?"

"I really think we should leave. I don't have a good feeling about this Alonzo. He sounds like a jerk."

I plopped down on the bed beside him, letting out a loud breath. "I don't get a good feeling about him, either, but we need Jerry. We need someone to protect us. My power is getting stronger every day, and I might need help controlling it. Plus, I have no skills. I wouldn't know the first thing about supporting us." I didn't tell him I really needed someone to protect him from me in case I went all demon crazy.

Henry placed an arm around me. "It will be all right, Ginny. You'll see. You're stronger than you think."

That's the problem. I'm a lot stronger than either of us knew. Gabriel claimed I was the strongest psy demon in the area besides him. Somehow, I didn't think that was a good thing. I leaned against Henry and smiled. "Come on. You have to love this dress. It's gorgeous."

Henry nodded. "If you like that kind of thing. Just don't let Jerry buy your trust."

I punched his shoulder. "He'll earn it. You'll see."

SIX

The pendulum clock in Jerry's drawing room marked five o'clock in the afternoon. The bong of metal rang against my ears like someone beat against the side of my head with drumsticks. Underlying the clatter, a loud voice boomed from the outside ordering people to pick up the pace and to be careful not to drop anything. Since I didn't want to remind Jerry about my inhuman senses, I resisted the urge to open the door until Jerry realized Alonzo had arrived. The buzzing of the intercom system as the butler announced Alonzo's arrival overlay the ringing still left over from the old pendulum clock. I shook my head, but it didn't make the pain any better.

Behind Jerry, Henry closed the notebook he'd been using to draw monsters and heroes, nudging it into a bookcase, out of sight, between aged volumes of Dante's *Inferno* and *Paradisio*.

I winced when the doorbell rang, putting my hands over my ears to protect them. All three of us started for the door like prisoners lining up for judgment. On my way out, I checked my reflection in the mirror, adjusted the shimmering blue dress that had crinkled as I sat waiting and fidgeting.

We followed the commotion echoing through the hallways.

The high ceilings, lack of rugs, and sparse furnishings made sound carry through this house. Jerry seemed to like it that way; the better to highlight the few pieces of art hanging on the walls, all of them signed by painters that were recognizable even to someone as uneducated as me. We stopped in the foyer built for the purpose of receiving visitors. A man I assumed to be Alonzo stood in the precise center of the Crane inlaid into the stone floor, the symbol of renewal, resurrection, and immortality.

At the sight of Alonzo, Jerry transformed into a man with a straight posture, a wide smile, and arms outstretched. His voice carried a hint of warmth and gladness. "My friend." *Neat trick. I didn't know Jerry could lie so well. I wonder what else he's been lying about.*

Alonzo pulled Jerry into a half handshake, half hug. Both of them acted like old friends, emphasis on old, yet they both looked twenty-five, their skin smooth, their bodies fit. *I wonder if the experiments done on me have something to do with that.* When they broke apart, they continued on their way down the hallways toward Alonzo's rooms without even looking at Henry and me. I had the feeling, though, that if we didn't follow, Alonzo would notice and he would make sure we felt his displeasure.

I fisted my hands while I thought about that paper I'd found in Jerry's office about the effects of demon blood. We followed the wave of cologne he left behind, and watched him. Chiseled jaw and high cheekbones complimented blue eyes the color of the midnight sky and blond wavy locks of hair smoothed into submission. His shirt and pants were starched stiff beneath his tailored jacket, almost as stiff as his posture. His smiles never reached his eyes, his laughter produced sound and nothing else, not even ripples in his aura. In fact, Alonzo's aura surrounded him in a thin sheet of serenity, devoid of doubt or guilt or happiness.

The butler dropped Alonzo's luggage in the closet and efficiently unpacked. Alonzo smiled widely and the butler's aura turned a deep warm shade of orange indicating he was pleased. "Will you require anything else, Mr. Nezmeth?"

"Please, call me Alonzo. The Lord made us all equal. There is no need to stand on ceremony."

Somehow, I think he only applies that rule when it suits him.

The butler inclined his head in a sign of deep respect. "Of course, Alonzo. If you need anything, I am at your service."

"Have a good day, my man, and may God go with you." Alonzo turned his perfectly smooth face to the butler and dismissed him with a thousand-watt smile that caused the butler to exchange his typical forbidding expression for an answering smile.

The butler bowed while murmuring, "And also with you," before closing the door and exiting without ever standing up from the bow.

No sooner had the door clicked closed, the smile fell off Alonzo's face like a mask discarded. "You really must hire better help. That man doesn't have the proper bearing."

I'm in way over my head. This man can slice into a person with his smile. What can he do with actual weapons meant to kill or worse?

Though Alonzo yielded charm and personal attraction like weapons, he had not yet turned it on Henry or me. Alonzo looked at us the same way he looked at the table and furniture, as though we weren't even human.

Jerry's smile never left his face, and since I couldn't see his aura, I had no idea how he felt about Alonzo's sudden about-face with regards to the butler. "He is a decent fellow. You will see." Jerry directed Alonzo's attention toward me. "This is Ginny and her brother Henry."

I waited for his judgment, hating the tiny part of me that wanted his approval, equated it with a measure of safety.

Alonzo spared me a glance, his aura still unchanged. "I'm

63

glad to meet you and finally get a look at you." He turned toward Jerry. "I'm rather tired. Can we be alone so that we can get business talks out of the way?"

Jerry nodded. "Of course. You must have traveled all night." He gestured for Henry and me to leave and we obliged. We couldn't walk away fast enough.

* * *

Henry and I arrived in the dining room as the damn pendulum in the drawing room bonged seven in the evening, dinner time. I massaged behind my ear as the metallic bong echoed inside my head.

Jerry, sitting at the head of the massive mahogany table fit for twenty, seemed happy to see us, but with his capacity for lying with his face and his voice, I couldn't tell if he was really glad or if it just suited his plans. Alonzo sat to his right, fingering a small gold crucifix he wore on a chain around his neck. He looked at Henry and me with horror. His entire body, aura and mannerism, united to produce a single sincere message: he didn't want Henry or me sitting at this table with him.

When Jerry stood to extend a hand toward me in welcome, Alonzo stood as well. "I have no desire to break bread with these demons."

And I have no desire to break bread with devils in human clothing, but here I am.

Jerry adjusted his suit and looked to his friend with a smile. "Alonzo, this is my home, and you are a guest and my friend. You came here to observe Ginny and Henry, yet you've avoided them at every turn. Are you afraid to sit across a table from them while surrounded by servants and eat?"

Alonzo scrunched his face like he smelled something disgusting rather than the sumptuous fragrances of cooked meat wafting from the covered plates. "I am not afraid. I simply have standards."

Jerry didn't say anything. He sat, shook out his napkin, and laid it on his lap. "You wanted to evaluate how Ginny and Henry are settling into my home. This is the perfect opportunity, don't you think?"

Alonzo watched Jerry pour a glass of wine, his gaze lingering on the label. Jerry took his time inspecting the wine, then smelling and tasting it. Alonzo huffed and sat, signaling a waiter to pour him a glass.

Jerry smiled. "Thank you."

As I watched Alonzo drink his wine, Henry touched my hand under the table and both of us waited in front of our empty plates while no one spoke, and the only sounds belonged to the water feature behind me, the waiters moving about, and Alonzo swallowing copious amounts of red wine. Alonzo broke the silence, saying a silent prayer to himself, "Our Father who art in heaven." I joined in the prayer, not sure if I believed in a Christian God, but hoping He existed, regardless. If there are demons, there must be a God, and whatever form God possessed, I had to be thankful. Henry and I had food to eat and a roof over our heads.

The servants placed soup in front of us first. The acrid scent was nothing like what I had smelled in the kitchen earlier. I took a sip off my spoon and put it down immediately. The lentil soup contained poison of some sort. I raised the napkin to my mouth and spit into it, placing a hand on Henry's arm to stop him from eating any of it.

Henry placed the spoon to his lips and sniffed, without eating any of the food. He placed the spoon back and pretended to eat. Thankfully, Jerry was too busy watching Alonzo inhale his soup to really notice the amount of food on our plates never dropped. For his part, he seemed revolted by the gluttony of Alonzo. Since no one but Henry paid attention to me anyway, I reached across and dipped a finger into Jerry's soup.

It tasted fine. I would have warned him if I thought he was in danger, but he didn't seem to be, which meant someone targeted only Henry and my plates. I didn't think Jerry would poison us, which meant Alonzo had plans for us this evening. I watched him and the way the staff making their way in and out of the kitchen interacted with him. Mr. Bartholomew wouldn't poison my food. People lied; auras didn't, which meant Alonzo's accomplice had to be amongst the wait staff.

Despite the fact my stomach grumbled in protest, I didn't dare eat anything for the remainder of the meal, which was a shame because the lamb looked and smelled amazing and I had eaten too little to support my metabolism today. I'd have to make something later for Henry and me. Mr. Bartholomew wouldn't mind.

For his part, Alonzo didn't speak much. He shoved four plates of food into his mouth without ever saying a word or looking directly across the table. When the beef arrived, he ate two servings and an entire serving bowl of potatoes to go with it. He also had a plateful of spaghetti and half a chocolate cake for dessert. When Mr. Bartholemew asked if he wanted to try the sweet potato pie, Jerry gasped in amazement at the man's positive response.

I wondered where Alonzo fit all that food and why he needed so much of it. I had never met a human who could burn through so many calories and not have four hundred pounds to show for it. At least the food seemed to improve his mood. By the time coffee service was placed in front of him, he had dropped the scowl of superiority and his aura had dropped the bluster of anger.

I dragged my attention away from Alonzo and back to Jerry. He sat with his back rigid, his gaze focused on Alonzo and his jaw slackened in shock. Apparently, I wasn't the only one surprised by Alonzo's appetite. Jerry must have seen me looking at him from the corner of his eye. He glanced at me showing a bit of guilt, maybe, but I had no idea why that would be. Jerry then cleared his throat and turned to Alonzo. "You seem rather hungry this evening. Is everything all right?"

Alonzo looked back at Jerry with defiance. "I have been under a lot of stress, physical and otherwise. I needed a boost."

Jerry glanced back at me. Again, I caught the look of guilt on his face when he turned toward me. I guessed whatever boost Alonzo had taken had to do with my blood, and the paper I had found on Jerry's desk. Or maybe Alonzo used one of the drugs that had been tested on me. I dropped my head and used my hair to hide the hatred for what had been done to me, for whatever vitality Alonzo had stolen at my expense or the expense of another demon. But, I had to get over it for now. Alonzo was up to something and I needed a clear head.

Jerry swallowed the remainder of his wine in a big gulp and reached to pour more into his glass. "We all do what we believe to be right."

Alonzo narrowed his eyes. Anger tinged his aura, as well as something else I couldn't quite decipher. Shame maybe, or righteousness. "You have no right to judge me. What I've done is not the same as you harboring demons as though they're equals."

"It is my home and I will do as I please and there is a difference in using DemB to continue our work and indulging in it to the point you become a glutton for food. What else are you indulging in, Alonzo? What do you do to satisfy your needs?" Jerry's accusation left me feeling cold and sweaty. DemB, they had a short cutesy name for my blood that they had stolen. What the freak was I doing with these people? I needed to get away, run out of there and never come back. I swung my leg to the side of the chair and I pulled Henry's arm, signaling that we should make a run for it.

He shook his head. He whispered while Jerry and Alonzo

continued to argue about Alonzo being out of control. "No, stay and get more information. If we leave now, we won't get far."

Alonzo looked directly at me and I dug my nails into Henry's hand to get him to stop talking. Few people looked at me the way Alonzo did, especially those that hurt and beat me. "What game are you playing, demon?"

I took a breath to steady my voice and smiled with as much serenity as I could muster. "I have no game. I want a roof over our heads, dinner on the table, a life where we choose when and where to go, a place where we don't have to fear the evil of men who hide behind piety."

Jerry looked at me in warning. Alonzo's visage didn't change, but the red tinge of anger intensified in his aura.

Okay, maybe I shouldn't have said that last part, but it's the truth.

"Tell me, Jerry, what have you learned from having this thing in your home?"

Jerry cleared his throat. "There isn't much you haven't learned in your laboratories. Ginny has behaved with decorum and hasn't done anything to harm me or mine. She is intelligent and has shown no signs of malice. It is my opinion she was treated badly and she isn't a danger to any of us as long as we don't threaten her or her brother. If we do, she'll do what any being would do for those they love."

"You mean she'll murder in cold blood anyone who threatens her."

Jerry glared at Alonzo, but smoothed his features when the other man glared back. "I don't think she's capable of killing anyone in cold blood. Look at her. She's a sweet young girl. She may be a demon, but she is also human. Perhaps she has the best of both of us."

Alonzo raised an eyebrow and Jerry did the same. They stared each other, having a silent conversation I couldn't decipher even with the ability to see Alonzo's aura. Finally, Alonzo unfolded all six feet of himself from the dinner table, turning over the chair behind him in his haste. "Matters are worse than I thought. You're besotted in less than two days. They need to be kept on a leash as I prescribed. Rick and Jessica understood that."

Jerry stood with a lot more deliberation than Alonzo had shown. His chair didn't make any noise. "I do not engage in torture. The treatment is unnecessary and I will not condone it." His tone was quiet, sure, and left no room for argument. I appreciated such vehemence.

Alonzo pursed his lips. Then, he deigned to speak to me. "Can you sense what I'm feeling now?"

"You're angry and determined. You hate me."

Alonzo seemed offended. "I am a man of God. I don't hate anyone. It is just my duty to take care of those under my care, and Jerry is one of mine. I don't like it when demons in pretty packages tempt him." The man liked to lie to himself. I filed the information away for future reference.

Jerry leaned toward Alonzo, his stance threatening. "She is not tempting me in the least, Alonzo, I assure you." Even though he'd just said I wasn't tempting, a small thrill of joy warmed my heart. I had been right to trust Jerry.

Alonzo laid a hand on Jerry's shoulder, but Jerry shook him off, which seemed to sadden Alonzo. In a conciliatory tone, he said, "I understand, old friend. She is beautiful, but don't be fooled by her exterior. She has no soul."

This was a new insult, even for me. "I have as much of a soul as you do."

"Do you now? I don't go around murdering innocents." Alonzo turned to Jerry, placing a hand on his shoulder again. "I think it's best if you take some time to clear your head, old friend. I'll be taking these things with me for a few days. Please pack whatever the female will need for its stay."

Jerry moved in front of me, stepping between me and Alonzo. "*She*'s just getting settled. She trusts me. I think she would do better if she stayed with me."

Alonzo stated in a smooth even tone that hid the angry dark emotions roiling through his aura. "That may be so, but I am more concerned for your well-being than the demon's. It's coming with me."

Jerry swallowed, but did not move from his position in front of me. "Please, Alonzo."

Alonzo looked regretful for the break between him and Jerry, but I could see no evidence of it in his aura. "Your behavior only confirms my suspicions. It's only a few days and look how you react. Move aside, Jerry. If you don't, I can take them both and make sure you never see them again."

"No. I think we're done for tonight. It's better if we separate before we say or do something we'll regret. I'll call a car for you." Jerry took out his cell phone. I wanted to hug him or kiss him or both in that moment. Instead, I moved to his side, a couple of steps behind his position, in silent support.

Alonzo's concern dropped like a curtain, to be replaced by anger. *There is the man you've been hiding.* Jerry looked stunned as Alonzo grabbed his shoulder swept his leg and rode him down, twisting his arm in an odd angle in the process. *Shit.*

I lunged forward to deliver a kick, hopefully giving Jerry enough time to recover. I smiled at Alonzo's grunt of pain when my kick landed on his thigh. Still, the man didn't lose focus. He touched a pressure point on Jerry that left him unconscious on the floor. I didn't know anyone could do that with such efficiency. The man had superhuman strength and speed.

When Alonzo started advancing on me, I backed up until I hit a corner. I kept his attention on me while behind him, Henry was unplugging a lamp, getting ready to hit him over the head. But Henry never got a chance. Alonzo smirked without taking his eyes off me, putting his hand inside his suit jacket. He kicked forward while withdrawing something. I instinctively blocked thinking he was about to strike me. Too late, I heard the bang of a gun, smelled the tang of salt and copper in air. Henry fell to the floor, red spreading from his leg.

I rushed to Henry, but Alonzo's arm closed around my throat, pulling my body back against him. I gasped for air. Henry tried to pull himself toward us. He didn't seem able to use his leg, but he wouldn't be deterred until Alonzo pointed the gun still in his left hand at him.

I stopped struggling, silently begging Henry to back off. His chest heaved with frustration and he panted in pain, yet he looked at Alonzo as though he would take him on for me. I loved my brother and was so proud of him in that moment. I couldn't lose him, not for anything.

"Even a demon can't heal a bullet to the head. As young as you are, it will probably affect you as it would a human. If you survive, you won't be the same—you'll be a mindless specimen for my laboratories, nothing more. How about you both stop struggling or die in the next five seconds. Five, four, three…."

"Please, Henry, do as he says," I shouted as much as the chokehold would let me. "Alonzo, I'll do whatever you say, just please don't hurt him."

Alonzo released me, stepping back and pointing the gun back and forth between Henry and me. Jerry's cell phone lay on the floor between us, ignored. I needed that phone so I dropped to my knees, not caring for the blood that stained my dress. Henry had bled too damn much. I knew in my head he was a demon like me, and I had healed worse wounds without medical attention, but the knowledge didn't make it any easier to watch him suffer.

I put my hands together in supplication. "Please, let me say good-bye to Henry." I didn't expect Alonzo to have an ounce of pity for me, but his vicious kick gave me the opportunity to grab the phone as I gasped for breath on the floor. Henry tried to pull himself toward me, but Alonzo pointed the gun to the back of my head.

Henry saw me pick up the device. "It's okay, Ginny. It's healing already. I won't die from this." I slipped the device into the bodice of my dress.

Alonzo yelled, "Enough. We're leaving."

"Make sure Jerry is okay, tell him what happened." I got up, not caring that the blood-soaked dress stuck to my legs. I walked out of Jerry's mansion with Alonzo and got in the car. Once inside, he tied my hands together in front of me with rope and secured his weapon in a panel on the side of the door, as though afraid I'd wrest it from him and shoot him. Sadly, I lacked the skill if not the strength for such a struggle.

I leaned back in the limo as it started to move. Alonzo's aura pulsed deep red beside me. Without taking my eyes off him, I tried to sink into that place of nothingness I'd found before when I had been scared and hopeless. Maybe I could use emotions as a weapon again if I needed to. I didn't really want to hurt anyone, even Alonzo that way again. Jerry would probably never forgive me, but I needed to do something. The way Alonzo looked at me, and the violence in his emotions, promised I might not survive a few days in his care.

I tried to look away beyond him, to the outside, to organize my thoughts, figure out my next step, access the demon inside. I turned my attention from him for a second, but it was enough for him to jam me in my left arm. I spotted the needle in Alonzo's hand as coldness spread from my arm to my chest. My thoughts slowed down along with my breath. My eyesight started to get blurry. I lost consciousness.

CHAPTER
SEVEN

I awoke unable to move my arms, my face plastered against a hard surface, much warmer than I was used to, a steady thump against my ears matching the heartbeat in my chest. I tried to move, but found I couldn't.

I kicked and pushed against the bindings, surprised when they disappeared, taking with them warmth and the comforting scent of coffee, sugar, and male. Strange, I hadn't noticed those before. I opened my eyes, my mind clearing of the grogginess that clouded it. Gabriel kneeled beside me, perfectly still, fading sunlight catching his blue eyes and making them glow and shine.

I suppressed a shiver. A predator lived behind those eyes and he had me in his sights. The sound of water crashing behind me made me jump. I turned toward the waves crashing and foaming a few feet in front of me. "What are you doing here, where am I?"

He didn't answer. Salt and brine and living things I could not name perfumed the air making it clean, beautiful, warm—promising long nights of leisure if only I allowed myself to fall on the warm sand and forget anything existed outside this place. I had never seen the ocean outside of books, had never lived farther than a two-mile radius around my once-prison and Jerry's home.

Growing up, there had been home and medical clinics, so many medical clinics and laboratories and testing centers, but never a forest or a park or an ocean. The beauty and vastness of the ocean knocked all thought out of my head, all fear from my limbs, and dropped to a whisper, the prickling warning that Gabriel had his own agenda, his own desires, and that I had no idea what those were.

In this place, as nature played a timeless symphony of color across the sky, as warm air caressed my skin and sunk its fingers through my hair, I let myself drop the burden of my own survival and just enjoy. I even suppressed the guilt that flourished at the thought of Henry. He couldn't be here and he was better off with Jerry than wherever I was.

Gabriel sat beside me. His perusal of me joined the thousand fingers of the wind, making my body flush and preen in appreciation. After the sun had set and millions of stars appeared with not a whisper of light to block the sky, he finally spoke. "This is St. Lucia as I remember it before electricity became so popular it outshone the stars."

"It's beautiful. Thank you for sharing it with me."

He shrugged, the corner of his mouth turned up the slightest bit. "Your blunders have bound us together. It is in my best interest to assure your safety and comfort, physical or otherwise."

"That's cryptic."

He laughed, a sound that rippled across me, sharp, but not unpleasant. My lips split to suck in more air. The temperature warmed, shifting with his mood and the smell of flowers underlying the ocean air intensified. "You'd better get used to it."

He stood, giving me a hand to help me stand with him while his face settled into a mask of blankness. I let him keep his secrets for now. I'd work on getting to them later, after I figured out other little things. Still, I couldn't resist. "I think you owe me more than that."

I didn't think it possible for moods to shift so quickly, but his face shuttered. The air that caressed my skin lost its warmth. His back rippled as though his wings fought to get out. I hugged myself and decided to do what I'd done my whole life when confronted with new people. I would pay attention, keep him calm and happy while I judged him for his actions, and then do whatever it took to protect myself and Henry.

Gabriel's right hand squeezed my wrist while the other opened and closed. Tension tightened his shoulders, his body poised for attack. "You are in a safe place for now and the drugs are fading from your system. I'm certain your captors don't expect you to be up for several hours given how many drugs they administered. Take whatever time you need to recover. Time moves more quickly in this dream than in reality. I am healing you for as long as you remain in this dream."

I couldn't tell him my location even if I wanted to, since I had no clue where I was. "Alonzo injected me with something that spread like a flash of ice through my veins. It affected my respiratory system and knocked me out in seconds." I waited for him to point out how he'd told me this would happen.

Gabriel stalked around me with the grace and menace of a large cat. He stopped his pacing in front of me, glaring down, challenging me. "I can't get to you, so I will teach you to kill him. He won't expect it. That's your greatest asset." His voice never wavered as he announced murder. He could have been talking about unwrapping a package of meat for dinner. I had to replay the words in my head a couple of times to make sure I heard him correctly.

I shifted back from him. "Did you suggest that I kill Alonzo?" At his nod, I took another step back. "I am *not* killing anyone."

Gabriel narrowed his gaze. "Do you think it's wrong to kill? That assassins are devils that forsake their souls for the sake of expediency?"

He stood frozen, unmoving, waiting for my answer. Nothing around me moved anymore. Even the breeze had fallen silent, stopped playing with my hair. I swallowed. "I didn't say that. I said *I'm* not killing anyone."

He smiled. "A diplomatic, if terrible response."

With all the attitude I could muster, I cocked my hip. "You'd better get used to it." His laugh this time reached across my psyche and made the energy inside me purr in time to his aura. It pleased me absurdly that he found me funny. I used my hair to hide my smile, and stepped back again. He stopped my backward progress by settling his hands on either side of my waist, and pulling me toward him. I twisted my head back to look up into his face.

"I don't think you quite grasp the gravity of this situation. You were injected with a liquid meant to incapacitate you, rob you of your strength and power. If I had not had a piece of my consciousness bound to you and your fate, I would have missed it. You would have been lost, alone, at his mercy. Alonzo is known to my kind. He hates demons, employs medieval torture methods, and always kills his victims after he is done breaking their minds." Gabriel pulled me closer. He leaned over me so that his breath warmed my neck. "I will not let you die."

His breath sent heat slithering from my neck down to my core. "I would rather die than kill again."

He whipped his upper body away from me while his hands held me still, our lower bodies too close for my comfort. Yet I didn't move back. "I need you to live, but you don't want to live badly enough. Let me change your mind."

He kissed me, not sweet, not promising, but rough and carnal, claiming me in a way I was just beginning to understand. He drank me in; his will suffused my every limb, washing away any objections I had. In return, he absorbed what I was, what he wanted. I would do anything to please him. I allowed his aura to pierce inside me, to rifle through my mind and memories, understanding by instinct what he was doing, and not caring.

I melted in Gabriel's embrace. I pressed my body against his trying to get as close to him as demonly possible. I wrapped my legs around him, my arms surrounded his neck. I kissed him back, slipping my tongue in his mouth and declaring war with it. I pressed myself against him, wanting to get closer, wanting to do away with every scrap of clothing or air or space in my way.

My skin itched for his. I felt his erection rub between my thighs and I pressed myself harder to him. His arms came around me and crushed me tighter. I wanted him inside me, around me, fused with me. I ran my hands down his torso and landed them on his pants. I'd never done this before, but figured out the mechanics. I fumbled with his top button.

He pulled away, his hands still attached to my waist, but holding me apart from his body. We both panted, our eyes locked together. I waited for him to rebuff me again.

He released me to cup my face. "You know incredible cruelty and yet possess the capacity to trust and forgive in spite of it. You need to live for yourself, for your brother, and for the piece of my psyche that is now tied to you. You will someday stand beside me. We can win many battles together. Don't ask me to let you die, to let that future die. I can't and I won't. I will do whatever it takes to convince you."

Breathless, I nodded and went back to working on his pants, but he cupped my hands within his and pulled them up to his lips.

He kissed my wrist, my palm, and my fingers. He seemed so earnest when he said, "That's not going to happen today."

I licked my lips, drawing his gaze. I confessed, "I want you."

He barked an amused laugh while he caressed my face, moving aside a tendril of hair the wind kept pushing onto my face. "That's hardly a good reason. Unfortunately, I don't know if you desire me because of the power I just poured through you or the bond. Either way, you can't trust your feelings where I'm concerned. The bond affects us both. I will push you to the brink of what is necessary to save you, but no further. You have my word."

I raised an eyebrow and waited for him to continue, swallowing the disappointment as his words sank in. He exhaled loudly while gently disentangling my hands from his shirt, stepping back and taking the scent of coffee and sugar and sweetness with him. Damn him, but I'd always think of this moment when I drank coffee. "You're almost healed now. When I finish, you'll wake up and you'll be in Alonzo's grip. We need to get you ready."

The mention of Alonzo sent a shot of acrid fear through me to chase away the pleasant sweetness of Gabriel's kiss. The crashing waves of the ocean no longer sounded like a song of peace, but rather a call to war to match the deadly expression on Gabriel's face. I touched my lips. "When you kissed me, you were in my head without my permission."

He didn't apologize or give any outward indication of how he felt about the intrusion. "I needed to know whether I could trust you. Your attraction to me, the bond, provided a helpful conduit for my power." He looked down and away from me. "I'm sorry I had to do that, but you're in danger and I don't have enough time to be polite."

I had endured too many indignities for this one to matter, but it hurt. "I thought I could trust you. Now you tell me I can't trust even my feelings where you're concerned."

He reached for me, but stopped short. "You can trust I will protect you now that I understand more about what you are."

"And what's that?"

"Innocent."

Maybe too innocent to survive. "What does that mean?"

"You didn't lie. Your bonding to me was an accident."

"What would you have done if it wasn't?"

He shrugged.

"Fine. I don't have time for whatever this is going on between us. Show me how to incapacitate him."

Did he look a bit guilty and unsure? Couldn't be. He pulled my hands into his. "Before we do that, you must understand what it means that we are bound. The attraction we feel is a part of the psychic bond you created when you reached out for my help and protection, and I provided it. It will help me keep you alive. It will help me teach you how to survive in our world, and when you are skillful enough and physically in touch, we can sever the bond safely and we won't feel this way anymore."

"How do you know it's just the bond?" I pulled my hands from his grasp, but he held me.

He put his hand on the side of my face, gently. I refused to turn my face closer to his touch, and watched him. "I've never been this attracted to a woman, this fast, without a psychic bond or *Persuasion* to help it along." He said persuasion like it was a filthy word. "I've never even met you and you don't have the experience I need in a partner. We are not meant for each other."

Too innocent to love.

I pushed away from his hands and his apparent kindness. I didn't even have a shroud of anger to soothe my bruised pride. Gabriel chased me and placed three fingers against the base of my neck. I swallowed, letting his warmth seep into my skin. Gabriel shifted his hand slightly, pushing into the circle at the base of my throat. Breathing got more difficult the harder he pressed. I could have stepped back, but I stayed rooted in place, looking him in the eye.

He smiled in approval. "This is the first lesson. You don't need to have more strength, you just need to use what you have more, and want to win the fight badly enough. If you can jam your nail and the pad of your finger into this spot, your target won't be able to breathe." Gabriel dropped his hand, allowing me to breathe once again.

I rubbed the hollow of my throat, where Gabriel had pressed. "Is that all he is to you, a target?"

"He is a direct threat to you and that makes him more, it makes him a man with the capacity to destroy something precious for the moment. It is my duty to ensure his destruction and your safety first."

"You mean you want me alive to break this bond thing. I'll bet it's painful if I die while still bound to you." I waited, stupidly hoping he would deny my claim.

"It would cripple me to see you die, but I'm good with pain. Place your hand here." He pointed to a spot on his chest.

I fought down a nervous giggle, sucked in yet another breath, and placed my hand on Gabriel's chest, caressed the muscles under my touch. He guided me to the spot at the hollow of his throat, placing my middle finger on it.

Gabriel commanded, "Push."

I bit my lip. "I don't want to hurt you."

"Push."

I pushed in small increments with the pad of my finger. Gabriel grabbed my hand and shifted it so that my nail sank into his trachea, leaving a tiny crescent-shaped bruise before I pulled my arm back.

"Again."

I didn't move to obey him. "I think I got it."

His anger surfaced like a flash fire. "You think you got it, but in a life or death situation, you need your body to know it, not just your mind, so you will do it again until I can't breathe, and only then will you release me. Is that understood?"

"No." *Why did I care if he thought me strong? Why didn't I pretend to be weak and pounce on him later? Why do I care if I hurt him? Stupid, stupid, Ginny. He told me not trust my feelings for him and still I do.*

Gabriel advanced on me, forcing my body back. When my back braced against a palm tree that had not been there before, he leaned down to whisper in my ear. "You can and you will, or I will make it my life's goal to hunt down Alonzo and your precious Jerry. I will gut him and torture him like an animal, and I will take great pleasure in doing so because you will be too dead to stop me. Ask me what I'd do with Henry?"

I swallowed. "You wouldn't."

"Ask me."

"You wouldn't hurt Henry, I know you wouldn't. You're too honorable." *Did I sound breathless?*

He smiled with absolutely no mirth. His voice dropped to a whisper of warning, his breath slithering fingers across my face and neck. "Do you *know* that or do you *feel* that? How could you possibly know what my honor demands?"

He hadn't touched me. He had not taken advantage of me so far. He was violent, yes, but he never hurt me without a reason. He was teaching me to protect myself, giving me strength rather than taking it from me. Everyone took from me, everyone except him. "I know."

He stepped back like I'd electrocuted him. Gray wings as large as me flashed behind him and disappeared, almost like an extension of his aura and his emotions. "To avenge what's under my protection, I'd kill a thousand humans without remorse. I would take my time carving their skin yet leave their faces intact so that no one doubts their identity, then I would parade my work before anyone who might someday think to hurt what I consider mine. If you have a problem with that, figure out how to protect yourself."

Looking at his glittering eyes, his aura's chaotic concern and vengeance telling me just how truthful his words had been. I should have been horrified at such a declaration, but what I felt was gratefulness and the first stirring of trust. He had said humans, and after ruffling through my memories, he knew Henry wasn't human. He would avenge me, but he wouldn't hurt those whom I truly loved.

I placed my hand on Gabriel's muscled chest, glided my fingers up the rift of muscle until I reached the hollow of his throat and pushed. Gabriel stood still, allowing my fingernail to sink into his skin. He stopped breathing for several seconds before he stepped back and pulled in air. "Good."

His praise made me feel like maybe I had a chance.

"Now let's try again."

I repeated the move a dozen times until I could find the hollow of his throat with my eyes closed, and use just the right amount of pressure to stop his breathing immediately. A large bruise flowered at the base of Gabriel's neck, and I could see a crescent-shaped burgundy scratch where I had pushed my nail repeatedly.

I reached up to run my hand over the wound. He put his hand over mine. "It will heal."

"I'm sorry I hurt you."

He only grunted his acceptance of my apology and kept working.

Gabriel showed me two ways to attack the wrist and the finger joints. He taught me a few ways to escape the most common ways men used to hold women down or to hurt them. He made me repeat each move at least ten times while he played the role of Alonzo.

After I got away from Gabriel's hold several times in practice, my lungs pulled in ocean air in tiny rapid breaths. My chest heaved and sweat coated every inch of my skin, making the thin film of the dress I wore stick to my skin uncomfortably. We'd been fighting for hours, but Gabriel seemed hardly winded. He had a preternatural fountain of energy. I wondered if with his help, someday, I could be half as deadly as he. If so, I could live my life as I pleased because no one would dare hurt me or Henry. I wanted that with the intensity of a river cutting through rock to reach the ocean.

Gabriel approached me and placed a warm hand around my neck in a touch that caressed and enticed. He used his hold to keep me immobile for his kiss. I made no move to fight him off, anticipating the gentle glide of his lips against mine, the duel of our tongues, the amazing connection I experienced every time our breaths intermingled. When he stepped back, I felt refreshed once again as though he'd fed me some of that boundless energy he seemed to possess.

"That's better. The physical touch helps ease the transfer of energy between us without altering the status quo of our bond. If you get in trouble, though, take whatever you need. We'll deal with the consequences later."

Maybe his kisses didn't strengthen the magical bond, but they bound me to him in a different way. "How do I take what I need?"

He ignored my attempt at flirting with double meaning. "The same way you did the first time."

"I don't like to think about that night."

He put his hand under my chin, lifting my face to his. The shade of his eyes matched the ocean behind him today. "There is no shame for you in surviving. You had no control. Besides, if you hadn't killed them I would have when I found them. You did them a favor."

"You're just trying to make me feel better." I studied his expression. The lines of his face stood out, the lips still glistened from my kiss. His gaze fixed on mine without a trace of a smile. Something shifted inside me at his words, at his utter honesty. "Good thing you didn't find them."

He smiled in approval then. "That's my girl."

That's all it took to make me feel like I wasn't alone. I hated the bond because I couldn't trust a damn thing that happened between me and Gabriel, but I was grateful that it would help me survive. Someday soon I'd have to suffer the pain of severing the bond, of going from having a mentor, a protector and an almost friend, to being alone again. But, for the moment, I smiled and flushed for Gabriel. I would worry about the consequences later. "Okay. I'm ready. Let's try again."

"Good. Now you know how to get him to back up enough so that you might be able to try something to hurt him or disable him. In the short time available to us, we'll go over some basics — breaking arms, collapsing tracheas, and gouging eyes." Gabriel's voice wrapped around the guttural sounds, an accent sneaking into his speech.

"Did you know your eyes gleam when you say that?"

He smiled. "That's because these are some of my favorite things."

I shook my head. "You are a bloody man."

He shrugged. "It is necessary, and you sound like you admire me for it." He studied my face.

I fought the shiver of want that spread throughout my body and the curves he seemed to caress with his gaze. "I do admire it, but be careful what you say. I might think you're a creepy old man."

He laughed. "In your case, I *am* a creepy old man."

He showed me the best way to gouge out Alonzo's eyes, how to collapse his trachea, and how to kick his privates and take him to the floor where I could gouge out his eyes or collapse his trachea. He finished his instruction with an arm-bar. Then, he showed me how to leverage the arm bar and hold onto it so I could use the power of my legs as I moved to break the arm.

After I had repeated each move another twelve times or so, he

84

stepped back. "I think you're ready. You've been with me for several hours. You'll wake up soon. How are you feeling?"

"I'm scared as hell."

Gabriel's hand reached out to cup my cheek, and I couldn't resist turning my face into his touch. "So honest, so exposed." He grabbed me and pulled me into the shelter of his body, then leaned down to kiss me. My body got lighter, my breath more even, my heartbeat matched his steady rate. When he withdrew, I was ready to tear down Alonzo with my bare hands. Aggression, strength, and power flowed through me as never before.

"What did you do?"

"I gave you my strength of body and mind. It will last for a little bit, a half hour at most, but it will help you through."

I caressed his face one more time. He grabbed my hand and held it as the ocean and the starry sky and Gabriel faded and were replaced by the back of Alonzo's limousine and the scent of alcohol, my own fear, and Alonzo's excitement.

Although my hands were tied in front of me, I held still and fought to keep my breath even despite Alonzo's hand stroking my leg. He did it so casually, not even bothering to look my way as he did it. *What a jackass.* I scanned my body for injuries. There were none. In fact, I felt great, if a little revolted by Alonzo's touch. My mind was clear of the anxiety that usually clogged it. I knew I felt fear, but didn't experience it with the same intensity I usually did. I could separate and act without any fear, guilt, or compunction to hinder me.

Alonzo drank from a glass of an amber liquid as he felt me up. Thank goodness for Gabriel's influence. I didn't have to fight to hide my instinctual cringe. Instead, I grabbed Alonzo's third and fourth fingers, twisting them in the wrong direction. I laughed at Alonzo's sudden intake of breath. High threshold for pain. Good to know. Alonzo tried to pull his hand back, exposing his body. I kicked his privates. He doubled over, letting loose a high yelp of pain. Alcohol splashed over the privacy shield as the glass tumbled to the floor. I enjoyed every grunt of pain my hits elicited, elated at the power that flowed through me.

I pulled my knee into Alonzo's face using my bound hands to grab his left shoulder and pull him down hard into the strike, breaking his nose. Alonzo's blood trickled down my calf, but I ignored the overwhelming urge to wipe anything of his from my person. I struck my elbow in the back of his neck, trying to render him unconscious.

Alonzo stumbled, but he didn't pass out. Instead, he reached up with his giant beefy hands and struck me across the cheek. I struggled to suck in enough breath. My eyes watered and my vision clouded as a thousand knives of pain radiated from my cheek. I lost track of Alonzo's movements for a few precious seconds. Gabriel's strength didn't teach me how to take a punch. Alonzo took advantage of the momentary shock. His body crushed me, his legs around my hips, his hands strangling me. I used all my strength to try to buck him from on top of me as I struggled to gulp enough breath to keep myself from passing out. If I passed out, game over.

Darkness ate at my vision. I couldn't let my life end like this. I couldn't let myself fall into the hands of another monster. With all my will, I called out to Gabriel. His strength infused my body with newfound energy that sifted through me like salt. Without air, I couldn't hold the energy he offered me. I couldn't even make my arms work the way I needed them to. My limbs grew heavy.

Then, something crashed against us and the car lurched, giving me much needed space. I sucked in great breaths, the oxygen flooding my body and giving me new strength. I was able to punch Alonzo's neck. It deflected somewhat from my intended target, but it was enough to get him off me. The car lurched yet again, giving my mind precious moments to clear. Another car sped beside us, hitting the limo at intervals. With a crash and a screech, my door dented toward me and the glass beside me shattered. Alonzo lunged at me once again. I grabbed a loose piece of glass from the window, ignoring the sting as it rubbed against my hand. I left myself open to another attack, but I needed to take care of him once and for all. The glass shattered in my grip into tiny useless fragments. Damn safety glass.

I spotted the crystal decanter Alonzo had been drinking from. I grabbed it and broke it against the side panel, leaving me with a sharp shard of high-end crystal. Alonzo's eyes tracked it as the crystal caught the moonlight. I tried to sink the shard into Alonzo's neck, but missed the mark and ended up with his shoulder instead. He loosened his hold around my neck and retreated, looking for something on the side-door pocket, probably his gun. I didn't have a lot of time. I went after him again, digging the crystal into his stomach and up toward his chest cavity. I didn't hit his heart. That was probably too far for the glass to reach, though I must have hit something. He started bleeding a lot, but he kept coming after me. His kicks and punches were a little slower, but they still hurt like hell. Finally, he found the gun and pointed it at me. Out of time and out of options, I plastered myself against the door opposite him and watched him, positioned to kick him if he came after me again. I had to get that gun off him. If he shot me, Gabriel might not be able to heal me before he restrained me for good. Alonzo wouldn't underestimate me twice.

The car lurched again, followed by a deafening crash jarring every bone in my body. My head bumped against the dividing glass, leaving me a bit disoriented. Alonzo grunted when his shoulder hit the same divider. He tried to shoot me, but his aim was off in the crash. The car flipped a couple times, throwing us both around, then it stopped with a loud screech. We landed upside down, Alonzo on top of me, the gun lost somewhere in the car. I hit my head again, leaving me groggy and stumbling. His blood oozed from the wound I'd caused, coating everything in bright shades of crimson and the scent of copper and gunpowder.

Alonzo's knee dug into my chest, holding me down. I pushed, the slippery blood making my movements awkward, my hands unable to get a good hold on him. I hated blood, its smell, its taste, its warmth. On the third try, I rolled him away from me. I pushed my hair off my face, leaving wet streaks of blood on my skin.

I scrambled around the car looking for the gun. Although he seemed out of it, Alonzo was doing the same thing. I found the gun stuck under a pile of broken safety glass in the far rear of the car. I scrambled to pick it up and pointed it at him.

He coughed, his eyelids drooping, his body swaying. I moved as far away from him as the small space would allow, pointing the gun at his forehead. I wanted to pull the trigger, but he didn't look like he had much fight left in him. Could I really shoot a defense-less man? Was that the type of person I had become?

I hesitated a moment too long. I knew I'd lost my chance when I heard Jerry's voice calling my name. I couldn't say I was sorry. I wasn't a cold-blooded murderer, not yet anyway.

CHAPTER
EIGHT

I had no idea what to do about the two men who promised to protect me but would kill each other if they ever met. I forced myself to gulp a large breath, trying to get my stomach under control as I looked over Jerry's Hummer. The scent of evergreens lining the walkways to Jerry's home mixed with the cold air helped to calm me. It would snow soon. I could taste it in the air.

The Hummer had been ruined. Big gashes and dents decorated the side where Jerry had rammed it against Alonzo's limo several times. Jerry had a few cuts and bruises that occurred when his body slammed against the steering wheel. I owed him a debt of gratitude, one I may never be able to repay. He had promised to keep me safe, and when I needed him, he came for me. I couldn't just tell Gabriel how to find him and hand Jerry over to him. I couldn't let Jerry get hurt when all he'd done so far is rescue me, twice.

Henry limped around the broken vehicle. He had refused to stay behind. I supported his arm as we turned toward the house, Jerry walking beside me. I didn't kill Alonzo, had chosen to endanger my brother in order to keep a bit of my humanity. And all for what, to prove a point? God, I was so screwed up, so confused. The longer I stayed near Jerry, the more confused I got.

An ambulance and a helicopter sounded in the distance. The sirens got closer, not farther away. "Aren't they supposed to take him to the hospital?" I spoke loudly due to the approaching siren and loud whirring.

"No. We can do more for him here. The Human Advancement Group head surgeon should be here in a few minutes." As if called by Jerry's words, a sleek black helicopter circled over the trees visible from Jerry's mansion. The paramedics in the ambulance wheeled Alonzo out and into the house, heading toward the forbidden wing.

I turned toward Jerry without letting go of Henry. "Is that what you keep in that wing, sick people?" I could have probably used a little less sarcasm in my voice, but at this point I was sick of being lied to and manipulated. Jerry wanted something from me and I wanted him to keep Alonzo away from me and Henry.

"Sometimes." Was that guilt I caught in his voice? If so, what could he mean?

Jerry kept his gaze on the paramedics preparing to save Alonzo's life. The look of concern on his face broke through my anger. I cleared my throat. "I'm sorry I had to hurt him. I know he's your friend, but he would have killed me."

Jerry turned toward me, compassion and empathy in his gaze, although I still couldn't sense what he felt. "I know you believe that. I'll check on you later." He patted my hand and left me standing on the lawn while he rushed to greet the helicopter landing in the front yard.

It was strange that Jerry would have such facilities in his home, but right about now, I was just grateful they might be able to undo the damage I'd done to Alonzo. Tomorrow, I'd think about the repercussions and figure out a way to get out of here, maybe steal some supplies for the house to keep us going until we figured something out.

Henry kept limping; he let go of me to try to walk on his own and screamed out. I rushed to his side to support his weight. It would take him at least a day to heal, maybe more. Then we'd leave.

"What are you doing trying to walk on that leg?" I looked at the paramedics hoping none of them decided to take a look at Henry and his magically healing leg, but they were all too busy trying to keep Alonzo alive. They rushed back and forth between the house, ambulance and helicopter getting supplies.

Henry shrugged and started tugging me toward the house. "The bullet went straight through. The rest is healing on its own. I guess being a demon has its perks, huh?"

I walked with him, leading him back toward his room, where I closed the door for some added privacy. "Don't say you're a demon so loudly."

Henry nodded. "It doesn't matter. I overheard Rick and Jessica complaining about their demon children. When I healed quicker than a superhero in a video game, I figured they didn't mean it metaphorically. I'm sure Jerry noticed, too. He's not stupid."

I wanted to ask him more about it, but I heard footsteps down the hallway. I didn't have time for this conversation now. I looked at my brother, making sure he understood I was serious. "Don't advertise that you're getting your powers early. Promise me, please. We will talk about this later. Just tell me, are you okay with it?" *Please, God, let him be okay.*

Henry nodded back, "I'm okay. We'll talk later." He sounded so sincere, I let it go until later when we were alone. At the moment, Jerry was approaching down the hallway.

Jerry's footsteps reached the door, followed by a knock.

"Come in," I called out.

Jerry opened the door. "Alonzo is in surgery. I have some time now. Can I walk you to your room?"

I hated to leave Henry behind, but Jerry seemed to have something important to discuss with me, so I hugged my brother, told him to keep his weight off that leg and left with Jerry.

Jerry helped support me as I stumbled through the halls toward my bedroom. Gabriel's strength had faded. I could walk, but the experience of fighting off Alonzo left me cold inside. Jerry's warmth helped, so I let him place his hand on my back and lead me toward my bedroom. When we walked through my door, he didn't stop. He kept guiding me until we stared at each other beside my bathroom mirror.

"You've been through a lot, let me help you get that thing off." There was nothing sensual in his touch today, at least not for me, as he peeled away my bloody torn dress. I put my hand up against the front, letting it gape behind me but still covering up a little bit. "I'll get you a new one to replace it."

The dress had seemed so beautiful that afternoon when I put it on. Now it was full of Alonzo's blood. "Thanks, but you don't need to do that. You've been more than kind. You rescued me, for God's sake." My voice broke a little. I turned away so he wouldn't see the tears threatening to spill. Despite everything, he'd kept his promise. He had come for me and that counted for a lot in my book.

He rubbed my bare arms and spoke above my ear. He seemed genuinely concerned. "What precisely did I rescue you from?"

I didn't look at him when I answered. "A fate worse than death or living, depending on your point of view." I couldn't confess I'd been about to murder Alonzo and he saved me from myself more than anything.

Jerry pursed his lips and nodded. "I didn't think he was capable of that. You are certainly beautiful, but we have a duty to control our baser urges, otherwise how are we different from the demons we pursue? I'm sorry you had to go through that."

I turned my back to him, then grabbed a bathrobe from the door and put it on, letting the dress drop away from me. Jerry didn't seem creepy, but I still felt weird being almost naked in front of him. "You pursue demons? Why?"

He turned sideways, took off his glasses, and rubbed them clean. "When we believe a demon to be dangerous, we take care of the problem."

My stomach clenched. I swallowed hard. I wouldn't panic, wouldn't throw up. I needed to be stronger than that. "What do you mean, you put them in a cage?"

Jerry cleared his throat. "Sometimes. Sometimes, if the demon is too powerful, we take stronger measures."

I rubbed the space above my chest, where it was suddenly harder to draw breath. I had to fill the awkward silence, but couldn't think of anything inane to say. "If demons are real, are angels real, too? What else is out there that I don't know about?"

"I don't know about angels. No one in our organization has ever met one, but I like to think they're real and they're on the side of humans, protecting us from the demons. I know vampires exist, but I've never encountered other creatures besides those, which doesn't mean they don't exist."

"Why do you keep saying demons are evil?"

His expression hardened. "They are. They live hundreds of years amongst humans, prey on them, and give nothing back."

"Prey? How?"

"Some pretended to be gods many centuries ago, some psychics and vampires fed on humans. Demons are too powerful, and power corrupts. My organization, the Human Advancement Group, is dedicated to serving humans, developing ways to protect ourselves from those who could manipulate or eradicate us."

I thought about it. I wanted to ask about my power. I wanted to share my fear that I might lose control, but what if Jerry feared me? Fear made people do strange things, even otherwise good people, so I shut my mouth. "Thank you, Jerry, for trusting me and protecting me, for giving me the benefit of the doubt."

Jerry looked at me. "My organization made you. You are our hope, our secret weapon against the demons. The least we owe you is some respect and a little trust."

I backed up, wrapping my arms around myself. "I don't want to be anything, especially not a weapon."

"You will be. You are part demon, part human. The H.A.G. made you in one of our laboratories long ago. Some wanted to destroy you, others saw an innocent child. They placed you with foster parents."

I pressed my finger into Jerry's chest, advanced on him, forcing him to back up until his back was a few inches from the wall behind him. "The H.A.G. grew me in a laboratory and put me up with possibly the worst human beings on the planet?"

Jerry stopped backing up. He looked me in the eye with his jaw set, his hands up to brace against me. "They are not the worst people on the planet. The worst are your people, the demons, the ones who live amongst us for hundreds of years, the ones who don't share the marvelous effects of their blood while humans die all around them, the ones who feed on our emotions and our blood. You're lucky we spared you from being raised amongst that."

"What do you mean by feed?"

"I meant feed. Demons who call themselves psychic or psy can feed on the emotions of others. Some have developed a taste for misery and they have no qualms in torturing humans to make a better meal of them."

"But I've never been hungry for emotions." Jerry's mouth

went slack, his face lost all its color and animation. Crap. I shouldn't compare myself to other demons in Jerry's presence.

To his credit, Jerry didn't lash out at me. He swallowed. "You're a psychic demon, but I think we succeeded in engineering that out of you. You should have most of the strength of your kind, but you shouldn't need to feed. If you do, if you feel hunger for emotions and find yourself absorbing it from those around you, I have medications to help you. I won't let you be like them."

Relieved I hadn't lost Jerry as an ally, my anger deflated even more. I thought of Gabriel and the first time I met him, how angry he seemed. I thought of how angry I had been only moments ago. I thought of myself ready and willing to shoot Alonzo even after I knew he was no longer a threat to me. "Are my people really that bad?"

Jerry placed his hands on my shoulders. His features softened with something akin to pity. "That and more. You don't want to know the atrocities I've witnessed." He smiled. "I wish I could tell you more now, but I can't. You'll find your place when the time comes."

No, I won't, I vowed to myself. I would choose my own path, neither human nor demon. For now, I needed to stick around to figure out what that path required and how to control my powers so that I could run when the time came. Jerry approached me from behind and folded me into his arms, caressing my hair. "Don't worry, Ginny. I know you're not evil and you deserve a say in your future. I'll protect you. I'll talk to Alonzo. I'm sure this is just one big cluster of misunderstandings."

I pushed him away. His embrace just seemed so wrong at this moment. "I think you should go."

Jerry's eyes widened in surprise. He didn't object, though. "Of course, you've been through so much. You need to rest." He kissed my forehead and stepped back. "I'll leave some tea out for you." He headed for the door to the bathroom, but stopped before closing it. "Don't leave this room. I'll post a guard outside to keep you safe, just until we sort this out."

He left the bathroom before I could reply. Nothing I said would have helped anyway.

I took a shower with the hottest water I could manage, letting it beat at me. I scrubbed my skin until all the blood was gone and kept going until my skin was red and sensitive. When I climbed out of the shower, Jerry was gone from my room. He left me a note in the mirror above the dresser and a cup of tea. The note said he'd come around later to check on me and that I should stay in my room, resting.

I put the note down, wrapped the towel around me and opened the bedroom door. The guard standing there turned toward me. "Can I help you?"

"No, thanks."

I locked the door behind me, blinking away the tears I would not shed. Now I'd also lost the trust of the person who'd promised me safety from Alonzo, maybe a few moments of normalcy. I didn't have the energy to ponder how to fix this mess, so I drank my tea and climbed into the bed alone in my room for the first time. I was so physically and emotionally exhausted, I fell asleep within minutes.

As the previous three times I'd fallen asleep, I visited the secret garden and Gabriel. I owed him big, but I didn't want to see him at the moment. I wasn't sure whether to protect myself and push him away, or plaster my body to his and swear my ever-lasting allegiance in this place with ever-shining sun and warmth.

He stood surrounded by red and white lilies, watching me with his arms crossed, his blue eyes gleaming, his face turned into a pleased smile. I didn't try to go to him right away. Gabriel made me feel safe, something new and more alluring than any drug. Yet he leached away my humanity, made me even more of a monster than I already was.

Gabriel sensed my mood because he made no move to get closer to me. "You survived. I'm glad." He modulated his voice, keeping it carefully neutral.

I turned away from him.

"You're not happy?"

I studied my surroundings and answered without looking back at him. "I'm happy to be alive. I owe you for that."

Gabriel approached, circled around me. He stopped a few feet in front of me without touching me. "But...."

"I feel like I lost something. I dug a piece of glass into Alonzo's chest. I was upset when it didn't pierce his heart. He's in surgery now and may not survive. I've killed two, maybe three people in less than three days. I should end this, but I can't. I should feel horrible, but instead all I want to do is hold you."

Gabriel smiled like he had a secret I wasn't privy to. "Only humans ever expect to hurt another and have no repercussions. It's a ridiculous notion. Someone hurts you, you crush them, you survive and make an example of them so no one else gets the idea to take their place. That's how the world really works whether you're demon or other. Your guardians trained you to feel bad about yourself so they could control you better. It's bullshit and it's about time you realized that." Gabriel placed his left index finger under my chin and used it to tilt my face up toward him. I didn't resist his touch or the caress of his other hand down my waist and my hip. "Tell me you understand."

I couldn't answer, couldn't tell him what he wanted to hear. When I opened my mouth to speak again, I got lost in his gaze, his irises a deep blue, so close to mine. His breath fanned across my lips. The demon inside me wanted him. I wanted to invite him to kiss me and do a whole lot more. Instead, I said, "What happened to me being too young for you?"

He stopped and smiled in a way that set off a line of volcanic eruptions through all my erotic zones. "I was being an idiot." He kissed me again and to my shame, I relented. I tasted his kiss while the man I'd hurt fought for his life.

When Gabriel pulled back slightly, so did I. The bond was working on both of us and I hated that some metaphysical thing controlled my actions, I hated he wouldn't want me if it wasn't for the stupid bond. "I need to go back. I can't stay here with you."

Gabriel's gaze swept up and down my body. I looked down to realize I was naked. Naked dreams were hardly news, but I stood naked in front of Gabriel and he's more than a dream. I covered myself as best I could and he laughed. His laugh was infectious and free. It stole all the lethal menace from him, turned his aura the same electric blue of his eyes and, impossibly, made him even more attractive.

I stood before him, feeling even more vulnerable than before. Gabriel swallowed his laugh, mirth still dancing in his eyes. He unbuttoned his shirt, making me clench in anticipation. His nostrils flared and he watched me as he slowly stripped his shirt off for me.

When he removed it, he revealed a sculpted chest and scarred shoulders that stole my breath and my concentration for a second. He approached me and wrapped his shirt around me, along with the scent of coffee and burnt sugar and male. Although grateful for the shirt, I was more than a bit disappointed he hadn't taken advantage of me. *Damn it. It's like I can't even control my own thoughts.*

He buttoned the shirt around me as I kept ogling him. The scars around his shoulders didn't take anything away from the beauty of his torso. I wanted to trace the contours of his muscles with my hands and started to do just that, powerless, a moth flying toward the sun.

Every time his fingers grazed my skin as he buttoned me up, a gnawing hunger deep inside me got stronger. When his hands lingered by my breasts, I slapped them away and finished buttoning the shirt myself. It fit like a dress. "Why didn't you tell me?"

Amusement still traced his features. "That you were naked?"

I nodded.

"At first, I wanted to know how badly you'd been hurt. I focused on that. Then, it was pretty funny how you kept talking without realizing it."

I had to admit, it would be funny if it weren't so mortifying. I couldn't look him in the eye anymore. I'd been feeling him up while fully naked. How easy it was to distract me from my responsibilities.

I cleared my throat. "Please, send me back."

He stepped back, folding his arms over his chest. "Why should I? You were drugged again. Alonzo couldn't have done it. When I find the person who drugged you, I'm going to take care of them."

His voice dropped to a low register such that I had to strain to hear him. The quiet menace chilled me. I scanned his face and aura looking for any trace that he was lying or exaggerating, but found none. "How do you know I was drugged?"

"I stopped fighting our bond. A piece of my mind attached to you. When you dream, I know everything about your body."

Holy crap. I didn't trust anyone, not even the man who had taught me to protect myself, to be in my head and my body. I'd been hurt too many times by the people who should have protected me. Why would Gabriel be any different? "Our bond can do that? How can we stop it?"

Gabriel shrugged. "We can't at this point. Maybe someday you'll have the skill to work with me and a witch to do it safely.

In the meantime, the stronger you become as a demon, the stronger our bond will be."

I backed away from him, wrapping my arms around myself. "There must be some way to stop this. I don't want to become more demon. I don't want any of this. And what will we do when this thing gets stronger? I can barely keep my hands off you now."

Gabriel shrugged. "There are worse fates than being stuck with you."

Incredulous, I advanced on him. "I'm glad you think so, but what about me? I'll be trading one prison for another. You can touch me, feel me, take me, no matter where I go. Every time I sleep, you're there."

His eyes narrowed. He advanced on me and pulled me up against him. I could feel every bump, including the one jutting into my belly. My traitorous body yearned to plaster itself to him, but I held still.

"Given your penchant for staying in dangerous situations, you're lucky to have me looking over you. If I could, I'd leave you to your fate, but our bond is beyond my control or yours. I will keep coming to this place every time you go to sleep. I will keep looking for you as long as I don't have you within arm's reach in the real world."

I hated how my body reacted to him. I hated how I didn't feel I had a choice. So many choices had been stolen from me already. "Fine. Under one condition."

He crossed his arms and waited.

I swallowed. "You have to leave me alone. Don't try to come for me."

He didn't say anything. Just kept waiting as though I hadn't said anything.

"Did you hear me?"

"I heard something, but I think it was just my imagination. No rational person would say what I think I heard, so I'm waiting for your real request."

"You heard right. I need you to promise not to come for me."

In a voice as serious as death itself, enunciating every syllable, Gabriel said, "I will always come for you. If I have to travel halfway across the planet, I will come for you. If I have to decimate an entire army, I will come for you. If I get my limbs sliced off and I have to crawl, I will come for you. That is non-negotiable."

I gaped at him. The man was temptation itself. What would it be like to have him watching over me, to not have to worry about anything, to leave all the hard choices up to him? If I allowed it, he would take over my life and I would go to my prison with a smile on my face. I couldn't allow that, and I couldn't allow him to hurt Jerry. My guardian wasn't my favorite person in the world but I didn't want him and Gabriel facing each other. One of them wouldn't survive, and I couldn't have that on my conscience.

"Promise me you won't fight Jerry, then."

He laughed. "Jerry works for the Human Advancement Group. He will kill me on sight. I won't make a promise that will put my life at risk, and yours. Try again."

I huffed at him. "What's the Human Advancement Group? Jerry mentioned them."

Gabriel's aura turned into black diamonds, sharp and foreboding. "The H.A.G. is our enemy. They hunt our kind and they use our blood for their benefit. What did Jerry say about them?"

I'd read the report about demon blood, but it still turned my stomach to have it confirmed. "He said that they made me in a laboratory."

"When you meet other demons, keep that information to yourself. They might decide to kill you for it." A breeze blew my curls around my face and Gabriel's expression softened. He reached out to touch me, but pulled back halfway through the movement.

Gabriel wouldn't' hurt me, but I still had to ask. "You would do that?"

"I wouldn't kill you or anyone else over an accident of birth, but not everyone feels the same." He ran his hand down my arm, comforting. His warmth seeped through my skin, leaving goose-bumps in his wake. "Demons are a complicated society; some are hardened by what we've had to do to survive through the centuries."

"Are you hardened?"

The color of his eyes shifted like an ice storm, mesmerizing me. I wanted to know his secrets, I wanted to know more about this man that I had bonded with, but could I trust he would be the same without the bond? *Probably not.* "I need some time, Gabriel. I can't just run off with you and despite what you say, Jerry helped me when I had nowhere else to go. I'm not the kind of woman who will betray him just because he's part of an organization, any more than you would murder me for an accident of birth. If you want to meet me, what can you promise me?"

"You really need to work on your negotiation skills. You have precious little to offer me."

Now that he mentioned it, I didn't think I had anything to offer him. I turned my face from him toward the great big tree shading a bench at the center of the garden. "I guess you won't find out where I am, then. Can I go home now? I'm tired and I need to think about everything that's happened. Otherwise, I'm going to sit here and wait until I die of old age."

Gabriel suppressed a smile, and I tried to not show how pleased it made me that I could make him smile.

"All right, I need your forgiveness."

All the warmth and comfort I had been feeling toward him vanished. "What did you do?"

Gabriel watched me. "As of right now, nothing. But, there will come a day when I will do something that you consider unforgivable. I need you to promise you will find a way to forgive me regardless, and in return, I'll do my best not to kill Jerry the moment I have the opportunity."

Gabriel was one of only three people I sort of trusted. I felt like my feet had grown roots into the ground. I couldn't move, couldn't think. How could I have been so stupid as to trust him so quickly? All the signs had been there. He'd freaking warned me. I counted my breaths, brought my heart rate down to a normal level and dry swallowed. "I need to leave, now."

"Not until you promise."

It was irrational to make such a promise, but I wanted to leave so badly, I figured I'd work it out when I got to that bridge. "I promise to try to forgive you, but I can't guarantee I'll succeed."

He nodded. "Very well."

Just like that, I was back in my room in Jerry's mansion, naked under the covers with a guard at my door. I jumped out of bed as though I'd never been drugged. I walked over to the tea and picked up the cup with my fingertips and sniffed so I could tell what the drugs smelled like in the future.

In the meantime, I had to make sure Henry was safe and deal with Jerry. I was running low on allies, so I really hoped he had a good reason to drug me, if he was the one to drug me.

CHAPTER
NINE

I put on the only dress remaining in my closet, a bright yellow sweater dress with white polka dots, no less. The dress hugged my curves and showed too much cleavage. It made me feel frilly and feminine, not ready to kick Jerry's butt the way I wanted to. Yet another thing to hold against him. I thought about Jerry as I pulled at a loose thread at the edge of the dress. *I'm not a pretty commodity to be dressed up and locked away.*

Jerry had rescued me and I would forever be grateful for that. When I first came here, I almost felt like I didn't have to be alone and on my guard all the time, like I'd found a friend, maybe more. But I'd been wrong, as usual. He'd drugged me, put a guard at my door. I wanted to wring his neck one moment and cry over the bed the next. Pushing away from the mirror, I headed for the window.

I'd get some answers just as soon as I got out of this room. I tried to open the window closest to my bed. Sealed. So was every other window in my bedroom, the gardens outside close but unreachable. Prettier than what I was used to, but still a prison.

I grabbed the chair from the reading nook in the corner of my room, and used it to try and break the window, but I might as well have been using a pillow for all the difference it made. I worked off some frustration swinging the heavy chair without leaving so much as a scratch on the glass surface. After I broke the chair and was left holding only the back of it, I admitted it was time to give up on that escape plan.

Unfortunately, I'd made enough of a racket to attract my guard. He stared at me from inside my bedroom door, smelling like he exercised in the morning and wore plenty of Axe. He should probably go easy on that.

His hazel eyes narrowed on me as he fingered the weapon in his shoulder holster, but he didn't draw it.

I guess a big guy like him doesn't need a weapon against a tiny girl like me. Machismo can get a man killed.

"Hold it right there." Even his voice was macho. Deep, rich, and baritone.

I assumed my best impression of a damsel in distress. "I'm sorry, but I don't like to be locked up. What woman does?"

The guy smirked. "I know what you are. Stop and put the chair down."

Did he think me an idiotic girl? I wasn't about to put down my only weapon. Instead, I rushed the guard with all the speed I could squeeze out of my body. The space between me and big macho guy blurred. I tackled him and brought the wood around, then the wood connected with the side of his head and the guy pitched forward like he'd been hit with a horse tranquilizer, weapon still in the holster.

I dropped the chair and stepped around him, closing the door behind me. Now, to get Henry.

I wiped my hands on the dress a few times as I navigated the halls. The scent of Old Spice and cigars and expensive cologne combined and wafted through the hallways before I reached

Henry's door, warning me to stay quiet and slow down. Another beefy macho guy stood outside Henry's room and I was all out of weapons. I started to backtrack toward my room, which was just a couple of corners from his. The farther I got, the more the air smelled like cigars and Jerry's cologne. Heavy footsteps approached. I couldn't go forward and I couldn't go back, so I held my ground and waited.

Jerry's voice echoed down the hallway, cursing lightly after opening a door, probably my bedroom. His steps quickened. When he rounded the corner, I pretended to be surprised to see him.

Jerry's thunderous expression promised trouble. "Hello, Ginny, what happened to your guard?"

I considered telling him a lie, but couldn't think of one and it wasn't my style anyway. "I hit him over the head with a chair and came looking for you. We need to talk about the drugs you put in my tea."

Jerry crossed his arms. "I drugged your tea so you could get some rest. If you have a problem with that, tough. You were safe as long as there was a guard looking over you. Did it occur to you to ask him to bring you to me?"

Crap, why didn't I think of that? I could be such an idiot sometimes, but I wasn't going to let guilt stop me from questioning Jerry.

Jerry didn't wait for an answer. "That's what I thought. You really need to stop making assumptions about my intentions. Come, let's see if you caused any damage. Branson is a good man. He doesn't deserve the headache you probably gave him."

A wave of guilt and inadequacy washed over me. I felt as low as the muck that grows in unseen corners of bathrooms. Still, unanswered questions pushed me to speak up. "What gives you the right to drug me? Why did you post a guard outside my room and what was in that tea?"

He looked at me, steady, sure, not a trace of the turmoil and the questions that I felt going through my mind. *I wish I could be that certain that I'm always right, that I knew what's going on, that I could trust my own instincts.*

"Not everyone in my organization wants you alive. Some may decide to take you by force. If that happens, I don't want you alone, asleep and vulnerable. I left a guard at your door in case you needed one, to protect you against other visitors to my home. As for drugging you, it is standard procedure at human hospitals to give sedatives to victims of trauma. I would do it for anyone I cared about. I decided to treat you the same way as anyone else under my care."

I recognized the bit about treating me the same as manipulation, but damn it, it still worked on me. "You could have asked."

Jerry nodded. "I could have."

How the heck do you argue with someone when they tell you you're right? "Is that an apology?"

He smiled. "Are you apologizing for hurting my guard?"

I dropped my head and tried to dredge up the indignation I'd felt moments before while I followed Jerry back to the spot where the guard still lay slumped on my room's white marble floor. Jerry got some ice out of the mini-fridge in my room and held it to the bump growing on the guard's skull.

He looked up at me. "Are you going to help?"

I bent down and picked up the man's legs while Jerry lifted his shoulders. I found him surprisingly light for his bulk, or maybe I was just getting stronger. Together, we lifted the unconscious man and laid him on my bed to recover.

Jerry sat beside him and glared at me while we waited for him to wake up.

"I really thought I was being held prisoner again. I panicked and I'm sorry, but if you want my trust, you have to give me yours."

Jerry didn't respond, which irked me, but I didn't say anything because he managed to make me feel guilty about hurting Branson. A few minutes later, when Branson started to stir, I heaved a sigh of relief. Jerry checked his eyes with a penlight, then suggested he go see the doctors for a concussion. Branson walked away on his own, so he couldn't have been too hurt.

I so didn't want to face Jerry right now and see the judgment there, but I did it anyway, and it was every bit as devastating as I had expected.

"In the future, try to think of the repercussions of your actions on others. With your penchant for hurting my friends and employees, I'll have to set up a permanent hospital."

I dry swallowed. What could I say to that? "I'm sorry about Branson, I really am."

"And Alonzo?"

A flush of heat pushed my shame aside enough that I could face Jerry head on. "What about Alonzo? He shot my brother, incapacitated you, kidnapped me, and shot me with some kind of tranquilizer. When I woke up, he was feeling me up, and then he attacked me. What do you expect me to do? Lie there and let him do whatever he wants to me?"

Jerry had the grace to flinch. "I'm sorry, Ginny. That's not what I meant. I know how it must seem to you, but you have to understand where Alonzo is coming from. He was afraid for me, that's all. I'm sure he would have just put you to sleep and kept you detained. Obviously, he didn't give you too much tranquilizer or you wouldn't have woken up so quickly. He never meant to hurt you."

I folded my arms. I was getting warmed up now. "Right. Kind of like you."

Jerry's face turned fire-truck red. A vein in his forehead pulsed with his anger, but at least, he kept his flexing fists at his side. "What are you implying?"

Shivers of dread scurried across my back. Some deep-buried part of me didn't want to make Jerry angry. I kept quiet while he waited for my response. A voice in my head urged me to tell him that he'd drugged me, that he had made me prisoner. But, what if he had good reasons for doing those things? What if I was overreacting because of Gabriel's influence? I really hated not being able to trust my feelings, not to be able to act on my gut.

Thank goodness, Jerry spared me the need to answer him and I was glad to let him. "I put a guard at your door for your own protection, and you went ahead and bashed the head of the man who was there to help you. I wonder if you'll do the same to me one day."

I rushed to reassure him. "If you don't betray me, I won't get confused. Rick and Jessica hurt me." I shivered, swallowing down the memories. "I don't give my trust easily. I'm not sure I would even if a good man came charging to my rescue in a black Hummer."

My gist seemed to placate Jerry's temper. He smiled a bit. "Well, it's an H2, actually."

Of course it was. I picked at another thread in my dress, leaving a frayed edge behind. "Why did you really drug me, Jerry?" I hated the pleading tone that sneaked into my voice.

He looked me straight in the eye. "You needed sleep and I didn't think you would get it any other way."

Well, I couldn't argue with that. I took a deep breath. "I've been drugged quite a bit. It bothers me that you drugged me without my permission. You could have just asked."

Jerry started massaging the back of my neck and shoulders. "I didn't realize it would cause you to panic. Please believe I had your best interest at heart."

Folded in the warmth of his arms, his hands caressing the back of my neck, I believed him. "I understand, but don't ever drug me again." I let a bit of threat slip into my voice.

Jerry mumbled into my hair. "I wouldn't do anything to lose you, Ginny. I promise I will keep you with me for the rest of my life if you let me."

I let myself take that as a reassurance and put my arms around him. I truly was a demon to be courting two men at the same time. I couldn't resist Gabriel, and I shouldn't resist Jerry. I just knew I'd end up heartbroken in the end.

Our moment was interrupted by the loud clearing of a throat. I looked to find a young man in nurse scrubs standing in the doorway. "Sir, Alonzo is stabilized and awake. He would like to see you now."

I couldn't stop myself before blurting out, "How is he awake?"

The nurse looked uncomfortable, but Jerry answered my question. "We've developed some drugs from our research into demons that helps humans heal faster. It's one of the more rewarding aspects of our work."

Right. The greater good in their work. I wondered who had suffered for it, against their will. Or maybe I was making assumptions. "Maybe I can help you sometime. I'm a quick study and I'd love to learn more about your work."

Jerry looked uncomfortable. "I don't think that will be necessary, but thank you for the offer. It means a lot."

He started walking toward Alonzo and I wanted to follow him, but the nurse stopped me, barring the door with his body.

"Excuse me. I would like to go."

The nurse looked at me the same way Alonzo had, as a piece of furniture making unwanted noise.

Jerry turned back toward us at my protest. "Let her come. I will make sure she behaves."

The nurse reluctantly stepped aside. I hurried to Jerry's side and walked through the halls into the forbidden wing. I took the opportunity to investigate everything since I didn't have to worry about being caught like the first time.

There were several rooms set up that could double as guest rooms or hospital rooms. Alonzo was in the largest at the end of a long hallway, overlooking Jerry's extensive gardens across from his office. The whole place had the look and feel of a clinic, but maybe it was the good kind—built to help people and not a place to run experiments on demons like me. I had to start thinking positive. Jerry had not done anything to make me think he was a monster, like the Blackwells.

I had to stop to take a breath before I entered Alonzo's room. The stink of ammonia and sanitizer mixed with Alonzo's grating laugh made my stomach clench. I refused to throw up. With effort, I pushed away the bad memories of Alonzo and the Blackwells. They'd done enough damage already. I wasn't going to let them ruin my future.

Alonzo had just made a joke to the staff. The laughter in their faces dropped away the minute I walked in. Alonzo nearly screamed. "What is *she* doing here?"

"She is here at my request. I'd like us all to talk while you're not holding a weapon so we can clear up any misunderstandings." Jerry responded with patience, absolutely no inflection evident in his voice. I found the effect more than a little unsettling.

I crossed my arms and waited for Alonzo to explain away his actions. Alonzo drew a deep breath. "Why would you bring the demon that left me in this condition to my sick room? Don't you have any respect?"

Jerry put his hands down in a placating gesture. "Calm down, Alonzo. I meant no disrespect. Ginny is here so we can get to the bottom of what happened. You haven't exactly behaved as a saint. You did leave me unconscious. If Henry hadn't called for help, I would still be passed out in the dining room."

Alonzo waved off Jerry's comment. "I didn't harm you. The pressure point I used wouldn't even give you a headache."

Jerry's voice didn't change, although he tapped his index finger against his leg, a nervous tic. "You still removed a guest from my home through the use of force. We don't do that to one another. We are better than that." *Great, it's not a problem to drug and kidnap a demon. It's only a problem if one is a guest in Jerry's home. I wasn't a living thing with rights to Alonzo, maybe not even to Jerry. I really needed to figure out how to take care of myself without Jerry or anyone else.*

"I thought we didn't choose the welfare of demons over that of our friends and superiors, either. You have been bewitched and all I have done is protect you, look out for your welfare and well-being."

"I can take care of my own welfare, thank you."

"No. I don't think you can. Your pet demon was in a car with me for less than four hours and managed to hit me and stab me with a slice of glass in the chest. She held a gun to my chest as I bled out. She would have shot me."

Jerry raised an eyebrow. "Why didn't she?" He turned toward me expectantly. "Tell me, Ginny, why didn't you shoot Alonzo?"

I swallowed, trying to get my thoughts together so I wouldn't screw this up. I still needed Jerry as an ally for the time being. "I didn't shoot him because I didn't want to. I just wanted him to stay away from me."

Jerry turned toward Alonzo with a triumphant smile. "I'm sure she only needed a few seconds to shoot you. She could have done it and yet, she didn't. Doesn't that mean she can rise above her birth?"

Alonzo harrumphed. "We are what we are born."

Sad thing was, I believed him, but I no longer cared if I was a demon by birth. Right or wrong, I deserved to live without persecution.

"If that is the case, we can hardly hold her accountable. And if it isn't, then she can be better than what she was born to be. Either way, she deserves our help. We are responsible for her birth, after all."

Alonzo studied his friend. I watched his aura, placid blue as before, but with the thinnest threat of guilt. Too bad I couldn't tell what caused that guilt. "I am willing to withhold judgment on what to do with her for the moment. She can stay here. Just, please stay away from her for a few days. See whether you feel the same. If you do, I'll reconsider my position. If you find I'm right, and she has you wrapped around her little finger...."

Jerry took a deep breath, visibly calming himself down. "I'm a grown man. I don't need you babysitting me."

"That thing can control emotions. Aren't you scared she's controlling you?"

Jerry smiled a secret smile. "I'm sure *she* isn't controlling me."

Alonzo narrowed his gaze at Jerry. I got the sense he didn't know about Jerry's immunity to me. Jerry didn't give him a chance to ask any questions about it. "Tell me what happened in the limousine. Did you drug her?"

Alonzo shrugged. "Of course I did. I'm not an idiot to make chitchat with a demon that can control emotions. I tranquilized her with a full dosage fit for a horse. Your pet is stronger than most. It should have been unconscious for at least ten hours and yet, she was up in less than four. I was drinking my whiskey when she attacked me, plunged a piece of glass from my own tumbler into my chest and grabbed the weapon I kept in the side door."

Jerry crossed his arms. "How did she get your weapon?"

"I took it out to defend myself, but was too weak to hold it after she hurt me."

Sure. Ignore the fact he intended to hurt me when he drew the weapon or while we're at it, let's ignore that he shot Henry.

Jerry took a deep breath, massaging his eyes. "You two need to both get over your issues." He turned to me, pointing. "I will protect you. Your argument and subsequent fight in the car was unnecessary. I would have come for you. I would have stopped it and gotten you back. Everything would have been okay if you had simply waited. You will refrain from hurting him or my staff while you are a guest in my home. If you have an issue, I will deal with it."

Alonzo smirked triumphantly. I wanted to put my foot in his face. Instead, I nodded at Jerry. He *had* come to rescue me from Alonzo and I didn't want to do anything to alienate him yet. "What about him?" I pointed at Alonzo.

Jerry smiled indulgently. "I'm getting to that." He turned to Alonzo. "Understand that Ginny is under my protection. She is not one of the demons who harmed you so long ago. She's innocent of those crimes. I will not let anything happen to her and I will restrain you if I believe it is necessary. If you value our friendship, please promise me you will not try to take her by force again."

With a resigned sigh, Alonzo said, "Fine. While we are both guests in your home, I promise not try to take her by force."

Jerry turned to me and held my hand between his. "He has never broken a promise. You will be safe for now."

Something told me that Alonzo would find a way to keep his promise and still force me out of the house. Jerry's trust in Alonzo's word was absolute, though. I could see that, so I'd have to figure out a way to protect myself and Henry.

With that thought in mind, I went to Henry's room to check on him. He opened the door for me and then limped to sit on his bed. Instead of sitting, he dropped down onto it, bouncing a couple of times with a grimace of pain. I had hoped he healed as I did, but it wasn't working out that way. Henry wasn't ready to leave and probably wouldn't be for a few days. I closed the door behind me and sat next to him, picking up an Xbox controller. "Looks like we'll be here for a while. Want to play a game?"

We played a racing game and laughed together all day, getting out only to grab food. We made the best of the moment of peace while the whole house was occupied with Alonzo. We created the memories that could sustain us when bad things happened, which they always did because that's the nature of life.

CHAPTER

TEN

The morning after my confrontation with Alonzo, I slept late. I felt like a rock was tied to every limb on my body, weighing it down, but I couldn't let the chemical weight and physical sloth keep me drowning in my pity party. I couldn't let them win; lie down while they did whatever they wanted with me, to me. I had more than myself to worry about. I also had Henry.

After literally dropping from my bed, I got up. The pillow top made the king-sized bed a little too high. The floor was white marble, really clinical, and cold and hard against me. Thank goodness my demon powers made it hard to bruise.

Padding to the bathroom, I shook out of the clothes I'd washed in the bathroom the night before to get some of the stiffness out of them. I didn't put on any underwear today since they had holes in them and it would embarrass me should Gabriel take me back to our garden and push off my jeans. *I really need to stop thinking about him. It wasn't right to picture him touching me, it wasn't right to think this way of two men. Wanting Gabriel could cost Jerry his life and me my humanity. You have to be better than this. Focus, Ginny. Get your hormones under control.* Just the thought of Gabriel made my whole body perk up, ready and alert for him.

I tamped down on that line of thought. I needed to make solutions happen in the real world. Still, I brushed my hair a little longer and applied the makeup Jerry had gotten me for Alonzo's dinner. I spent entirely too much time primping for a man I may or may not see today, and it was only morning. *I need to stop focusing on sexy demons and start focusing on taking care of myself.* Disgusted with myself, I washed the makeup off.

In Alonzo's limo, I had gotten a taste of what it was like to not be prey, and I wanted that with every fiber of my being. Until I escaped Jerry's estate, I was going to learn how to fight beyond the few moves Gabriel had shown me. I barged out of my room dressed in the jeans and T-shirt I'd worn the day I arrived at this place. The hallway outside my door sat empty save the Renaissance portraits Jerry favored, with not even a hint of sweat or male. Only the fading scent of jasmine lingered in the hallways. Strange. Jerry hadn't posted a guard at my door since I'd beaten Branson over the head, unless the new guard was female.

My stomach growled, sealing my decision to turn left toward the kitchen instead of right toward Henry's room. As my demon powers grew, so did my metabolism. No matter how much food I consumed, I still felt hungry.

Next time I saw Gabriel, I'd ask him about it. Or maybe Jerry would know something. While at it, I had to figure out why I got my powers at twenty, but Henry got his at sixteen. It didn't make any sense, unless different demons developed at different times.

The scent of jasmine followed me. I turned back toward the hallway to scan it for the source of the scent. Standing in the door of the room beside mine stood a woman in blue slacks, white starched shirt buttoned up to her throat, no jewelry, and a tablet clutched in her hand. Her aura seemed chaotic, with curiosity, fear and determination ruling over her emotions.

Her gaze followed me. I waved at her, trying to put her at ease enough to start a conversation, but she pursed her lips and looked down at her tablet. Weird. I got a few steps beyond her, then turned back to introduce myself in what I considered a friendly, non-psychotic way, but she just disappeared into her room. I winced when I heard the lock click into place. I really wanted to knock on the door, but the memory of the fear in the woman's aura stopped me. Maybe she feared demons, and I had no desire to confront her on an empty stomach.

When I got to the kitchen, yet another woman sat on a stool by the kitchen island. Glad for another opportunity to make a friend, I smiled and said, "Hello. I'm Ginny and I'm happy to meet you."

This woman looked a little less scared than the other with her golden hair tied in a ponytail, beige slacks, and white starched shirt. She, at least, had a couple of buttons undone and wore a thin gold chain of St. Jude, the patron saint of lost causes, my favorite saint. She smelled like baby powder. Maybe I did the whole thing wrong. It's not like I had a lot of practice. So I just talked to her the way I would Henry. "I'm sorry. I didn't mean to scare you."

Uncomfortable, the woman smiled weakly, but at least she didn't leave. Instead, she used her tablet to ignore me. Well, if it's okay for her to ignore me, then I could ignore her too. I started cooking for myself and Henry. I meant to surprise him with a tray of eggs and bacon and buttered toast and French fries. We could dip the fries in the eggs or we could use them as weak tiny swords before holding a mouth-tossing contest. I'd been getting good at those since moving here.

I finished cooking under the glaring gaze of my nameless companion. The knot of hunger in my stomach helped fight the unnerving effects of being scrutinized in silence. I made a dozen eggs, a pack of bacon, half a bag of French fries, coffee, and eight pieces of almost-burnt toast before I packed two trays and balanced them while nearly running out of the kitchen.

I stumbled when the weird lady got up behind me and headed in the same direction. Okay. Maybe I was being paranoid, so I slowed down. She slowed down with me.

Not paranoid. She really did follow me while taking notes on her tablet. I sped up until she had to run to keep up. I took the longest route possible, but she stayed behind me. The woman hadn't made any moves to hurt me. Giving up on escape, I turned the corner to Henry's room thinking if we were going to have it out, I needed to eat first. I hate having confrontations on an empty stomach.

Henry opened the door before I even knocked, taking the tray of food from my arms. The smell of bacon must have called to him. He sat down to eat on the floor by his bed without so much as a hello. I smelled baby powder coming from around the first turn in the hallway, telling me the weird woman with the St. Jude medallion hid just out of sight. I put down the tray with coffee and orange juice, then closed and locked Henry's door behind me. I went over to the radio to turn up the soft rock station.

I grabbed a piece of toast and worked hard to control the tremor of my voice. "You know, you didn't even say hello. With such a lack of manners, no wonder I can't make any friends around here."

Henry put down the bacon and swallowed, thankfully sparing me one of his worst habits. "You can't make friends anyway, and it has nothing to do with manners."

I rubbed the ache somewhere in the vicinity of my heart and plopped down on the carpet beside Henry, grabbing a piece of bacon off his plate. I figured it was okay since they were all on his plate.

"That's true. I don't have any friends besides you. What's wrong with you?"

I took one bite of bacon followed by a piece of bread dipped in egg yolk. I alternated between both, savoring each morsel.

Henry shrugged. "I don't get out much."

I sensed the sadness that followed his statement, but didn't comment. Time to drop the news about the stalkers. "You know there's people out there."

"I've heard rumors." He stuffed an entire egg into his mouth.

"I meant there are people following me around with tablets. If I didn't know better, I'd think they were taking notes on their little lab rats, otherwise known as us."

Henry choked on the last piece of his toast. I pounded his back, then handed him a glass of juice to wash the massive amount of food down. When he got himself back under control, he said, "What the hell?"

I popped another piece of bread into my mouth and chewed, the food eased my hunger, but not enough. I couldn't eat enough. Henry watched me and waited, making waving movements with his hands, telling me to hurry it up.

I kept my voice low, steady like a ticking clock. "On the way here, two women completely ignored my attempts at conversation while watching me closely. One followed me through the halls in circles until I came in here and is currently standing behind that door trying to listen to everything I say." We both turned as something thumped against the floor followed by a muted female curse, proving my statement was right on.

Henry took another gulp of orange juice. I watched his breathing even out, his face don a mask of control that didn't reach his eyes or his aura. "What are we going to do?"

I shrugged. "I'm going to go out there and figure out what's happening. You're going to stay here and play video games like a normal sixteen-year-old and pack."

Henry put a hand over mine. "I want to come with you."

"Absolutely not. Just get ready in case we have to leave. I want to trust Jerry, but we have to be ready in case he betrays us."

Henry studied me with more knowledge and understanding than should ever live in such a young body. "Okay. I'll stay here, I'll pack, but I want to see you before lunchtime or I'm coming to get you."

I agreed, I couldn't ask him to not worry. It would be like asking the sun to not set. I ate a few more pieces of toast and two more eggs, then made a lot of noise as I stacked the dishes back on the trays, giving my stalker enough time to scurry away. The watcher woman made more noise than I expected.

I figured out why when I stepped outside the door. I found not one, but two strangers in beige slacks and starched shirts scribbling notes. They were multiplying and freaking me out more than a little.

I extended one foot to pull the door closed behind me, delivering one last glare at my brother to keep him in his room. Both women followed me to the kitchen and hung back as I unloaded the dishes, leaving them for whomever to clean. I didn't have the patience to put dishes in the dishwasher right now. I rubbed my stomach. The hunger had lessened, but wasn't completely satisfied. I needed air, some space to think. Maybe this was the right moment for a walk.

On my way out of the kitchen, I stopped myself, took a deep calming breath. I looked straight at the woman who didn't have her head down; and who had only thin streaks of malice staining her aura. "Hello. I'm Ginny."

The girl with the St. Jude necklace extended her hand. "Matilda." The other girl cleared her throat, but didn't pull Matilda away or run screaming. It helped put me at ease that they weren't going to hurt me. After all, who smiles at their experiments or victims? Matilda's hand was warm and I noticed a thin thread of energy leaving the girl when I touched her, like I pulled it into myself. It relieved some of the hunger I still felt even after the large breakfast. I quickly dropped Matilda's hand, freaked out by it. Was I feeding?

"Would you like to walk with me?" I asked. "It's better than stalking, I assure you." I regretted my remark immediately as a bit of shame rushed through Matilda and she bit her lip.

"I'm sorry, but I was told not to follow you outside the house or into Jerry's work wing."

Unbelievable and more than a little concerning. "You were told to follow me around taking notes and then given limits."

Matilda looked down and wrung her hands. "Yes."

"Who gave you those limits?"

"Alonzo."

Of course, who else?

"Do you know why you can't follow me outside?"

Matilda shook her head, her blond ponytail bouncing with her movement. She seemed like a nice girl. A little weird, but nice. As I turned away, Matilda called after me. "Just be careful. You don't seem evil, and I have a weird feeling about all this."

"Take care of yourself. It was nice talking to you." I shared Matilda's bad feeling and didn't relish the idea of walking into Jerry's office to start screaming, which is what I wanted to do. First, though, I needed to think about what I could say that wouldn't make me sound like a paranoid psycho. Alonzo was having me monitored by a bunch of geeky scientist types. I alternated between laughing at the absurdity and marveling at the sheer genius of it. I rushed through the house with its pretty marble floors and its mahogany woods and colorful art that reminded me of exotic birds kept in cages until they didn't know how to fly.

I stepped outside the door, leaving the two women following me behind. The sun warmed my skin despite the cold weather and the fact I wasn't dressed for it. I didn't worry about that since I'd warm up as soon as I exercised, and the cold bothered me less than it used to. I gulped a big breath and sprinted without knowing how far Jerry would let me go without sounding the alarms.

I circled the garden. No one stopped me and as Matilda had predicted, no watchers followed, either. I ran in ever larger circles while I tried to figure out why Alonzo would leave the outside of the house unguarded. It made no sense whatsoever.

I eventually ran out of room to expand my circle and followed a little path that wound through the forest-like area behind Jerry's estate. The grounds were huge, several acres at least, plenty of space to run around without running away. Since it was cold, most of the trees were bare except for the evergreens, firs, and pines. Those perfumed the air and littered the running path with pinecones. The path wound in a circuit through the trees, to a little brook with an empty cabin beside it and then back toward the house and Jerry's gardens, which were surrounded with hanging vines and rose bushes that had dried up and lost their leaves in the cold. At the end of my fourth circuit, I stopped to stretch briefly. I turned to run around a fifth time, not even a little winded and loving the physical perks of being a demon.

"I'd rather you didn't make me run after you. I'd hate to scuff my shoes."

I turned. Jerry stared at me, wearing black shiny leather boots not fit for dirt, let alone the gravel surrounding his garden. Just the man I wanted to see, but later.

I turned to Jerry again, gritting my teeth in a semblance of a smile. *No need to be rude.* "Good morning. You're just the man I wanted to see."

Jerry turned his head sideways, studying me. His smile actually reached his eyes. "Does that mean you missed me?"

The display of emotion unsettled me. I was angry at Alonzo,

not Jerry, but still he watched me expectantly and I didn't want to disappoint. "I guess I did, a little bit."

Jerry moved toward me slowly, as though afraid I might bolt, and then encased my upper arms with his hands. The warmth of his touch penetrated through my sweat-damp shirt, like a brand. I squirmed, not liking the feeling at all. Then, he looked into my eyes with that gentle way of his and my discomfort vanished. This was Jerry, who had picked me up from a police station less than a week ago and given me a home, who had rammed a car into his friend's limo to get me, who had forgiven me every transgression. His only crime so far was being too naive to see Alonzo's true intent. I couldn't hold that against him and so, I settled down and accepted his touch, looked up into his face, and waited.

"You know, I was raised within the organization. I've spent a significant portion of my life hating your species, but I can't hate you. In you, I see such beauty, such innocence. In our ignorance, we may have performed a miracle. We made you a demon and raised you a human. You are one of us with the strength that they possess. I promised to protect you and I will, because to me you are precious."

His words were a mixed compliment, at best. *I lost my innocence a long time ago, and I'm not anyone's miracle, not even my own.* I never got to respond to him, though. My thoughts scattered when Jerry kissed me. This wasn't one of the tentative kisses he'd shared with me before. This was more carnal, more possessive, hotter. It wasn't "singe you with fire" hot like Gabriel's, but the kind of heat you get when you drink a cup of hot milk in winter. The kiss made me feel like I'd earned a reward of some sort. I was good; Jerry liked me, everything was right in the world, as it should be.

Some small part of me deep down screamed that it wasn't right, that I should be with Gabriel, with my kind, but I shushed it because Gabriel's kisses burned away the part of me that made me human, that knew right from wrong. When he kissed me, I lost all sense of shame, all sense of self-judgment and humanity. I needed to hold on to that humanity.

I hugged Jerry and he put his arms around me, just holding me. "You wanted to talk to me about something?"

I nodded and stepped out of his embrace. "I wanted to talk to you about a couple of things, actually. Can you get someone to teach me how to fight, and tell me why you let Alonzo put people around the house to watch me?"

Since I went ahead and said two completely unrelated things in the same sentence, I had no idea which surprised Jerry.

"The watchers are there to keep you safe."

Fingers of doubt loosened their hold on me, but didn't vanish. "How are a bunch of people following me like a lab rat going to make me safer?"

"I know Alonzo will keep his word, but if he doesn't, they'll alert me. It's a win-win. He gets to see you're not evil, and I get satisfaction that there's someone verifying your well-being."

His reasoning made sense. "Who are those women looking after me?"

"Some of our brightest researchers. I picked them myself for their open-mindedness and thoroughness." He seemed proud of himself, pleased perhaps that he had twisted Alonzo's little project.

"What are they studying?" I held my breath, hoping he would say something that wouldn't disappoint me, make me feel less than human. Perhaps I expected too much.

"You, they are studying a demon without any drugs or restraints. They are studying what you could be, if we engineered and raised you." He spoke fast, animated, excited. Jerry believed in his cause. I should be grateful it provided an ally who would protect me from the H.A.G., help me in walking the razor's edge between being demon and being human. But, all I felt was a vast chasm of disappointment eating up my hope for the future. With Jerry, I would always be other. He loved his cause more than he could ever love me. If he ever could love me. *And why do I want that anyway? I don't know if I could ever love him, so I guess we're even.*

"If that's the case, then why can't they follow me outside?"

Jerry shrugged and offered me the charming smile, the one that said he was about to say something I wouldn't like. "We have cameras for that and I thought you'd appreciate some space where Alonzo can't follow you. You get a little…defensive about him."

My gut churned. What he said made sense, but it felt off. Then again, I don't think the same way everyone else does, and what Jerry said was plausible. "I guess you're having a hard time trying to balance both my needs and Alonzo's."

"I'm grateful you understand that." Jerry wrapped me in his arms again. I didn't feel comforted, rather, I felt claustrophobic. Speaking into my hair, he said, "Both of you are challenging, although you're a heck of a lot more fun."

I stepped away from his hold and Jerry let me go, but placed a hand on my shoulders, his gaze flitting around my face. "Are we okay?"

I nodded. Why had I been so angry? Why did I always have to assume the worst? Alonzo would have a hard time kidnapping me again if his own people sounded the alarm as soon as he tried, but I still needed to know how to protect myself and Henry. I cleared my throat. "What about my other request?"

Jerry played with my hair. "What other request?"

"For training."

He let go of my hair. I held my breath, waiting for his response.

"I don't think you need it. I'll protect you as I have done so far."

What I really need is to not depend on your protection.

"Please, Jerry, I need this. I need to know that if you're knocked out on the dining room floor, I'll still be able to do something, maybe help you out."

Jerry stepped back from me, his face a mask of fury. "You are my ward and I have taken care of you. I will continue to do so. I can't have you learning to become more lethal, more scary. It will make you less safe, not more."

He stepped away from me, but turned around after taking a step. He extended his index finger in my direction. There was nothing romantic about his nearness, nothing to indicate he would ever kiss me again. His face held the kind of emotion that made me want to curl up into a ball and protect myself. But, he didn't hurt me. He never hurt me. With his fist opening and closing beside him, Jerry said, "Quite frankly, it rankles that after everything I've done for you, you trust me so little."

Jerry reminded me I was destitute when he found me with a teenager in tow and now I lived like a princess in a castle. All he asked is that I follow his rules and let him take care of me. How many times did I wish someone would take care of me growing up? Guilt rose in my mind like a giant wave, washing away my doubts and leaving me floundering to remember why I should be angry and scared, why I planned to run away as soon as Henry was healed. I had thought myself the one being hurt. I'd misinterpreted all the signs around me, as usual, where Jerry was concerned. I'd messed up and I wanted to set it right. I rushed to assure Jerry. "It's not that. I trust you. It's just that I feel so exposed, and I hate that feeling."

Jerry eased up a bit on the anger. "I don't want you to feel exposed. I'll tighten up security. I'll make sure you're not alone or unguarded. Would that make you feel better?"

No. Not really. I struggled to swallow my anger and my pride. I could see this was the best deal I could get at the moment from Jerry. He didn't want me to be more lethal. "Okay, Jerry. But, if

Alonzo tries anything and I survive, promise me you'll help get me trained."

Jerry nodded. "I promise."

Fat lot of good it would do me after Alonzo hurts me again. I'm going to have to get that training elsewhere and figure out how to not lose myself to my own demon nature and Gabriel. It would be so easy to lose myself in Gabriel, too easy.

Jerry kissed my forehead, and all traces of anger vanished. "Would you come inside with me?"

Even without my demon senses, I could tell there were layers to Jerry's invitation. There was a hopefulness in his voice, and then there was that kiss we'd just shared, but I didn't want to follow him. I wanted his protection and although nice, his kisses made me feel like I was payment for his continued protection. I didn't want to go there. "I think I need some space now."

Jerry stepped back slowly, dropping his hands behind his back, as though waiting for me to change my mind. But I wouldn't.

I ran three more circuits, navigated the labyrinth in the garden and the hallways mulling over the conversation, certain I missed something, but unable to put my finger on it. When I made it to my room, I went to the en suite bathroom and turned on the shower. My stomach growled again. I was always hungry now, more evidence of my demon attributes taking over my body and my mind, more each day. *God, if you're up there and you listen to demons, I could use some help. I'm bonded to a demon I crave like a drug. I'm living with a human who fears my kind. I have no idea how to take care of Henry or even myself on my own. I don't expect you to solve my problems, but I could use some guidance.* I waited for some kind of mystical answer that would tell me what to do, but none came. I'd have to figure things out on my own for now.

I hand-washed my clothes again, laid them on the towel

warmers to dry and inspected my naked body in the mirror. Not a single bruise remained from Rick's abuse or my fight with Alonzo or even the limo accident. Being a demon did have some benefits.

I got dressed in the ugly yellow dress again. I needed to get to Henry's room and tell him I was okay, but stopped when I heard a whirring noise coming from the corner where Jerry had placed my TV. It was off and I'd never set up the DVR for recording. I grabbed a chair and climbed on top of it to investigate the corner shelves filled with electronics. Not a speck of dust marked the area. Shelves high in the corner of a room should not be this spotless. I wondered at what kind of man kept staff that would bother with this level of detail. I had never even seen anyone entering or leaving my room. It just seemed unnatural.

The whirring started again, mechanical in nature. A human probably wouldn't have picked it apart from the background noise. I followed the sound to a tiny button-sized sphere and gasped at what I found.

A camera. Someone had placed a freaking camera in my bedroom.

ELEVEN

I stomped through the hallways toward Jerry's office. After finding the camera in my room, I'd checked Henry's and found a camera there, too. I ripped the thing from Henry's room to pieces and now carried what was left of it in a little sandwich bag. The secret wing was locked, but I used my considerable strength to pull the lock mechanism apart. Although I knew it was probably a mistake to show Jerry my strength, I just didn't care at that moment. I wanted to rip a lot more than a lock apart. The idiot mistook my caution for weakness. *Well, screw him and the Hummer he rode in on.*

As I approached the office, I heard Alonzo's voice from within joining the soft cadence of Jerry's speech. Alonzo and I were currently at a standstill. No matter how angry, I couldn't just barge into Jerry's office with Alonzo there. He would just use my outburst to take away the headway I'd made with Jerry, and I'd be damned if I gave that old man the upper hand, so I stopped outside the office to take a few breaths and calm myself down.

When my heart rate came down a few notches and I felt like I could think before I said something regretful, I knocked on the door and entered. "Can I talk to you?"

Jerry smiled at me with warmth. He approached me, placed a hand on my back, leading me to a plush leather chair beside Alonzo. His touch didn't make my hunger any worse and I was grateful he was a blank slate to my demon senses. "Please, sit down. Alonzo and I are almost done. I'll be with you in a minute."

I resisted his guidance and stepped back toward the door. Jerry let me be and sat at his desk again. He seemed at home in his study, filled with dark woods and with books lining the walls. An artificial fire crackled on one side beneath a mantel filled with statues in various styles. They looked like they came from different cultures, several Madonnas, ballerinas and milkmaids, eggs, carved females in crystal or porcelain or wood. I studied the art, turning my back to Alonzo's scowl of disapproval while I waited.

I couldn't help but feel menace coming from him and I relished it, soaked it up like a glass of warm milk. Alonzo's nearness made my psychic hunger worse. A dark part of me wanted to grab hold of him and pull at all of his anger and fear and loathing, drink it down and gorge myself. I resisted the urge, stepping farther away from him and slipping my hand into my jeans. I fingered the folding knife I kept inside my left jeans pocket while Jerry sipped fragrant amber alcohol, whiskey I think, across the table from Alonzo.

Alonzo recovered miraculously fast, using treatments developed by H.A.G. and probably a little demon blood. Considering how much the man ate, he probably had been consuming demon blood even before the accident. It would certainly explain a lot. Maybe it was my blood running through his veins making him heal so fast. Maybe it was someone else's, and the sad part was, that bothered me more. I could handle what I had suffered. I deserved that and more, but it seemed wrong to let him sip whiskey and smoke cigars off the suffering of other demons like me, or Gabriel.

I shut down that train of thought. Gabriel led my mind along paths I'd rather not travel. He made my synapses misfire and brought to life a deep part of me that wanted to fight and lash out at the world, that didn't care who got hurt in the process. I couldn't afford that. In my life I had committed few sins, but biggies. If I spent the rest of my life living like Mother Theresa, I still wouldn't make up for it all and I was deathly afraid of divine retribution.

Still caressing the knife in my pocket, I closed my eyes and prayed silently to the powers that be. *God, if you're listening, what do I have to do to keep them all safe? I'll do anything. I'll walk out of this room without stabbing Alonzo in the heart again. I will do what I'm supposed to. I'll be Jerry's girlfriend. I will forgive Alonzo for trying to kidnap me. I will live and let live. I'll be perfect if only you don't take my sins out on my loved ones. Please, all I want is for Henry to live a good life, for Jerry and Gabriel to not kill each other, for them both to die in their beds of old age.* Who was I kidding? God wouldn't listen to the likes of me. Still, when Alonzo got up to leave, I dropped my hold on the knife and put both hands in plain view on the baggie I carried.

On his way out, Alonzo let his arm rub against the side of my breast. He did it in such a way that it looked like an accident— nothing to notice—but his wink gave it away. I pretended to be startled and pulled my hand behind me to remove the temptation of stabbing him. In my haste, I dropped the bag containing the evidence of cameras in my room. Ever the gentlemen in Jerry's presence, Alonzo kept walking out the door.

I bent down to pick up the bag, fully aware of Jerry's focus on my breasts, the hitch of his breath, the appreciation of his smile. He didn't even look at the plastic container. I sat down, folding my legs at the ankles, smoothing my dress, my face forcibly relaxed, not showing any of the loathing I had for Alonzo. I shifted so that I hid the small bulge in my pocket from Jerry.

I didn't bother exchanging pleasantries. Jerry was not going to sweet talk me out of this. I took the little baggie and dropped the contents all over his desk. "What the heck are cameras doing in mine and Henry's bedrooms?"

His eyes widened, and his lips thinned for a moment before he caught himself and a smooth mask of nothing slid over his face. He ran his hand down the front of his lapel, as though smoothing it. "Can you show me where you found these?"

I expected a lot of things: a little anger, a flat out denial, righteous indignation, but none of them was a straightforward question. It defused all of the steam I'd built up for the confrontation I expected. Instead of saying the speech about privacy and boundaries I had prepared, I heard myself say, "Let me show you" with such pleasant tones I might have been discussing sunny May weather.

Jerry followed me a little too closely, the scent of cigars and cologne he always carried surrounded me. He made no effort to talk to me as we navigated the hallways of his mansion. No matter how fast I walked, short of running, he was right there beside me, and I was not going to run. When I reached my room, Jerry stepped around me and opened the door himself. He stood in the center of the room, an eyebrow raised as if questioning my sanity. I wiped the smug look off his face when I pulled a chair, climbed on top of it, pinched the cables and the camera mount between two fingers and pulled, ripping them from the wall, along with a bit of sheet rock.

Maybe I didn't need to show off my strength, but the moment of shock before he made his face a placid mask again gave me a small thrill of pleasure. He inspected the tiny device and then asked, "How did you find it?"

"I heard it whirring, so I searched for it."

Jerry nodded. He didn't say anything else.

As he turned to leave, still holding the camera, I got up the nerve to ask, "Did you do it? Did you put that thing in my room?"

He smiled sadly. "If you believe that, you're getting paranoid. Take your pills and take a nap. You'll feel much better."

And with that, he turned the winding mechanism of my mind to spin all evening trying to figure out what the heck had happened. Was it a denial? Was it an admission? Was he just deflecting the question? I had no freaking clue, and it both drove me wild and drained me. I needed to sleep, but I didn't want to because I wasn't ready to face Gabriel. So where did that leave me?

Exhausted and frustrated, that's where. I tried to spend a few minutes with Henry playing video games but I kept getting distracted by my own inner thoughts so after an hour or so, I went to the kitchen in search of Mr. Bartholomew. Alonzo was nowhere near there and Mr. Bartholomew wasn't in the kitchen. Matilda followed me around today, which reminded me yet again of why I was angry at Jerry.

I made myself a peanut butter and jelly sandwich with a glass of milk. When that didn't fill me, I made another and another until I had put away six of them. Matilda didn't say anything about my hunger, but I did notice the curiosity in her aura. I wanted to pull at it, eat some of her emotions – the curiosity, the compassion, the love that sometimes flittered across her aura. The love coincided with a small smile, like she thought of something funny. I wanted that so badly for myself, I took a step toward her. I extended my hand, pulling a small delicious thread of it to me, tasting her.

Her taste changed as I pulled. The smell of baby powder mixed with anxiety as I got closer. The scent was enough to shock some sense into me. Without saying a word, I turned and almost ran out of there toward the library, looking for a distraction. Thankfully, I didn't find anyone in my path.

In the library, I warmed my hands on the fire Jerry always kept running. I felt feverish, as though the cold and hunger had become a part me, fusing to my bones. I wanted nothing more than to hide but I really needed something to keep my mind from Matilda's taste. I picked up a romance novel, a Regency about a Scottish man and a runaway bride, then headed to my room. I avoided talking to Matilda or even looking at her. When I got to my room, I locked the door behind me and settled under the covers to read.

I couldn't retain what I read. After reading the same chapter five times I put it down and stared at that damned pill bottle Jerry sent earlier. It was filled with pills that would supposedly suppress my demon side, maybe suppress the rising hunger that food couldn't satisfy. Jerry had said psychic demons needed to feed. I didn't want to feed. Jerry hadn't mentioned the subject again, but he'd had the pills delivered. He must have noticed my eating habits or maybe something else. Regardless, I was grateful to have a choice, a promise of relief, if I could just trust Jerry for a little while.

I stared at the tiny pill bottle long enough for the writing on it to become fuzzy. If I took it, it meant I trusted Jerry and I wanted to trust him. I didn't want to be a paranoid demon who found cameras in my bedroom. I wanted to be someone who *could* trust. Funny thing about trust—sometimes you force yourself to jump off a cliff because you want to believe this time will be different.

I grabbed the pill bottle and dry swallowed one of the pills before I changed my mind. Sleep came within a few minutes after that. There was no Gabriel, no dreams of any kind, just nothingness.

In the morning, I awoke well rested and more than a little sad.

I got exactly what I wanted, but it would take some getting used to.

CHAPTER
TWELVE

I struggled to keep my eyes focused on my romance novel as the bed shifted and Henry shouted triumphantly. He seemed healed up, ready to leave so why wasn't I packing? It was the right thing to do, but Henry and I had enjoyed the last few days and I was afraid of what lay outside this house in a world full of humans and human emotions. So I procrastinated and I needed to stop that.

Henry jumped up on the bed and pumped his fists. Definitely healed. I put my book down, and leaned back on the pillows, savoring the look of joy on my brother's face. He seemed to fit in this place. He'd even gained a little weight, his bones didn't protrude as much, and once in a while after a hard day of gaming, he smiled and laughed and celebrated. His bed was a queen-size with pillow top, a green bedspread and surrounded by signed posters of various sports stars. Henry never got a chance to watch sports, but Jerry had decorated the room for a typical teenage male. Henry loved the room, not just the video games, which he had been playing all day and most of the night. The clock on the bedside table marked nine in the evening, the twelfth hour of game play for today. I needed to go to bed soon, but I had only slept in my room once since getting here. I didn't want to leave Henry alone and unprotected, at least not while Alonzo was alive. And I didn't want to waste these few days of calm and games. Jerry had left us alone for the few days since Alonzo got hurt and I avoided walking around since the watchers creeped me out. Henry and I had huddled in this room and ignored the world, happy to be ignored in return.

I started arranging pillows and blankets on the carpeted floor in what was becoming my nighttime ritual. Henry had offered the bed many times, but I simply waited him out until he gave up on the idea. I wanted him to enjoy this room and the luxuries it offered. He really liked the space. He took as much care of it as he did his video games, most of the time. After I talked to him about the coke bottles, he started to keep his bedroom immaculate and sprayed eucalyptus air freshener every few hours. The scent soothed the headache that started two days ago when I started taking Jerry's pills. At least, I didn't feel the disturbing psychic hunger. As side effects went, a headache wasn't too bad. I had to make sure to take the rest of the pills with me when we left. They could help me keep control of my abilities around Henry, especially if we ended up in a city with big crowds.

Henry punched my arm in commiseration. "Did you see that? I kicked GTA ass."

I rubbed my suddenly sore arm. Ever since I'd taken the pills two nights ago, I bruised a lot more easily.

Henry looked at me quizzically. "Are you okay?"

I cleared my throat, folding the corner of the page and putting the book away. "Yes, I'm fine. I'm just a tiny bit disturbed by my little brother's cursing and I have no idea what GTA stands for." From what I'd seen, it was full of guns, cars, and pornographic images, a sixteen-year-old boy's dream. Henry loved it, even though he was an otherwise gentle soul. The games provided a much-needed outlet.

"Fine. I kicked major Grand Theft Auto butt. Take that, suckers."

I laughed at Henry's exuberance and hugged him.

Crack!

Crack! Crack!

Crack!

I released Henry, annoyed at the gunshot sounds. "Seriously, Henry. Can you put that thing down for one moment and hug me back?"

The hitch of Henry's breath sent a sliver of unease through my mind. "I did put it down. That sound isn't coming from the game."

Instinctively, I pushed him behind the bed, away from the windows, ignoring the slight tremor in his voice and my own. "Stay here." I approached the window to investigate further, knowing from previous experience they were made of bulletproof glass. My senses weren't much beyond human with the pills, so I had to strain my sight and hearing to figure out what the heck was going on outside.

The moon shone over the labyrinth of Jerry's garden just as it always did. I heard nothing out of the ordinary, just running water from the fountain over the pool to the right.

Crack!

I yelped at the gunshot, but got myself under control. Light flashed behind Jerry's azalea bush, highlighting a man jumping clear across the width of the pool. Impossible for a human. My thoughts raced. *Has Gabriel found me? Will he be angry at me for abandoning our shared dreams? Would he hurt Henry or Jerry? What if it isn't him? What if it's someone else?*

Outside, shadows moved so fast I couldn't count them. I pulled the curtains closed, stepped back from the window, praying I didn't give away our position through the movement. I had a sense of foreboding that the people outside were no friends of ours. It wasn't an absolute knowing like what I sensed before taking the pills, but more mild, a whisper in the wind. Maybe it was Gabriel, but something didn't feel right.

Swallowing down my fear, I burst into motion, turning off the lights, locking the door. I then joined Henry beside the bed to worry and wait. *God, I hate waiting. I hate not knowing what to do, but most of all, I hate being powerless. If we get out of this alive, I'm flushing those damn pills.*

I dug into the pocket of the jeans I wore, checking my switch-blade knife. I then pulled up Jerry's mattress and took out the hunting knife I had hidden. I slipped the switchblade back into my jeans while keeping the hunting knife in my hand. "Henry, I need you to hide in the closet."

Henry ignored me, looking at me as though I'd grown two heads, or pulled a knife as big as my forearm out from beneath the bed, glad I had had the foresight to steal it from Jerry's weapons room. "Do you seriously believe I'm going to hide in the closet while my big sister takes care of business? I don't think so."

"I'm your big sister and I've always taken care of you."

He snorted. "Look where that's gotten us."

I didn't have time to argue or explore the hurt that bloomed at his comment, so I did the next best thing, act. "Fine. Barricade the door with anything you can find. There's people outside with freaking guns and I don't think they're friends."

Gunfire sprayed the house. I pulled Henry to the floor and waited. The bullets bounced off the windowpane leaving spider-webs to mark where they'd hit, visible from the very top where the curtains gapped. I heard the sound of glass cracking but not breaking. I had no idea how long the glass would hold, but was thankful for Jerry's paranoia in having it installed.

I looked to Henry, crouched beside me with his eyes closed, his breathing labored. I realized if those whatever-they-were came through the doors, I couldn't protect him because I'd brought a knife to a gunfight. Not my brightest moment. I would have had a better chance to protect him with my demon power, if I had a demon power. I cursed my decision to take the pills yet again.

Crack!

Another ping hit the glass. I grabbed Henry's hand and pulled him into the bathroom. He wouldn't let go of my hand once we were inside it. A tingle of energy crept up my arm and I pulled away from him, not sure what caused it. I opened my mouth to ask, but he cut me off.

"You're not going out there without me. Either we go out together, or we stay here together." The determined glint in his eye told me it wouldn't do me any good to argue with him, so I settled beside him to wait.

I waited, holding unto the knife until the design on the hilt had imprinted onto the skin of my hand, listening for the results of whatever conflict played outside, counting breaths to mark the time.

After one thousand breaths, gunshots led to shouts, then grunts, then dead quiet.

Fifty more breaths.

Shouts and orders rang through the night. I focused on the curlicues of my hunting knife to help me vanish the dread that I might soon see Jerry's body bleeding at Gabriel's feet and the disturbing hope that I'd glimpse Alonzo facedown in the pool lifeless with a little cigar floating beside him. *Okay, that wasn't a nice thought.*

One hundred breaths.

Two hundred.

The air stank of sulfur, acrid and awful, intermingled with the screams of pain. With every grunt, I grabbed the knife tighter and prayed. *God, please protect us. I know we're demons, but please don't forsake us now.*

Another thirty breaths.

A single shot, followed by more than I could count. An execution?

Twenty breaths.

Fifty.

Despite my prior reticence, I would have given my humanity for the certainty that I could keep my brother safe, that I could do more than hide in this bathroom while men fought for ownership of me outside, and who was I kidding? They all wanted me for their own reasons. *I was so stupid to have taken those pills. I would rather deal with demon hunger than this damned helplessness.* The anger I felt at myself helped me deal with the terror, and I held onto it like a lifeline.

Two hundred and fifty breaths.

I lost feeling in my hand and the knife I gripped within it. Were the attackers my friends or enemies, or both? I prayed that Gabriel had nothing to do with it, that he was somewhere far away safe and maybe a tad bit angry, but alive and not planning Jerry's death.

Eight hundred and seventy-three breaths.

My hold on the knife slackened. My muscles cramped, shook. I fought to rise above it, maintain my hold on the weapon, stay crouched beneath the level of the windows so that I could jump at anyone who walked through the bathroom door.

Footsteps echoed through the hallways, tightening the band around my chest, adding weight to the dread in my stomach. Adrenaline had drained away, leaving me to experience all the aches that had accumulated during the long minutes crouched on the cold bathroom floor awaiting our fates. I tightened my grip and kept my eyes fixated on the door handle.

The footsteps stopped, the locked handle vibrated. Through the space beneath the door, drifted the odor of male sweat, whiskey, cigars, expensive cologne, and gunpowder. The lock jiggled and stopped resisting the pressure being placed upon it, fighting valiantly for just a few more seconds until it couldn't fight anymore and the mechanism broke.

I wasn't sure whom I wanted to see. The door swung inward. The light showed manicured hands with a few scratches, followed by blond hair and dorky glasses. I didn't feel relieved to see Jerry standing there instead of a faceless attacker. In fact, I felt nothing.

Jerry rushed to me, running his hands over my body, presumably looking for injuries. "Are you okay? Did anything hurt you? They came so unexpectedly. Alonzo and I were caught in the crossfire and I couldn't get to you."

I grabbed his hand and held it. The gesture seemed to set him more at ease than my words. "I'm okay. I'm more resilient than you might think."

"I'm not so sure. I don't know how strong you are anymore."

I couldn't bring myself to respond to him. I couldn't feel much of anything except tired now that the fear started to drain, leaving behind a strange lethargy and numbness. "Are we safe now? What happened?"

Jerry didn't answer right away. He ran his thumb over the back of my hand while he thought about his words. The movement served to soothe me too. Eventually, he said, "For now, we're okay. We need to find a safe place before they regroup. We had a vampire attack, but something about their attack doesn't seem right. I think they found out about you. They went straight for this room. Did you talk to someone, send a signal?" He looked at me suspiciously.

I pulled my hand away from him and rubbed my chest. I couldn't have given away my location to Gabriel, since I had only a vague idea of where we now lived. Jerry had made sure of that, and I hadn't pushed for fear I would betray him. The way he looked at me made me think maybe he didn't deserve my loyalty. Miffed, I blurted, "How would I reach anyone? We have no phones or friends outside. You've kept us in this house with watchers following our every move. I have only gone to the kitchen and back in the last twelve hours and we stayed here during the whole attack, waiting for you. Could it have been one of your staff?"

Jerry rubbed his eyes, his shoulders dropping. "Perhaps it was one of them. I'll have everyone checked, especially the new staff hired for Alonzo's stay. We need to find out how vampires found this place within a week of me having you. Unfortunately, none survived our guards."

So he thought someone betrayed him. I didn't know how to reassure him, and I needed to for my own sake. It wouldn't do to have a paranoid Jerry making calls about my safety. "What are we going to do now? We can't stay here."

A shadow behind Jerry combined with the metallic scent of blood announced Alonzo's arrival. He emerged from the darkness behind Jerry, glaring at me like the boogeyman in a horror film looking at his next victim with glee. I tamped down on my flinch. Jerry's hand slipped up to me and remove the knife I still held.

Alonzo, not Jerry, answered my question. "We are going to a safe place, my home. You don't need to know the details. It's safer that way." Adrenaline rushed through me once again. I didn't want to go to Alonzo's home. I knew in my gut he couldn't be trusted.

Jerry didn't contradict him. I studied Jerry, looking for any sign he disagreed with Alonzo, but found none. It seemed I had gained and lost more in the past week than I had in my entire life before that. I might yet lose my life, and Jerry seemed unwilling or unable to protect Henry and me anymore.

How would Gabriel have handled the situation in my place? He probably would have gutted Alonzo already and left him to freeze under the moonlight. I wasn't made of the same stuff and I'd fought hard for that. I'd have to pay the price now. Gabriel wouldn't be around to help me anymore. I'd made sure of that when I took the drugs Jerry had offered.

Once again, I was on my own and I was out of time. Placing myself under Alonzo's control without Jerry's trust and protection was a bad idea. I didn't have many options left. Even though I had avoided being on my own until now, I felt it was the only option left to me. I'd do what needed to be done and endure whatever life threw at me. The idea solidified in my mind and in my heart. I would escape with Henry tonight. I'd learn to survive, whatever it took.

Alonzo blocked our path out of Henry's room. He commanded Henry to pack, even though he had already packed when I told him to a few days ago. Henry pursed his lip and fisted his hand, an obstinate stance I recognized all too well.

When Henry made no move to obey, Alonzo stepped forward, his arm poised to slap Henry. Before I could think about the consequences of my actions, I jumped in front of Henry and took the slap for him. I felt the sting of that slap through every bone in my body, through my soul. Jerry made no move to intercept, no knee-jerk response. He watched, with no emotion evident on his face. He abandoned me to Alonzo's whim and that hurt like a physical assault that went straight to my chest, a bone-deep disappointment.

As I rubbed my face, Jerry said, "That's not necessary." His tone of voice never varied from the calm I would expect if he had been asking Alonzo to say "Please" and "Thank you." I shouldn't feel the sting of betrayal, but I did.

I started picking things from the closet and throwing them on the bed, trying to hide the fact that Henry had already packed. Jerry instructed Matilda and Branson to wait for us outside the bedroom door and then left to do his own packing.

THIRTEEN

The night after the vampire attack was one of the longest of my life. Jerry and Alonzo didn't let Henry or me out of their sight, insisting we all remain together in the library. None of us slept, just looked at each other with suspicion and a building tension I could taste in the air. By morning, I could read it in Alonzo's aura, sense it inside myself. I missed my pills last night after the attack and had no intention of making up the dosage. My demon senses recovered slow as slugs, but at least I hadn't done any permanent damage. I could, for instance, see that Alonzo was curious as he studied me, that there was a trace of lust in his aura to match the look on his face every time his gaze dropped to my chest. I was so tired I had no filter left between my thoughts and my mouth, and I was hungry, so very hungry for food and emotions. "Why do you keep looking at my chest? Aren't I supposed to be beneath you?"

A tinge of red crept up Jerry's collar. Alonzo didn't bother with embarrassment or indignation. Maybe he was too tired to bother with bluster and lies. "I don't hate you, but I'm certain you had something to do with the death of Rick and Jessica. Unlike Jerry, I don't think you have risen above your birth. I think maybe my organization failed you when we let you live long enough to stain your soul. Maybe God will let you into his kingdom if you repent and die now, before you commit any more sins."

The fact he was right about Rick and Jessica made me feel dirty and guilty, but not enough to accept his judgment, not enough to think I didn't have a right to live. "Isn't there something in the Bible about not throwing the first stone?"

He laughed. "This wouldn't be the first stone in the war between demons and humans. Your people sinned first, and often. I have the marks seared in my flesh. I was your victim first."

I fisted my hands to resist the urge to touch him and absorb all the emotion he was just throwing out into the world. *Why couldn't I absorb it at a distance?* No sooner than the thought crossed my mind, a thin tendril of his emotion started to drift toward me, feeding my starved mind.

I looked him in the eye. "I am sorry for whatever you suffered. I really am, but you weren't *my* victim and I am not responsible for the sins of my people."

Alonzo looked away from me and didn't reply. Jerry refused to look at me or speak on my behalf. *So much for being my protector.* Alonzo's aura changed with guilt and remembered pain. Whatever demons had harmed him, he was determined to pay it forward with my pain and maybe my death. Even if he wanted to, Jerry couldn't stand in his way forever. No one could stand in the way of such blind hatred. I really had no choice but to escape this place. In the meantime, I fed on him, which made me feel a little guilty and a little dirty, but at the same time, it seemed to calm him. Unfortunately, it also made me remember Rick and Jessica. It made me remember every pain, every painful drug I endured. I stepped back and away from him, breaking the connection and walking to the other side of the room, as far as I could get. I had no idea what I just did, but Alonzo seemed calmer and I more rattled. Henry took a step toward me, but I signaled for him to stay. The last thing I wanted was to harm him inadvertently.

I tried to focus on anything but the pictures running through my head. Around the room, half a dozen men with guns surrounded us, their gazes darting around, landing on Jerry every few seconds. All the emotion in the room melded to make one gooey mass of impatience suffocating me with each breath. They melded with the memories of my past pain and with the fear for the future.

Jerry's phone rang. All eyes shifted to him, praying we could finally get out of this room cramped with eight people that didn't like each other.

Jerry announced, "It's here."

Alonzo sighed in relief. "At long last."

Relieved, I approached Henry, grabbing his hand in my own and squeezing, reminding him to stay quiet and let me handle this.

The guards moved to surround the group, three guards walking in front of us, three behind. Jerry placed his hand on my back to guide me toward the front door. Alonzo stood behind me, which freaked me out, but I didn't have much of a say in the formation we followed.

As we walked, Alonzo bent down to whisper in my ear, his breath sending dread and revulsion skittering across my back. "Try not to wreck this car or I'll take it out of your hide, one strip of flesh at a time." The way he said the word strip, drawing it out, lashed with malice across my skin.

I couldn't stop my shiver of revulsion, but didn't give him the satisfaction of a verbal response. Jerry noticed, though. He stopped, turned toward me, and placed a hand on my cheek. "You seem flushed and tired. Have you taken your medication today?"

I plastered a smile over the disdain I wanted to show. My palm itched with the desire to slap his hand way. My voice breathless, I nodded. "I think I'm just having trouble adjusting to the new regimen. I'll get used to it."

Alonzo laughed with bitterness. "Careful. Never forget she's a demon, and frankly, beneath you."

Henry opened his mouth, but I squeezed his hand again in warning to let me handle this. Jerry's jaw ticked, but he ushered me beside him, followed by Alonzo chuckling behind. I took a deep breath and prayed for the opportunity to get the heck out of here soon. Alonzo's emotions swirled within me, filling me and spilling out through my pores. I let go of Henry's hand for fear I infected him with what I felt.

The guards remained alert, searching for threats coming at us, yet not paying any mind to the little woman and her brother.

Alonzo raised his voice. "If I were you, I'd shoot her with a tranquilizer and throw her in a sack for the help to carry in the trunk. What in God's name are you thinking?"

Jerry rotated toward Alonzo. *Thwack*. His fist connected with the wall beside Alonzo's head. For a moment, I bemoaned that Jerry deflected his punch at the last moment. Then, I realized how unlike Jerry it was to lose control. *Crap. Did I pass Alonzo's emotions to Jerry? Isn't he supposed to be immune? Why the heck isn't there a manual for this demon thing?* I wrapped my arms around myself and looked down, trying to seem as small as possible. Jerry's eyes almost bugged out, his face red and mottled with anger. He looked comical and weak, and more than a little pathetic as he muttered his apology over and over.

Alonzo's voice turned soft as if he were sorry to see his friend fall so low. "See what she's done to you."

Jerry didn't say another word. He turned toward me and barked. "Pick up the luggage and meet me at the car."

I did as I was told, grabbing two heavy bags and struggling down the stairs with them while Alonzo smirked in satisfaction,

Jerry still apologizing repeatedly beside him. I really hoped he wouldn't figure out I was to blame for his loss of control.

As I struggled with the weight of the luggage, I cursed myself for screwing myself over with those pills. My strength returned too slowly. I could use all the power I could get in my escape.

Henry carried his bags beside me as though they were filled with pillows instead of weapons and medicine and Alonzo's precious shoes.

From above, Alonzo surveyed the peons as we lugged the bags to the limo parked out front. Jerry still muttered apologies beside him. Henry carried the heavier bags despite the fact he wasn't much to look at in the muscle department. Henry had confessed to me he had demon powers already. We had spoken about it in hushed tones in his room while the TV blared in the background, afraid Jerry would find out. Henry's powers weren't psychic, they seemed to grant him control over the body instead of the mind. He felt none of the hunger I experienced with my powers, and I thanked the heavens for that every minute.

I hoped Henry would have an easier time living around people once made our escape. I didn't have much hope for myself. I would be fighting hunger and the overwhelming influence of human emotions every moment of the day, but it had to be done. I stumbled down the last few steps with the luggage, biting back a curse as the corner of the red hard case landed on my foot.

Alonzo's voice rang through the front yard. "Hurry up, demons. We don't have all day." Jerry stood beside him, looking down now, thinking and maintaining a blank expression. If he had any reservations about how Alonzo talked to me, or suspicions I had prompted his earlier outburst, he didn't show it.

What the heck had made me think I was safe? Hope really was a total b-i-t-c-h, making me ignore the evidence before my eyes. Jerry was nice, but he couldn't protect me. No one could.

The guards had spread out farther trying to cover a bigger area and giving Henry and me the chance we had been waiting for.

I whispered to Henry, "Ready?"

There was a driver in the car, but other than that, everyone was too busy preparing for our leave and protecting the perimeter to notice us. I headed toward the driver with stumbling steps, exaggerating my struggles with the luggage. Henry didn't bother with any type of pretense. He walked up to the driver, tapped on the window and touched him when he rolled it down a bit. The driver collapsed on the spot, although I could still hear his heartbeat. *Holy hell. What did Henry do? Is that guy okay?*

Henry winked at me, pushing the man off the driver seat, his body as pliant as a rag doll. "Come on, we don't have much time."

I snapped out of my shock and checked on the driver, relieved to find he was just sleeping. I grabbed Henry's arm, pulling him toward me with little to no effect. "Get in the back seat. I'll drive."

He didn't move so I repeated myself with a little more force. "Get in the back seat now and don't forget your seatbelt."

Henry did as I asked, pushing the seat belt with a harsh jerky motion. "Please try not to break the seat belt."

I had never been allowed to drive except for using simulators in laboratories to test my reflexes and my attention span under the influence of certain drugs. I now thanked goodness for the experience, something I thought I'd never do. I put the car in drive and tapped the accelerator.

The car lurched forward for about ten seconds. I maneuvered between topiaries and an SUV the guards had brought with them. I crashed into the corner of the SUV, but lucky for me, I'd only been going about forty-five miles an hour at the time. Alonzo and Jerry were now done arguing with each other and were racing toward the limo barking orders.

It took me a moment to get the reverse to work and then I shifted and lurched forward again. Driving wasn't much different from one of Henry's video games, although I wouldn't be telling him that. He might get ideas.

I swerved my way down the long winding road and made it to the front gate, which was closed. I put my foot on the gas like I'd seen people do in Henry's video games. Unlike in the games, I only succeeded in denting both the car and the gate. The crash created a tiny gap between the metallic doors, caving the metal, but not anywhere near enough to let the limo through, but Henry and I could make it through on foot.

Behind us, Alonzo had managed to turn the SUV around. It moved slowly forward since the front left tire wobbled and flopped where I had hit it. The guard from the little house beside the gate came out pointing a gun at my head. I climbed out of the car and rushed to the passenger side. Henry's seatbelt was stuck, and the release mechanism wasn't working. He reached down and pulled at the belt. It started to fray, but not enough to break open. I planted my feet shoulder-width apart, grabbed the belt, and helped Henry pull himself free, trusting the guard wouldn't pull the trigger as long as I didn't pull a weapon on him. The belt frayed further, but didn't break all the way.

Henry dropped his hands, his face contorted into a mask of fear. "Watch out."

I pulled one last time, snapping the damn belt at last. At the same time, I heard a whoosh behind me, followed by the press of cold metal against my temple and a muscled arm pulling me back against a hardened warm body.

Henry reached out to touch the arm currently snaking around my neck. The weight of the guard pulled me back and down, choking me. I couldn't breathe and I fell. I panicked and started pulling at the arm wrapped around my throat, surprised when it came away easily. The guard had passed out beneath me.

I jumped up, not as fast as usual, but I managed to climb over the wrecked car and avoid most of the twisted metal near the bumper. I bent my body and followed Henry out through the odd-shaped hole the crash made in the gate. At least our accident would keep any other vehicles from making it out of the property in pursuit before they cleaned up the mess. Hooray for my lack of driving skills.

Henry and I emerged through the twisted gate onto a long stretch of road surrounded by trees. I could hear the faint zing of cars in the distance so we headed that way as fast as we could. After a while, my thighs burned in protest, but I forced my legs to keep moving. I struggled to breathe, resorted to counting breaths, steps, anything to keep my mind focused on the price—my freedom and Henry's.

Behind us, Alonzo pulled himself through the same opening between the gates. He ran behind us with far more strength and endurance than a human should have. We kept going as fast as we could manage, using every ounce of our demon strength to keep Alonzo from reaching us or getting within shooting range of the gun he still clutched in his fist.

An eternity later, Alonzo started to fall behind. We kept running for a few minutes longer. I ignored the burn in my thighs and lungs, sucked in air through my mouth. I had far less endurance than my brother. He still ran at full speed while my head felt woozy and I had to slow down to keep from stumbling through trees in the surrounding forest.

A road and headlights were visible through the edges of the trees now. The sound of Jerry's goons struggling to move the limo had long faded in the distance. Alonzo's steady steps had faded as well. All we needed now was a ride. I doubled over, my hands on my knees, and sucked in a few breaths until I no longer felt like I was going to vomit my drumming heart.

I wiped myself down with a piece of my shirt so I didn't look like I was about to pass out and started walking while making the universal sign for hitch-hikers. Car after car ignored me. Morning rush-hour traffic provided a lot of opportunities for drivers to ignore hitchhikers. Everyone was in a hurry and no one cared about a couple of people stuck in the middle of nowhere. I wasn't even sure how I looked at this point, probably not very good. I had no money and Jerry's people would have cleared the wreckage and would be looking for us near the roads by now. I had very little time left before Jerry or Alonzo found us. It didn't look good. Time to put on my big-girl pants. I dropped back into the cover of the forest and took a breath. I wasn't sure I had enough strength for what came next.

"Why are we stopping?"

"I don't think anyone will help us."

"I know. So much for human kindness."

I shook my head. "It's okay. As dangerous as the world is, I'm not sure I'd take us in if I were in their place, living their lives."

Henry sucked in a few more breaths. "You're too easy on them. What are we going to do if no one helps us?"

Henry tried to sound normal, but I heard the apprehension hidden in his voice. I squeezed his hand in reassurance.

"We have to stop waiting for help and figure this out ourselves. If we hide in the trees, it will make it harder for anyone to see us."

"We won't get very far," I said.

Henry shrugged. "We will get as far as we need to. We just need to make it to a town, then we'll figure out what we can do to get someone to help us. Our chances are better one-on-one. Worse case, we can steal what we need."

I swallowed down my objection. We had to survive and stay away from Alonzo. We might not have the luxury of my morals, not that I had many. I was a demon, after all.

* * *

I listened for any clue Alonzo or one of Jerry's people had gained on us and we would have to go back to Jerry's gilded prison or Alonzo's unknown one. The limo had to be out of the way, since at least an hour had passed judging by the height of the morning sun.

Afraid Henry and I wouldn't make it out of the forest, I weighed our options. On one hand was letting Alonzo and Jerry catch me and let Henry get away. On the other was giving up what little of my dignity I had left and seeing this escape through.

In the end, it wasn't a hard choice, after all. I had already committed murder for our freedom. This was nothing compared to that. I started working on the jean jacket I wore and dropped it in the dirt.

"What are you doing?"

I smiled to try to put him at ease. "What do you think I'm doing?"

Henry gulped. "Is that really the type of person we want picking us up?"

"How much worse than Alonzo can he or she be? Just stay hidden behind the trees."

Henry turned from me. A sting of shame tried to get a hold of me, but I pushed it to the back of my mind, behind guilt and horror, covered with a mantle woven of my will to survive. Down to my open jacket, bra, jeans and boots, I let my hair down and stepped out onto the side of the road, ignoring the cold that nipped at me. Within three minutes, a silver Nissan Maxima squealed to a stop, filled with three boys about my age wearing sports team jackets. The boys in the back stank of beer at nine o'clock in the morning on a Sunday. *Classy*.

"Hey there, beautiful, where are you going?"

I smiled and imbued my voice with a suggestive swag. "Wherever you take me?"

They smiled lasciviously, anticipation and lust dripping off their auras in waves. They opened the back door for me. I hopped in and held it open for my brother to follow.

The driver sputtered. "What the fuck? That's not what I signed up for."

The jock beside me tried to pull the door closed, but I shoved him back long enough for Henry to get in and touch him. The boy fell asleep beside me, his hand dangerously close to my crotch.

I shoved him off while Henry put one of the boys in front down to sleep. I raised an eyebrow at the driver who now held a cell phone in his hand.

"Put that down or I'm going to have to leave you out here and I really don't want to do that. We just need a ride."

The man looked at his two sleeping buddies and nodded. Fear wafted through him. "What did you do to them?"

I shrugged. "A new drug, transmitted through the skin. We can always try it on you, and dump you in a bad part of town. Would you like that, or would you like to start driving?"

Without any further comments, the boy put the car in drive and took off. "Where to?"

I sat back, resting my forehead on the back of his headrest. "Just keep driving. We'll tell you when you've gone far enough."

The sun rose high above the mountains and snow drifted around us, not too heavy. Despite the worries cycling through my head, I couldn't help but notice how beautiful and peaceful it all looked. Pristine, pure, undisturbed. I let the boy drive another three hours past several towns before he started running out of gas. I instructed him to pull over on the side of the road beside a sign announcing the mall. I didn't really want the driver to figure out where we were headed, so I thanked him. "Thanks for the ride." I fished out the wallet of the jock still sleeping beside me in the back seat, took out all the cash he had, ten dollars, and returned the wallet to him. I left the credit cards because I figured I couldn't use them anyway and he needed something in case he ran out of gas. "Your friends will wake up in a few hours without the hangover they would have gotten if we hadn't interrupted your day trip. If you tell anyone about this, we will find you and we will do a lot worse than drug you. Are we clear?"

The driver nodded. "You know, for a beautiful girl, you're scary."

I showed my teeth in a feral smile that I hoped imitated the one Gabriel had given me the first day we met. In my sweetest voice, I replied, "Thank you. I'm working on it."

Henry and I got out of the car and started walking toward the giant seashell spires shining in the sun that I assumed belonged to the mall. I walked for over a mile, dodging cars that took the curve a little too fast.

I almost cried with relief when we reached the parking lot of the shopping mall. Henry and I picked up our pace, fueled by hope.

I'd never been to a mall, but I'd seen plenty in movies at the laboratories. I couldn't wait to get out of this stink, sit down in air conditioning for just a couple of minutes while we hid in the bathroom and figured out our next steps. We ran through the empty parking lot and approached the giant glass doors, covered by metal grating. Closed. What kind of place closes their malls on a Sunday?

I sat on the sidewalk outside the doors and took a moment to cry and scream a few choice words into the cold empty parking lot. No one responded. No one cared. I just had to accept there would be no washing our faces in the bathroom or drinking from the water fountain or sitting in the food court. I had to move on, except I had a sixteen-year-old boy looking to me for safety and I had nothing, no money, no talent, no resources, no friends and no clue of what to do next.

Relax, Ginny, think.

What do humans do when they're in trouble? I have no freaking clue, but maybe if I could find a desperate human some place in this damned closed on Sunday town, he or she can tell me.

My mind made up, I dusted the dirt from my jeans and started walking, sending my demon senses out looking for the poor, the homeless, the desolate. If their emotions drowned me, then I'd just have to deal with it. Henry was my first priority and I'd do anything to keep him safe.

CHAPTER

FOURTEEN

About four hours after leaving the closed mall, I waited in line outside a youth shelter. An African-American woman of healthy weight, a kind gaze, and a sticker that said "Wanda" stared up at me. "Your name, dear? I have a dozen kids to get processed. I need something to call you."

Before I could really think about it, I answered. "Hope. My name is Hope Freewoman and my brother's name is George."

The woman smiled, scribbled Hope on a ledger and a number. "Your cot will be the second one in the fifth row in the Woman's room, number 52. Do you have ID?"

I shook my head.

Wanda nodded. "That's okay. We'll set you up with a worker to talk to you Tuesday morning, 11 A.M. Put together whatever you have for your interview. You can stay until then."

I smiled my best harmless smile. "Thanks."

"Don't thank me. Thank the taxpayers and the Church. Dinner is at seven, lights out at ten, breakfast at seven, service at nine in the morning." The woman shoved a bunch of papers into my hand. "In case you want more permanent help. Your case worker will go through it with you."

I looked down at the papers for the Welfare-to-Work program, waiting for Wanda to process Henry.

"How old are you, dear?"

Henry lied. "Seventeen."

Wanda pursed her lips and handed him a thicker set of hand-outs. "You're in 33, third cot in the third row, men's side. The rules are in the handout. Read them."

Wanda dismissed him and started processing the next person in line. It was too late for dinner, so Henry and I would have to wait until morning to get something to eat. We went and found our cots. The shelter had a few offices in front and two large rooms with cots in the back. On the left were a cafeteria and a community room with a TV, a few board games, and a bookshelf. My cot was a basic wire bed with a mattress, clean linens, no pillow. A lot better than what I had enjoyed at Rick and Jessica's home. I plopped down the bag I'd carried from Jerry's throughout our escape. In it was a switchblade, a bottle of water, a change of clothes for each of us and two apples. I handed one of the apples to Henry and ate the other. Henry seemed reluctant to leave my side, and I was glad for the company, so I didn't complain when he sat on my bed.

The light dinner did nothing to settle my stomach or my cramped muscles. I massaged my temples. With so many emotions, I had trouble sorting through all the inputs. My mind felt like there was a huge weight pressing down on me, squeezing my brain. I struggled to breathe and gain some semblance of control.

Henry touched my arm. "Are you okay?"

I pulled away from him. "I'm sorry, but I'm not doing so good. The emotions here are so loud they're giving me a headache."

Henry looked at me with compassion. "Can I try something?"

What the heck. How much worse can it get? "Just be careful. I don't want to hurt you, but my control right now sucks."

Henry smiled and touched me. My headache eased, tension draining out of my tired muscles and my scalp. I felt better able to handle the stress, although the emotions remained just as loud as before. I detected an undercurrent of compassion and community strung through all the other crap humans were putting out in the world. If I focused on those emotions, the psychic cacophony seemed almost bearable. "Thanks, Henry. That was pretty awesome."

He smiled at my praise. "Yeah, I think it's pretty cool that I can help you for a change. You've always taken care of me. It feels nice to be able to do something for you. It makes me feel useful."

The happiness and self-assurance spilling from him made me think maybe I needed to praise a little more. Everyone needs to feel needed, even younger brothers. "You've never been useless. I can't tell you how many days I would have given up if it weren't for you. We take care of each other."

On the cot beside me, on the other side of Henry was a girl a few years younger than me, with bottle-red hair and artfully torn clothing. I smiled at her and was surprised when the girl smiled back.

The girl stuck out her hand. "I'm Brenda."

I waved at her without touching her, more than a little afraid of losing control of my ability with all the emotions constantly beating at me in this place. Brenda frowned and dropped her hand. "Okay, be like that."

Better to hurt her feelings than something else. Henry extended his hand to Brenda. "I'm George, that's Hope. Don't worry. She's just afraid of touching people."

Brenda's demeanor changed as she looked to me. "I didn't

know. I didn't mean to make you uncomfortable, but you could have said something."

I nodded, crossing my arms around myself. "I'm sorry. I'm just not good with people."

Brenda laughed as she rifled through the bag she carried with her. "I don't know anyone who is." I glimpsed a blue wrapper inside the bag, nothing dangerous. Brenda pulled out two black Oreo cookies and held them out to me. "Here. Have a treat on me."

There was no subterfuge in Brenda's aura, nothing but kindness. Everything she had in the world probably fit in that bag and yet, she'd offered me something. Carefully, I took it, making sure to avoid touching her in any way. My gut feeling said that bad things could happen if I touched anyone with all the emotions coming at me. My power behaved unpredictably at the best of times. I swallowed a couple of times to clear my throat of emotion. "Thank you. That's one of the nicest gifts I've ever gotten. We just had an apple for dinner."

Brenda huffed. "You look like you're new, but you'll get the hang of it, figure out where to go for meals and when. Were you in the system?"

I shook my head.

Brenda kept talking, filling in the silence for both of us, which I appreciated it. "Well, I was. I left after some bad stuff happened. I'd rather be here with a group of strangers, than alone with one or two." Brenda shuddered.

Brenda's aura seemed lonely, maybe as lonely as mine. Maybe it was stupid, but images of BFFs on television flashed across my head, fueling a longing so deep it made my heart seem hollow and empty.

"They gave me drugs and they hurt me," I blurted out.

Brenda didn't push or pry or give platitudes. She nodded,

accepting what I told her with grace and empathy. "If you ever want to talk, let me know."

When I didn't say anything after a few seconds, Brenda said, "Want to watch TV?"

I nodded my agreement, pulled Henry behind me, and the three of us sat on the floor of the community room in front of a television. Henry sat beside me, but didn't say a word the whole time. There was a horror movie on where the thin, prepubescent heroine walked outside to face off against a predator in a black garb dressed as death. Brenda turned to me. "Horror movie heroines make us girls look bad. I'd never be so stupid as to go outside when I know there is something scary out there, and who thinks kissing a boy is worth risking your life."

I laughed. "Very true. Although, I can think of one boy worth any number of dangers."

A hungry look of interest stole across Brenda's face. "Oh, this should be good. Do tell."

Brenda was careful not to touch me as we sat side by side running a commentary and laughing at the horror flick.

Lights out happened before the movie ended, but neither of us really cared about the end. As I watched Brenda praying, I wondered if it would help. I still didn't feel safe, but I'd found something I hadn't known I needed, a friend. "You're religious."

Brenda shrugged. "I guess I am. I like to think that someone cares if I live or die, if I eat, if I'm cold, or if I suffer. God seemed like a good choice."

I liked the idea that someone cared too. "Good night, Brenda, and thank you."

Brenda didn't ask what I had thanked her for. She just said, "You're welcome." And lay on the bag she used as a pillow right before the lights turned down but not completely off.

Eventually, I nodded off and landed in the dream garden again.

I looked around trying to locate Gabriel, but he wasn't there, so I sat on the bench under the tree. In this place, I was alone and finally, I didn't have to worry about what anyone saw, what anyone thought, what anyone would do to me if I showed one iota of weakness. I didn't have to worry about Henry and think that I was being selfish just by letting go of all the pretense and stopped having to be strong for one minute. I gave myself permission to let go and once I did that, it was like all the layers of cement I'd placed on my emotions cracked all at once, and all the stress and fear and uncertainty of the last weeks spilled out of me. I cried for myself, for my lost dreams, for the pain I'd suffered, and for the hopes that had evaporated under Alonzo's attack.

In this secret garden, I was safe, free to be as miserable as I wanted with no dangerously attractive male pushing me to be strong, to learn, to kill, to survive. I was alone, and I didn't let myself feel sorry for it. Rather, I took advantage. I cried, and when I tired of that, I punched dents into the tree at the center of the garden, stomped until I was too tired to continue, and then I lay down hoping to sleep or return to Henry and the shelter. Neither happened. The tears dried, but all the crying left my throat scratchy and my body heavy. I lay down to rest. Not long after, warm arms encircled me, lifting me up from my perch on the bench.

Gabriel cradled me to him. "I thought I'd never see you again."

I let myself sink into his warmth. I hadn't lost him. I hadn't screwed up to the point of losing the man who had not let me down yet. "I doubt that will ever happen. I can't seem to get rid of you."

Gabriel's laugh held an edge. "You managed to disappear yesterday, left me to wonder what was happening to you."

I twisted to look at him, but only managed a sideways glance since he was so close to me. My lips were inches from the stubble on his jaw. I wondered what would happen if I tried to kiss him. He'd probably turn away. So far, he'd only kissed me to get information or transfer energy, or to get me to do something I didn't want to do. "You found me and tried to take me by force. I know you meant well, but all it did was get some of your people hurt and make things worse for Henry and me. Jerry freaked out to the point that he was willing to take me to Alonzo's to keep me safe. I couldn't allow that, so we escaped."

Gabriel studied me without confirming or denying my accusation. "What happened?"

"Jerry and Alonzo were prepared for your attack. They shot everyone or they ran off, I don't know for certain." I reached out and put my hand over his, giving silent support. "Your vampires put up a fight, but Jerry and Alonzo choked them off."

Gabriel kept his gaze steady on a point in front of us. He placed his hands on my upper arms. "No demon has attempted a rescue mission since you went missing, and we sometimes protect vampires, but we never work with them. Whoever tried to breach Jerry's compound, I had nothing to do with it."

Gabriel didn't say another word. He stood up, pulling me up with him, put my head against his chest and gave me comfort. The silence and his hard body around me helped me get myself under control. I was so ignorant of this world, I didn't know how I would survive or protect anyone else.

I pulled back and looked up into Gabriel's eyes. "Teach me."

"What would you like me to teach you?"

"How to feed."

He looked at me sharply. "You've experienced your first hunger?"

I nodded, pulling from his warmth and wrapping my arms around myself to keep from reaching for him again. "I fed on Alonzo, but it wasn't enough. I'm always hungry."

Gabriel shuddered. He placed his hands around my arms, but

didn't pull me back against his chest. Still, his warmth seeped through me, calming my mind and my hunger. "Don't ever feed on a person like Alonzo, his darkness will infect you, remind you of every bad thing that ever happened to you. It's best not to feed on such individuals. If you can, find a place where humans go to have fun or to seek solace, a place that brings out the best in them, and let their emotional energy into you."

"How often do I have to do that?"

"Depends on the size of the crowd. The bigger the crowd the longer it will be between feedings. I like to go to concerts. A single event will feed me for weeks."

I could not suppress a laugh at the thought of serious, intense Gabriel in the middle of a concert, surrounded by humans swaying to the music or maybe teenage girls shouting at the stage. "What type of concerts?"

"Many types. Rock and Gospel music are my favorites. The energy such music evokes is the strongest."

He made it sound so practical, but the sparkle in his eyes betrayed him. He enjoyed concerts, and not just for the psychic sustenance they provided. I tried to picture Gabriel in a rock concert, his body banging away to the music, his face glistening with sweat, a tight black T-shirt clinging to him. My libido awoke with a vengeance, tightening my nipples and sensitizing every other part of my body. I needed to focus on getting information, not this attraction between Gabriel and me. I stepped away from his hands, his warmth, and the temptation he represented. With Gabriel, I wanted to give up everything I was, everything I could be, and just let him take care of me. I couldn't let that happen.

"Tell me about demons and the Human Advancement Group, and how to keep my ability suppressed enough that I don't start killing people or going mad from too much input. Help me survive."

Gabriel's grip on my arms tightened slightly. "Are you sure you want to know all that?"

No, I wasn't sure, but I was tired of being a puppet. Swallowing hard, I nodded.

"In a single afternoon, you think I can teach you that?"

"Isn't there some magical way you can share with me?"

"No. There is no magic pill. Every power, every move, every expenditure of energy has a cost. Otherwise, there is no balance. I beg you, tell me where you are. I will protect you."

It would be so easy to let him protect me, to give up all responsibility, but if the past few weeks had taught me anything, it was to depend on myself. "And what happens if you can't?"

He didn't make fun of me or show any hint of anger as I expected. He didn't even assure me that he could handle anything. "I can't always be there, but I promise you I will honor you and do my best to prepare you for everything."

"That sounds tempting." And it did, so very tempting.

Gabriel's eyes shone with promise. "It should be. I'll protect you, introduce you to our world."

"How do you know I want to be introduced to the demon world?"

He looked away from me, as though accessing a memory deep within, one that made the corner of his lips twist up in pleasure and his eyes gleam with a far-off fondness. "It's beautiful, glittering, old, and full of history. There are so few of us, we're like a very powerful family. We have the power plays, and arguments inherent in all families. We're not perfect, but I think you'll like it. We can give you what you need."

"You didn't answer my question."

He made me wonder what put that smile on his face, he made me want to give up the version of myself I was just discovering to be with him, to let his strength and his intensity dominate the woman I would become. It is a desire I fought because he'd warned me it was a lie, the product of a psychic bond. I needed to put some distance between us. Maybe that's why I sounded so prickly when I said, "And who are you to determine what I need?"

Gabriel ran his hand through his hair, leaving his locks mussed. I curled my fists to stop myself from reaching for him. Letting out a deep breath, he said, "I'm no one and I'm your bonded mate. Perhaps I'm projecting my own desires on you. I hope that our world can be what you need. I wish to see you by my side. Even though I know it's the bond making me so… attached, I can't seem to care anymore."

I tossed my head back, trying to dislodge the inconvenient attraction between us. *I have nothing. It would be so easy to fall in your arms and let you take care of everything, too easy.* "I want, I need to protect myself. You're so strong and you have your place in the world already. You won't mean to, but you'll still end up taking my choices away because you have a strong base and I have none. I owe myself better. I deserve to choose, to learn to take care of myself and Henry, to not have to depend on you or anyone else for my safety."

"Even if you get hurt in the process?"

I didn't want to get hurt, but I willingly risked it. "Even if I get hurt."

Gabriel leaned into me, his breath a whisper against my sensitized skin, his warmth seeping through his hold on me. "I hoped you wouldn't say that. Please, don't make me do this. Don't make me watch you suffer."

"It's not your choice. I know it's difficult for you to understand, but I've lived my life surrounded by people who hated me. The only thing I have is the belief that they were wrong. Despite everything they've done to me, I'm not a monster. I don't ever want to feel that it's okay to kill my enemies. I don't want to be so cold, and getting closer to you, it makes me want to survive at all costs, not for Henry, not to protect you or Jerry, or anyone on this planet except myself. With you, I'm selfish because I want to live to enjoy another kiss, and I don't care who gets hurt." I took a steadying breath. "So I'm choosing that, if that is the way of things, the person who should get hurt, the person who should pay for my survival is me. I don't want you to stand like a shield before me. Not you. I couldn't survive it if you got hurt trying to protect me." I tried to shake free of Gabriel's hold, but he held me tight enough to bruise. My heart sped up a few notches, but I had nothing to worry about. Except for the flames from hell that first day, Gabriel never hurt me. He did everything to make sure I learned to take care of myself. "Let me go."

Gabriel's irises had turned to ice storms, spreading across his sclera until they encompassed his entire eye and scaring the hell out of me. Gray wings tipped with purple spread behind him and around us. "Please understand," he begged. "You are in danger of losing not only your life, but your sanity. Alonzo Nezmeth uses faith as a shield to ward off any kind of morality or ethics or compassion. He is merciless because he believes he is right. To him, you are a commodity at best, something to be crushed at worst. I have seen what remains of his victims after he's done with them. I care for you. Let me protect you. Let me take care of you."

"At what price? I'd rather be a victim than a killer like you. Better to be innocent, than a monster." He flinched. Maybe that's why he looked so hurt and guilty and angry all at once.

He opened his arms, releasing me as though I had struck him, and in a way I had. I almost reached out to him and took back my words, but it was too late. Once you hurt another, the hurt can never be undone. It can be repaired, but the break will always be there. I'd spoken harsh truth. I was sorry for the pain I'd caused him, perhaps all the more because I'd spoken the unvarnished truth.

Gabriel tucked his wings away, advanced on me again, and pulled me into his embrace, kissing me. I let go of my control for a moment and melted into his kiss. He stepped back, holding my hands between his. "Forgive me."

I had no time to understand his apology before my world exploded in pain. Every cell in my body burned from the inside out. My heart beat ever faster, drumming ever-stronger blasts of fire into my head. My vision blurred, I screamed, but no one heard me except the man who betrayed me. I lost track of time, lost track of everything except the burning flames wracking my body and my heart.

Eventually the pain ended, as all things end. I looked at the latest of a long string of betrayers, my voice a hoarse whisper, my throat raw from all the screaming. "Why?"

I sensed remorse from him and something that resembled love, but that didn't make sense. He'd caused it. "I couldn't dull the pain. I'm sorry for that."

I shoved him away and he let me. "I asked for your help. I trusted you. I'd never done that before with anyone. Why betray me?"

Gabriel kneeled before me, his hands folded in supplication to me. "Forgive me. I only did as you asked. You said you'd try to forgive me."

Confusion stirred. The pain was too raw, too recent, making my thoughts sluggish. "What did you do?"

"I made you stronger, strong enough to survive."

"That pain is not what I asked for."

"Strength has a cost. Diamonds are forged by pressure, swords by fire, you by pain. It was the only way I could think of. Perhaps, if we had more time, I would have found another way to grant your wishes."

Gabriel made a gesture to touch me, but I flinched. "Don't touch me."

He looked down, still on his knees, his head dropped, his shoulders defeated. "I've sacrificed something precious between us. I did not give it up lightly. You asked me to make you stronger, to help you. To make you stronger, I had to bend you, break you. You are a stronger demon because of what I did. You lack knowledge, but not power. I gave you everything I could give, made you faster, stronger than even I can be." He reached for me again, but did not touch me this time. "You promised me once a single act of forgiveness. I am calling in the debt."

I heard him, the rational part of my brain understood, but the part that ruled my emotions had been wounded by him and I couldn't turn it off. "I will keep my promise, but I need time."

Gabriel nodded. He faded from my vision, still kneeling, his face hidden by black locks I wanted to yank back to expose his face, his lips, the truth of his intentions written in his eyes. But I didn't need his eyes to know he spoke the truth. He'd done it for me. He'd done everything for me, and even though I hated him for the pain I had suffered, for breaking my trust in him, I understood.

FIFTEEN

I watched over Brenda as she shuddered and moaned in her sleep, debating whether or not to wake her. Breakfast would be served in ten minutes, and most of the homeless residents were up doing chores in the lunchroom and cleaning the common areas. Although the sleeping area was almost empty, I could still feel the energy of people through the walls separating this room from the lunch area. This morning, their energy had turned from desolate and exhausted to purposeful, much easier for me to handle. Henry woke up a while ago and stood beside my bed fully dressed and smiling, as though he had complete faith in the world to keep him safe. I wish I could still believe the same, but it was my job to know better so that he didn't have to.

Brenda whimpered a bit, her hands clasping the covers, her body huddling into a fetal ball. I wondered what hurt my friend, and whether it would be a good idea to wake her. My hand hovered over Brenda's shoulder, but I pulled it back. Instinct warned me not to touch her. I had no idea what would happen now that Gabriel had boosted my volatile powers.

I felt Brenda stir to consciousness, and turned away seconds before the other girl would have woken up and found me looming over her. Brenda rubbed the sleep from her eyes. When she saw me, she smiled with a joy that invaded my heart and filled it with an answering joy and hope. "Hello."

"Good morning. Is it time for breakfast yet?"

I nodded. "It'll be served in about ten more minutes, I'm told."

Brenda jumped out of bed with more energy than anyone had a right to before coffee and grabbed an overused toothbrush out of her bag to head toward the washroom. She changed her mind halfway there and came back for her bag, taking it with her to the washroom.

I busied myself with finger-combing the tangles out of my long curly hair. I'd have to wash it soon or risk looking like I carried a bird's nest on my head. Beside me, Henry took a hand-held gaming system out of our bag.

Brenda came back with a big smile full of newly brushed pearly whites judging from the scent of mint wafting from her. I managed a closed-mouth smile back, sorry I hadn't been able to properly brush my own teeth with my fingers.

Brenda didn't seem to notice or care, and led the three of us to the long line in the cafeteria. We passed Wanda's desk in front of the cafeteria. Behind it, there was a plastic fold-out table with a bunch of books arranged neatly. Curious, I asked Brenda, "What are those?"

"Wanda and some of the volunteers drop books there. You can pick one up if you like. She's got some juicy ones."

I turned. "You've read them?"

"Of course. I'm too poor to afford any other hobbies. Between this place and the library, I get to live the high life and meet hot men with hero complexes every other day."

I laughed. "It sounds like you've been holding out."

Brenda picked one book out of the pile with an H on the cover encased in a white diamond. "These are the best. You can always count on Harlequin for a steamy read."

I took the book from Brenda, making sure not to let our fingers touch. I inspected the book, *Possessed*. Sounded promising, if the muscular man and barely dressed woman on the cover were anything to go by.

"Sounds like a horror flick."

Brenda winked. "The only horrible thing about that book is that you can't jump in the book and seduce Charles away from the heroine."

"Sounds tragic." I could use a distraction, especially when my psychic hunger acted up.

Brenda giggled. "You have no idea. That man is hotter than anything you'll ever meet in real life."

Thinking of Gabriel, I doubted that, but kept the comment to myself. Brenda would only dig to learn more about Gabriel.

Henry interrupted our banter. "As much as you ladies seem to like Charles, some of us are hungry for food. Can we go?"

I performed a bow in the style of a King George era heroine. When I stumbled a bit, I laid a hand on the wall for balance and pronounced, "Of course, your majesty. Let us go."

The line moved like slugs in molasses, so both Brenda and I whipped out our books and immersed ourselves in the wonderful world of romance heroes. We lost track of time and didn't mind the long line. When my turn came, I regretted having to put down my book before I found out whether the heroine was going to accept Charles's proposal of seven nights of sin in exchange for not turning her into the sheriff. But physical hunger won out and so, I held out my cracked blue bowl and collected a tray filled with hot oatmeal, crackers, and a hard-boiled egg.

Brenda, Henry, and I sat together at a table near the front to eat our food. I sat on a corner with only Henry beside me to make sure I didn't accidentally touch anyone. I focused on my food. First, I ate a hard-boiled egg in two bites, then I attacked the oatmeal without saying a word. That first bite of warm liquid filling my belly almost made me moan in pleasure.

I shoved the rest of the food in my mouth, not bothering to talk, the cessation of physical hunger too good a thing to pass up. Unfortunately, the psychic hunger was another matter altogether. It gnawed, eating at the corners of my mind as a physical thing that pressed upon me, affecting my balance and concentration. The fork in my hand shook and I had to make an effort to keep it steady. I did my best to ignore it and wished like Hell it would just go away, however unlikely that might be.

When I was done eating, I said, "That glue-like stuff tasted better than most gourmet meals at Jerry's house. I guess there's no better seasoning than hunger."

Henry laughed. "The company is way better."

Brenda said, "I don't know this Jerry, but I can imagine. So, what are you guys doing today?"

I shrugged nonchalantly. "I'm going to help clean the dishes and then I don't know. We'll come back here tonight, but we have no place to go this morning after service."

"It was the same way for me my first day," Brenda said. "Want to hang out with me? I'll show you the ropes."

Henry looked at Brenda with suspicion. "What kind of stuff do you do?"

"Oh, I hang out at the mall and assault helpless shoppers with my unvarnished opinion and substandard food. I got a job there a couple of weeks ago, but I don't make enough to get my own place and I have no money saved up. You guys are welcome to hang out with me. I'll put a good word in with my manager. He's a decent guy, doesn't hit on me or anything."

The table standing in my way stopped me from making a fool of myself by hugging Brenda, which was fortunate because in my condition, I would almost certainly feed on her. Henry hugged her instead. Brenda closed her eyes and hugged him back for a brief moment. Excited about our day, I stood up and piled three trays, three plates, and three bowls on top of one another. The trays had been slightly warped from use so they didn't fit together quite perfectly. Still, it was only three plates and three cups, so I packed everything on top of the stacked trays and picked it up. "Come on, let's get chores over with."

Brenda eyed the mountain. "You want us to get the cups?"

My coordination wasn't the best at the moment, but it didn't seem too bad, and I didn't want Brenda accidentally touching me, so I shrugged. I stacked the cups on top of the plates and went on my merry way. I got about four paces before the whole stack in my arms started tottering. Brenda rushed over and placed her hand beside mine to steady the pile.

I focused on our joined hands for a fraction of a second before a flurry of images dripping with terror and fury rushed at me. A slap across the face, a belt to her back, a kick to her stomach, a two-by-four breaking over her crouched form, a caress that hurt worse than the beatings, choking on her own sobs, not being able to breathe, not being able to get up, not being able to escape. She morphed into me and I screamed, "Get away from me, Dominic! Get the fuck away!"

I kicked, pushed, did everything I could to get away from the images, to get away from Dominic, to get away from the forced intimacy with him, with Brenda. Glass bit into my legs, my butt, and my hands. The pain of my body focused my mind away from the images my power forced upon me, images from Brenda's life.

I took a breath, then another. My sight cleared of the normal-looking home of horrors. The plates I'd been holding lay shattered about me. Broken porcelain dug into my skin. Trails of blood marked the suddenly vast space between Brenda and me. Brenda stood frozen, all signs of friendship drained from her face and her aura, replaced with disbelieving horror and hurt and fear. "How the fuck did you know? What the fuck just happened?"

I just lay there, looking up at her, waiting for the slap in the heart that I could see forming in Brenda. She tried to speak a few times before she managed to make sound come out. "I can't fucking deal with this right now." Brenda walked off, leaving me on the floor alone, surrounded by the mess I'd caused.

Henry knelt beside me, careful to avoid the shards of porcelain. He picked out a large piece of glass that had lodged in my forearm. I stared at my hands, letting the blood run before I snapped out of it and picked at a few pieces.

Wanda rushed to me with rubber gloves and inspected my hands. She handed me a tube of Neosporin and some bandages.

I smiled up at the older woman. "I don't know what you did, but I believe in the good Lord and that people are innocent until they prove otherwise. Go on and get yourself cleaned up, honey. I'll get someone else to clean this mess."

Henry grabbed a broom and got to work while I walked to the bathroom with half the residents of the shelter staring after me. I held the tears in until the door closed. Still, I kept my hand over my mouth so my sobs wouldn't escape. I didn't want or need anyone else's kindness. It hurt too much when they found out who I was and withdrew that kindness, or when I fed on them against my will. The psy hunger had melted to the background. I fed on Brenda and her god-awful memories, and I didn't know what to do with myself to stop it from happening again.

I indulged my crying for a bit too long. Wanda knocked on the door. "Are you okay in there? Do you need anything else?"

"Just a few more minutes. I'll be right out." My voice trembled a bit, but Wanda didn't question it. I thanked God I'd met someone like her, even if it was in passing, even if our acquaintance lasted one night. At least now I knew for certain genuine and kind people existed, even if I couldn't stay near them for very long.

I quickly washed away the rest of the blood on my hands and ran a wet towel over my butt and thighs to remove the pieces of glass that had snagged at my jeans. Henry had picked out the pieces on my back. The cuts and scrapes were already beginning to heal. I'd be fine in a few minutes, but my shirt would have stains and I didn't have anything to replace it with. Finally, I washed the evidence of tears from my face and took a few calming breaths.

Henry stood outside the bathroom right next to Wanda. The rest of the occupants of the room had left to perform their chores in the kitchens or start their day.

Wanda smiled. "You okay?"

I nodded, not yet trusting my voice.

She handed me an old white T-shirt and a piece of lined paper with an address scribbled on it. "I've seen strange things in my life, and I've made a lot of friends, all kinds of friends. I don't know what you are or what happened back there, but I know you are not a regular human and that means you need a little special help."

My breath hitched, but Wanda put out a gloved hand to soothe me. "Don't worry, it's okay. We're all God's creatures. If the story of what happened here gets out, some folks won't want to know you exist, let alone have you around. Don't worry about them. You know what's in your own heart. You can come back tonight, but if you need a job and a warm place for the day, go talk to my friend Paul Reilly. Tell him Wanda sent you."

I nodded. "I don't know how to thank you."

"No need. It's my job." With that, Wanda turned around, her good deed done.

I turned toward Henry.

Henry asked, "What now?"

"I don't know. I guess we go find Paul Reilly."

* * *

From the outside, Paulino's Brazilian Bar & Grill was a cozy kind of place with a log cabin look and feel to it. Chimney smoke wafted from the roof, carrying with it the delicious scent of roasting meats even at ten o'clock in the morning.

The three-mile uphill trek through foot-thick snow had been well worth the trip. Inside, Paulino's bar dropped the log cabin façade. Large screen TVs framed like paintings decorated the space above the bar at the center of the place and modern booths made of worn wood and leather surrounded that. The scent of meat and burning wood, combined with a warmth and lingering energy of leisure, set me at ease. This was a shelter from cold and hunger and loneliness, a place to relax.

I had never been to a place with such effortless class. The King of England could dine here in the booth next to a local family of four and neither would look out of place. It was a neat trick and I liked the owner all the more for managing it.

The front was empty, so Henry and I were led by the nose toward the kitchen. The kitchen was dominated by a large fire with racks of roasting meats turning over it. The rest was a mass of stainless steel, with supplies stacked neatly on shelves above the countertops, and a mountain of cooking bowls and utensils filling one of several sinks.

A man with glistening muscles and a face permanently marked by laughter worked the meats. A tiny patch of gray decorated the sides of his black wavy hair, giving him a distinguished look that complemented the kindness in his forest-green eyes and his aura. "Hello, menina. What brings you here so early?"

I resisted the urge to look down and smooth my worn jacket

and jeans, not that it would do me any good. "Are you Paul Reilly?"

The man's lips thinned. "*Paulino* Reilly. Who's asking?"

"We…I am here for a job. Wanda sent me."

Paulino raised his perfectly formed eyebrows and gifted me with a sun-bright smile in a sun-tanned face. The effect was stunning. "Ah, you are from the shelter, no?"

I nodded, cleared my throat. "Yes. I'm strong and fast. I'll do whatever you tell me and never give you any trouble."

The man currently holding our fates in his hands stared at me, measuring me, then Henry. "And the menino? Does he mind doing dishes?"

Henry shook his head, stood a little straighter. "No, sir, I don't mind work."

Mr. Reilly nodded. "Then we have no trouble. I have three rules."

He held up one finger. "If you decide to leave, you give me at least a day of notice."

Two fingers. "Do not give me attitude or I will have to put you in your place."

Three fingers. "If you see something out of place, ask me about it before you go off telling stories."

I asked the obvious question. "What kind of strange things?"

"I did not say strange. I said out of place." When Henry and I just looked at him, Mr. Reilly shrugged. "Do you want the job or not?"

Of course I did, so I nodded, incredibly grateful and not at all weirded out by the strange things comment. I was a little strange myself, so who was I to judge? Mr. Reilly led both of us farther into the kitchen, gave us burgundy aprons decorated with black script letters for *Paulino's Brazilian Bar and Grill*.

I tied the apron on while Mr. Reilly talked. "The dishes are there. I trust you know how to wash them, vegetables are going to be set in this area for cutting. He pointed to an empty counter far from the meats. You can get started setting tables based on these instructions."

Mr. Reilly handed me a detailed instruction manual and pointed me toward a large box filled with silverware and salt shakers. "There are your supplies. When you get through setting the tables and folding the napkins just so, come and find me."

I swung Jerry's bag onto the floor and tucked it by Henry's side. Then, I picked up the box with little effort, maybe too little since I felt the bottom start to give out almost as soon as I lifted it single-handed. I let the weight plop down on the table again with a heavy clatter of metal and filled a plastic tray with the silverware instead.

Still heavy, but at least the container wouldn't warp. I propped the burden against my right hip and was able to keep it balanced with one hand. Mr. Reilly watched me with a little too much curiosity as I worked, so I quickly got out of his line of sight and went about getting my work done.

I struggled with the first two tables, shifting the settings a few times before I got them right, but got the hang of it after that. By the time I finished, my hands moved through the motions without thought. I may have cheated a little and used demon speed to help me along. It had been over thirty-six hours since I'd last taken Jerry's drugs. I just hoped I could handle all the crowds that would invariably invade a place like this without losing control. Maybe Mr. Reilly would let me stay in the back cooking. I made a mental note to ask him about that later.

* * *

When I asked Mr. Reilly about working in the back, he didn't even raise a black brow at my request. In the musical lilt of his voice, he pronounced, "I've got enough pretty girls out front. You can cut vegetables with your brother."

I smiled at the compliment and thanked him. Then, I grabbed a knife and started to work on the onions with gusto, but Mr. Reilly grabbed my hand to stop it from coming down on the third chop. I tensed, pulling my hand away from him. Paulino picked up the knife as if I hadn't dropped it. I waited, but no memories hit me at all. Confused, I started to say something, but then shut my mouth. *What if some people are naturally immune? What if I give myself away by saying something?* Paulino acted nice but I just met him today.

"Are you trying to punish the vegetables? Take it easy." Paulino went on to demonstrate how to chop, sliding the knife instead of whacking with it. "See? Go easy on the onion and my knives. If you keep whacking things, you'll end up cutting through the cutting board. You are too strong for that." He positioned my fingers on the cutting knife and then watched for a few minutes before harrumphing for a moment. "Good. I think you got it."

He turned his back and went off to work on the meat. I kept chopping things while Henry did dishes, cleaned surfaces, and picked up a few messes. Mr. Reilly had a calming effect on my power with his easy laugh and his kindness. I decided to watch him and try to figure out why he didn't affect me like Brenda did.

He didn't raise his voice even once during the night, not even when a waitress spilled a plate of lobster and beef on the floor. He simply shrugged and pronounced, "See, everyone. In my restaurant, even the garbage tastes good. The bugs will eat well tonight." Henry cleaned up while everyone else continued doing their jobs, and Mr. Reilly turned back to roasting a lamb chop over the fire.

What impressed me the most about him was that his kindness and good humor went deep, as deep as his aura, at least. There had not been a hint of anger when the waitress had dropped that plate.

The rhythm and feel of the restaurant sank into my psyche, stealing away the fear I'd lived with for so long. As the anxiety fled, energy from the kitchen, the restaurant, and the bar drifted to me and through me. Somewhere around nine o'clock at night, after eleven hours in this place, the dinner crowd faded. I had no more vegetables to chop. Mr. Reilly told me to take a break, which I didn't want to do, but he still made me stand in a corner and drink a coffee he made for me himself. As I sipped the hot liquid and took in the people around me, winding down, I realized I felt content, safe, and that my psy hunger had faded. Somehow, without realizing it, this place had fed me, and I didn't have to hurt anyone to do it. I jumped at the realization, splashing coffee all over my shoes. A few drops landed on the bag we carried with us, now tucked into a corner of the kitchen. I put the coffee away and took the bag into the bathroom so I could clean it off before it stained.

I smiled while I scrubbed the spot in the bag, content. I understood now what Gabriel had said about feeding from crowds. Just being in this place soothed my mind, made me feel inexplicably relaxed. The horrors that lived inside me shied away from such an environment. Nothing here could be confused with a threat. Joy bubbled through my body, buoying my heart. Maybe I could build a life here with these people and I wouldn't have to fear myself or Alonzo Nezmeth.

The thought of Alonzo sobered me right up, staining my joy with ugliness, but not able to take it away completely. I went back to put away food in the refrigerators, humming to myself. An hour later, I graduated to rubbing meats with seasonings for the next day. I looked forward to tomorrow for the first time ever. Mr. Reilly promised he'd teach me how to rack the meats and turn them the next day. He left me to work while he took his break.

After I finished with the last rack, I looked around for Mr. Reilly, but he wasn't anywhere around. Henry was still drying dishes, and I didn't want to bother him, so I stepped outside to look for Paulino and ask him what to do with all the cooked meats and sides left over from the night.

The full moon lit my way to the back pretty well. I took a moment to enjoy the view of the town spreading before me. Paulino's Brazilian Bar and Grill sat on a mountain, and with the moon shining on the rooftops and the snow covering all the little imperfections, the view was breathtaking. I loved it, but I couldn't slack off on my first day of work, so with reluctance I turned from the view and headed toward the storage shed about two hundred feet from where I'd been standing. I could hear Paulino's heavy breathing in there. He probably needed help with something.

The minute I walked into the shed, the scent of copper and roses assaulted me. It was dead winter, but inside this room, steam condensed on the windows. The scent of roses wafted from a woman who was responsible for most of the heavy breathing going on. She was wrapped around Mr. Reilly, one leg hoisted against his butt. He had his hands on her buttocks and her dress wrapped around her waist. Her arms curled around his shoulders while he nuzzled her neck.

When I gasped, both turned toward me. A single drop of blood dripped from the corner of Mr. Reilly's mouth. "I'm sorry. I didn't mean to—" I fought to control my shaking voice. "I'm just going to go back." I ran as fast as my demon body could go, rushing breathless into the restaurant a fraction of a second after seeing whatever it was I'd seen.

The bar remained open even though the restaurant had closed. A few men and women sat drinking and talking. I gulped a few breaths to steady my speeding heart and did my best to pretend to be a normal girl in jeans and jacket, walking around in a bar where everyone else was dressed up.

I walked at a normal pace toward the kitchen, each step seemingly taking forever. I was halfway to my destination when Mr. Reilly came in from the outside. He made no effort to look normal as he rushed toward me and grabbed my arm. "We need to talk."

I shook my head. "No need. I'm just going to go back to the shelter and live my life. I'm tired after a long day of work and my mind is playing tricks on me."

He laughed, drawing my attention. Against my will, his laugh wrapped around me, set me at ease. I really looked at him for the first time since witnessing that drop of blood on the corner of his mouth. I expected to see anger, fear, determination, but none of those colored his aura. He smiled and his eyes glowed with the ever-present mirth.

I couldn't see him killing me and burying my body under the snow down the side of the mountain. "What's so funny?"

"You. You're not the only one who saw strange things tonight. I should know who you are given how fast you ran out of that shed, but I don't, and that means something is very wrong."

Before I could think about my response, I said, "Nothing is wrong, Mr. Reilly."

"Either you are very ignorant or very stupid. Either way, it is in your best interest not to lie to me."

"Mr. Reilly, what are you?"

His eyes widened just a smidgeon before he narrowed his gaze. "Ignorant it is. I'm a vampire, my dear, and you should know that. The fact that you don't, tells me you were not raised with your people, the demons. Life is dangerous for a beautiful girl as young and ignorant as you."

"Can you stop calling me ignorant?"

He raised his brows. "Why? It's what you are. The sooner you realize that, the better off you'll be."

He pulled me to a private room reserved for parties and closed the door behind us with a thunderous click. I swallowed, but I stayed put. I wasn't afraid of what he'd do to me anymore. I was more afraid of what he'd do about me. "I just want to be left alone. I was raised by humans and want nothing to do with them or the demons."

Mr. Reilly smiled in approval. The man had a thousand different smiles and each one put me at ease. "That makes you smarter than most. I'm not a fan of either. You'll get no trouble from me. You're welcome to work here and live at the shelter or you can stay at my place. Oh, and call me Paulino. Mr. Reilly makes me sound almost as old as I really am."

I got the feeling he didn't go around advertising his age and it wasn't my business anyway. Getting into a conversation about it just seemed too intimate at the moment, especially after he offered me a place in his home. "No, thank you."

"Excuse me. Don't I get to choose how you address me?"

I blew out an exasperated breath, no longer worried about being murdered. "Not that. You've been kind, and we love working here. I'd love to come back, but I don't think we should stay with you. It would just be…weird."

Paulino shrugged. "The offer is open should you need it. The world is dangerous for one such as you. You should take me up on it."

I shook my head of the foreboding he elicited with his words. "Thank you, but I've imposed on you enough."

He gifted me with another of his easy smiles as he drew a card from his back jeans pocket. There was nothing on it but a number. "Should you ever get in trouble, call this number. It cannot be traced, but should you call, I'll come get you."

I smiled, truly grateful for the thought, slipping the card into the left pocket of my jeans next to the folding knife I'd stolen from Jerry. "I am grateful for everything you've done for me, and whatever you are, your secret is safe with me. That woman didn't look like she was complaining."

He laughed, delighted. "No, her only complaint is that our time was cut short tonight. But don't worry. I'll be taking care of her later."

I just bet he would. "Well, that's a little too much information for me. I'm just going to get Henry and we'll be on our way."

He laid a hand on my arm, warm, comforting, and not at all suggestive of anything beyond friendship. "I'll drive you. I have to drop off leftovers tonight anyway."

CHAPTER
SIXTEEN

Being trapped in a pickup between my little brother and a laid-back vampire I just witnessed screwing a stranger wasn't just a little awkward. I had trouble not thinking of Paulino's assignation. He still reeked of sex and roses and blood. The eucalyptus that clung to Henry's skin and clothes did little to soothe me in the small space. I sat sandwiched between them while Henry studied our surroundings, quiet.

The vampire's eyes gleamed green in the night, reflecting the light of the dashboard. Leaving the car in park, he pulled out an envelope from his jacket and passed it to me. "What's this?"

"Your pay for the day's work."

I opened the envelope and counted out three hundred dollars in cash. "This is a lot of money for a single day's work."

Paulino shrugged. "I pay fairly and the staff uses communal tips. You did well tonight, menina."

"Are you sure that's all it is?"

He bristled with irritation. "Don't worry, I wouldn't lie to spare your ego. It's not worth the effort."

"Glad to hear it." I split the money, giving half to Henry and keeping half to myself. He'd worked for it and deserved to hold on to it.

Henry smiled. "Thanks, Mr. Reilly." He returned his attention back outside.

The crisp paper of the bills left a phantom imprint on my fingers. I wanted to keep touching it, looking at it. It was mine. I'd earned it and that made me unspeakably proud. "Thank you."

Paulino put the pick-up in drive and pushed the accelerator. The light highlighted the too-perfect angles of his face, the ink-black waves of his hair. The man really was beautiful, preternaturally so. I didn't want to jump his bones the way I did Gabriel, but I could appreciate him like the work of art he resembled.

"Were you born the way you are?"

His lips curved, the light spreading shadows across the planes of his face. "I don't usually answer questions like that, but seeing as your ignorance is a threat to your continued survival, I'll make an exception."

"Gee, thanks." I felt Henry's attention shift to me and Paulino, but he still made no move to join the conversation, leaving the information gathering and decision making up to me for now. I appreciated his vote of confidence.

Paulino ignored my attitude as he navigated the dark empty snowed streets. "I'm a hybrid. My mother is a Brazilian vampire who should have known better than to get involved with a high-ranking American demon. But she did, and I was the result. He acknowledged me and gave me his last name before his family pressured him to walk the dotted line and the rest is history. My mother raised me and did a good job of it. The vampire community is full of people who don't stick their noses in other people's business."

"Sounds awful. I'm sorry." Vampires sounded okay, but Paulino's opinion seemed to be a bit biased by his deadbeat demon dad. Maybe demons had all the same types of issues as humans.

"Don't be. It was long ago. I didn't tell you all this for my benefit. I told you for yours. You're a demon and the Demon Council doesn't know about you, or they'd be hunting you, judging by the power I can sense radiating off you. Whoever sired you was really high up in their aristocracy. You're going to be a bleeding fish in a shark tank if and when they find you. It's a feudal society and the aristocrats run the show. Psychics like you are rare and owe service at the Defense Council unless one of the aristocrats grants you reprieve. If living like that is not what you want for yourself, stay under the radar. You can work for me. You can build a life."

I warmed at his repeated offer to work for him and build a life in this place. I had no desire to owe service to a Council I never even heard of until today. I imagined what it would be like to get an apartment here, go to work each day, feed on the patrons of the bar each night without ever harming anyone. I imagined what it would be like to have a friend in Paulino and my heart filled with hope. "I like it here, but I'm not sure how I feel about vampires. A few invaded the place where we were staying a few days ago. There was a shoot-out."

Paulino didn't immediately deny my claim. He remained quiet, humming softly in thought. "Did you see the vampires or did someone tell you there were vampires?"

Henry spoke behind me. "Someone told us."

"Vampires are loners. We don't do missions or group things. It's possible there is a mercenary group, but if they operated locally I would have heard about it. I think someone's been lying to you."

Henry gave me an I-told-you-so look, which I did my best to ignore. Paulino didn't say anything for a while after that and neither did I. I hadn't planned on running to Gabriel, but now I had even more reasons not to. I had escaped a life where all my choices had been stolen. Even after Gabriel's betrayal, my skin itched, my psyche wanted to call to him. The farther from Jerry's drugs I got, the more suffocating the need, but I liked making choices even when I was scared of making the wrong ones.

"What time do you want us here tomorrow?"

"Ten o'clock will work. I'll come get you."

"Thank you." And with that, I sealed our fates and pinned my hopes on this little town and a vampire-owned bar.

The car turned off the expressway. I walked this way just a day and a lifetime ago on the way to the shelter. Even though we were still a couple of blocks away, I could feel the pull of humanity, although a little darker than I remembered from last night. I could almost separate the feeling of Brenda from the others, a bundle of nerves and need and guilt, which concerned me. Taking deep breaths, I made an effort to pull back my power, imagining a block of ice surrounding me. It helped a bit, but I'd have to work on the imagery to keep my power under control. I'd worry about it later. I didn't want to deal with it yet. I wanted the peace I'd found in Paulino Reilly's bar and car to last a little longer. "Can you drop us off here?" I pointed to the big red 24-hour pharmacy sign just off the expressway.

Paulino turned into the parking lot and shut off the car. "I'll wait." His tone brooked no argument, and I didn't mind an extra person watching our backs. I still got a little nervous when I was alone with Henry, like maybe Alonzo was just around the corner waiting to kidnap me. I shook off that train of thought. I needed to learn to live my life, choose to live it in spite of what I feared.

Henry followed me into the pharmacy. I walked through gleaming aisles filled with all kinds of knick-knacks and vitamins and glittering beauty supplies. I turned into the oral health aisle and stared at the wide assortment of personal hygiene products. I picked out a delicate pink toothbrush with a blond princess carved into the handle. I had never owned anything so beautiful. The Blackwells had always chosen utilitarian things with no decoration. Jerry had picked fancy things to fit *his* taste. I put the pink princess toothbrush back and eyed a Hello Kitty one instead.

It seemed so over the top to spend five dollars on a toothbrush instead of ninety-nine cents for the utilitarian kind, but I could live a lifetime without seeing one of those again. Plain things reminded me of Jessica Blackwell and her insistence that I live an austere life free of temptation. Pretty things, comfortable things, warm things were all temptations, at least where I had been concerned.

The money Paulino gave me begged to be used. I picked Hello Kitty and dropped it into the basket I carried.

Henry stared wide-eyed beside me with a little smile on his lips that warmed my heart more than my threadbare jacket could. He picked up a Hulk toothbrush. "You know, that's the first thing I think I've ever chosen for myself."

I squeezed his hand. "Me too." We looked at each other, the bond between us vibrating with thankfulness and hope, and in this little thing, my psychic energy made it so that I could almost taste his love for me, and I was grateful. Not all things demon were bad, after all.

I dropped his hand and proceeded to the lotion aisle. I spent eight dollars on scented lotion and another fifteen on underwear and plain clean white T-shirts for both of us. Henry insisted on paying for the lotion and I took care of the toothbrushes and the clothes.

We walked out of that store with more than pieces of plastic, cloth, and scented lotion. We walked out having reclaimed another small part of ourselves.

* * *

The TV in the shelter's community room hurt my ears all the way from across the room, but I didn't mind because it was the only discomfort I suffered. After my first day of work at Paulino's, I sat on a warm cozy couch with money in my pocket, far away from Alonzo, my belly, and my psyche full. With my psy hunger satisfied, I could almost pull my power snug around me like a blanket, ignoring most of the emotions in the room. Most of the people closest to me were having a good night, and the satisfaction in their auras infected me and added to my own. The pressure of their minds seemed a lot easier to manage after feeding on the energy and food at the bar. In fact, the entire shelter had dined on Paulino's leftovers, and they had been delicious.

I rubbed my full stomach in remembrance. Henry and I huddled on a couch in a corner by the library Wanda had set up, the only two people not interested in watching the season finale of a reality TV show to find out who would be the next whatever star. I was a heck of a lot more interested in finding out how to stay here working at Paulino's and maybe getting a studio for us. I studied the forms Wanda had given me the night before. I could get government help to get us on our feet if I had a social security number. Problem was, neither Henry nor I had any record of our existence except for our bodies walking around, of course.

This place with its walls filled with bulletins, bland oatmeal breakfasts, and rows of beds was quite possibly one of the best places I'd ever lived. I was certain of it, even after Brenda started heading straight in our direction with guilt and anger choking her aura. Maybe in time, she and I could build that friendship we started yesterday. Given the emotions storming through her, it seemed unlikely we would make up today.

Brenda stepped right up to me so that the hole on her left shoe lined up with the papers I held in my hand. I put the papers down, but didn't say a word, and neither did she. I just waited, suddenly having the patience of Mother Theresa. Maybe I should have taken Paulino up on his offer. If I had, I wouldn't have to worry about Brenda or about psychic meltdowns. On the other hand, I was kind of tired of depending on the kindness of men. So far, it never ended well.

I figured Brenda wasn't going to go away until we rehashed the morning's occurrences and I'd better get it over with. I stood up intending to face her down like she was the enemy, but she bit her nails and shuffled her feet. For some reason, I still wanted her to like me, I still wanted to be friends, wanted to at least not be hated, so I smiled as best I could under the circumstances and ignored the streams of guilt oozing from Brenda's every pore and every movement. I wanted to get this over with and stop with the standing around so I said, "Hello."

Brenda narrowed her eyes and then exhaled a great big weight. "Look, I was freaked out this morning. That stuff about Dominic was a shitty thing to be reminded of. I didn't handle it well, and well, I did something I'm not proud of."

I really didn't want to know, but I went ahead and asked anyway. "What did you do?"

"Well, there was this alert on television I saw at work. I thought you were in trouble." Dread grew in my chest, so heavy it kept me frozen in position so I couldn't have throttled Brenda even if I wanted to. I wasn't even sure if I wanted to kill the girl or cry.

Brenda continued, oblivious to the war going on in my head. "They had pictures of you, and they said that you were a runaway and that your guardian was looking for you, and I know I shouldn't have believed them, but I...I wanted to. I wanted an excuse to get rid of you and I'm so sorry, but I think I fucked up."

I didn't have the energy to make Brenda feel better. I kept my voice steady, even, like the voice of the computer on the GPS module Jerry used to get around. "What did you do?"

"I...I called the number and I told them I met you and I knew where you were. Then, this man got on the phone and I knew I fucked up because he sounded so charming, but I got this dirty feeling just from sitting there listening to his voice, and I didn't tell him where I met you, but the phone booth was only a couple of blocks from the shelter, and if he's as bad as Dominic he'll figure it out, and I'm so sorry, but I think you should go."

The dread in my gut turned to something else, gasoline lighting a fire under me to get the heck out. I sprang for my cot and picked up my bag, pulling Henry behind me. I hadn't stayed here long enough to know anyone, but apparently some people had been paying attention. Two girls split themselves from the television and approached. One was a pink-haired girl that kept mostly to herself. The other—a young girl with black braided hair, olive skin and a little-girl voice—asked, "What's going on? Do you need help?"

I swallowed the lump forming in my throat. "I'm fine, really."

The olive-skinned girl folded her arms and pursed her lips, showing disbelief. "Girl, don't you know fine is what we say when things are really fucked up. Let us help you."

I shook my head in denial. The girl was just trying to be nice, but my legs itched to run out of here and away from danger. Maybe I could go to Paulino's for now, just until we figured out what to do next. I still had his number in my jeans, and in any case, we could walk up the side of the mountain like we did this morning. I refrained from using my power on the girls to get them to leave us alone. If I hurt one of them, I'd never forgive myself.

Brenda stepped in. "She's feeling a little sick. We're going to go to the hospital and see what's up."

The lie did the trick. The girl who'd spoken stepped back a little bit and said, "It's not contagious, is it? Let's get you out of here. Do you need us to call an ambulance? They take forever to come this way, especially with the snow. If you want to walk, we can go with you."

Brenda stepped in again. "It's okay. Her brother and I can

handle it." The girls didn't ask any more questions, happy to let someone else handle it.

We headed out the door. The wind howled and even more snow fell all around us, muffling sounds and lending the almost empty streets an eerie feel, like the whole place howled in warning. Two SUVs idled at the curb, releasing fumes and leaving a thin stack of smoke lifting from their mufflers. No sound besides the wind and the rumbling engines disturbed the night.

I pulled my thin jacket tighter around me, wrapping the sleeves over my bare hands. I could see the hills that would eventually lead to Paulino's Bar & Grill off to our right, a few hours walk in this weather. Henry jogged in place ahead of me, trying to keep warm. I turned to thank Brenda for warning me at least, even though she'd been the one to call Alonzo in the first place. I barely opened my mouth when five bulky men stepped out of the SUVs and I recognized them as Alonzo's guards.

Brenda couldn't look me in the eye, and I knew why guilt had been oozing from her. Brenda had betrayed us. I don't know why I cared but I asked her, "Why?"

For whatever reason, Brenda answered, and my pathetic heart was grateful for so little. "After I hung up on him, he showed up at the shelter, and he knew all about everyone logged for the night. He figured out who I was. He said he'd call Dominic if I didn't help and you were right there with me this morning, I never want to go back there again. I'm sorry, but I can't."

I believed her. It didn't change what Brenda had done, but a small part of me sympathized, until I saw one of the guards lay a cloth over Henry's mouth. The wind carried with it the scent of chloroform. I ripped away from Brenda's mumbling apologies and ran toward my brother—too slow. Two bulky guards stopped my forward trajectory. Henry kicked and struggled while the two men holding him dragged him to the SUV. He tried to reach toward their faces, the only piece of exposed flesh, but he didn't get that far before his struggles slowed, the chloroform doing its work to incapacitate him. They had him for now.

I pulled, trying to reach Henry, but two guys held my arms, while another injected me with a cold liquid, probably the same one Alonzo used to incapacitate me the last time he'd kidnapped me. Even though the men holding me each weighed twice what I did, I budged them a few inches. Adrenaline countered the effects of the liquid injection, leaving me feeling tired but awake and mad as hell. Still, I couldn't move fast enough before the SUV sped away from the curb leaving me bound and facing a smirking Alonzo. He had me and he knew it.

SEVENTEEN

S hackles and darkness pressed upon my sanity. No matter how many times I blinked, how much I told myself it was all a horrible nightmare and I needed to wake up, it didn't change. With every moment that passed, my panic grew as did my hunger, my thirst, and my dread.

I couldn't move my head even an inch. I was freaking naked, but didn't feel any soreness between my legs. I'd been spared that, at least, so far. I tried to take deep breaths, keep calm, figure out where I was and what Alonzo wanted from me. My arms and legs were secured with coarse rope, probably. I could hear flames crackling nearby, but couldn't see their shadow. There must be a fire or something, keeping the air reasonably warm. At least I wouldn't freeze to death, but why couldn't I see? Why couldn't I sense anything psychic?

Alonzo must have done something to me so I couldn't see, but it wouldn't do him any good. I'd get through this. I'd gotten through endless painful drug trials. I was a pro at this.

Alonzo's voice echoed around me, kicking my heart rate up a few notches. "Good, you're awake. We can begin."

I pulled harder, trying my damnedest to bend my elbows and knees, testing my bindings.

He waited. His steady breaths marked time as I struggled; only succeeding in cutting my wrists and ankles against the rope. Wetness trickled around my wrist, blood. The metallic smell mixed with ammonia. I wanted to throw up, but ended up swallowing my own bile. I couldn't scream, since all it would accomplish is to give Alonzo extra pleasure.

Fabric slid against fabric. A shoe thumped against a cement floor. Alonzo recited the lord's prayer before saying, "Before we begin, confess your sins."

I stammered. "I don't know what you're talking about. Where's Henry? What's going on?"

The air around my leg warmed up a bit. "Your brother was sent to Jerry. He hasn't displayed many demon qualities so far. He's a little faster and a little stronger, enough to be of use to my organization, but not enough to be a threat. Despite what you might think of me, I don't torture innocents out of spite."

I didn't antagonize him, not now. Instead, I silently thanked God for my brother's safety, glad Alonzo had not learned the extent of Henry's power.

"Last chance before I begin. I spared your life long ago, and now I know that it was a mistake I have no choice but to rectify. Jerry cares about you and I owe him the chance to cleanse your soul before you die. He's right, that I have a duty for having created you, and I will not shirk it."

"Why kill me? I've done nothing."

He exhaled. "I suppose you deserve to know why you must die. You see, it's not about what you've done, although I know you for a murderer. Even without that, I'd still have to kill you because it's really about what you are. When we made you, we mixed different species of demons. We used genetic techniques and gene splicing, and we broke checks and balances built into the DNA of other demons. To them, you will be a prize to breed for them to use in ways I can't understand. I'm told every demon in the world will want to bond with you, use your power for his to destroy humanity, and I can't let them have you."

For a moment, I remembered Gabriel standing over me as I burned from the inside out. For just a moment, I doubted everything he'd ever told me, but then I remembered the hate in Alonzo's aura when he said similar things at Jerry's estate, smelled the stink of his excitement even now as I heard his movements about my prison. Perhaps what he claimed was true, but it wasn't why he prepared to hurt me. Alonzo used logic to justify what he wanted to do, and nothing I said would dissuade him, so I shut my mouth and waited while my pulse drummed ever louder.

Searing pain speared through my thigh. The pain was so sharp I couldn't catch my breath enough to scream. I couldn't process, couldn't understand. When I would have screamed, I bit my lip, tasted my own blood, but did not cry out.

"Demon blood is strong in you. No human could withstand that." He rubbed his hand along my arm in a mockery of comfort that sent shivers of revulsion through me. "Don't worry, my child. You will be whole, cleansed from the demon within, in the Kingdom of Heaven."

Alonzo removed the object that burnt me. I tried to control my breath, but it came out as panting. I couldn't see, I couldn't move, I had no control here. In the past, I hated being a demon, but right now, I'd give just about anything to be able to shove whatever he put into my leg up his anus. I should have shot him when I had the chance and screw the guilt afterward.

"Repent," he demanded.

I bit my lip and braced for the pain. He struck again and again. It was more than I imagined was possible. Bile rose in my throat, and I threw up all over myself, choking in the process. I couldn't breathe with the disgusting liquid swimming around my face, clogging up my nose and my mouth. I inhaled the stuff into my lungs. With each breath, I drowned in my own vomit, and I couldn't even move my head to help myself.

A wet rag rubbed away the worst of it. I inhaled and despite the stink, despite the pain, it was the sweetest breath. The bindings around my head slackened and all of a sudden, I could move it. My upper body jerked as I tried to cough the inhaled vomit from my lungs. The rope still pulled at my wrists. Alonzo continued to wipe at my face, his movements almost gentle.

He smoothed back my hair. "You are beautiful. I can see why he's so taken with you. You seem so innocent; Rick and Jessica kept you pure as long as they could, and you repaid them with murder. I don't know how you did it without touching them. I wanted to split you open and find out how you worked, but Jerry wouldn't let me. He thought it would be cruel. Cruel, I think, would be to let you live, to let the stain of what you are seep through to your soul, eroding all the good Rick and Jessica did."

He believed it. That was the worst part of it all. He was torturing me, so excited I wouldn't be surprised if he took a break to relieve himself of the tension soon, as Rick often did. Yet, I was the evil one, the one stuck with a murdering demon inside her. "Fuck your sanctimonious ass."

"Such language from such a pretty mouth," Alonzo said. Cold metal pushed between my legs, growing and pushing at my inner walls and blowing me apart. I smelled copper and salt, my own blood wetting my thighs, spreading warm and sticky under me. When he removed it, releasing the pressure, I could feel the pain of the tears inside me even more. My insides bled more and I cried out, no longer sure I could survive this torture.

"You can stop this any time. I'll give you last rites and you can be at peace."

I should repent my sins and die. The trouble was that when faced with the prospect, I didn't want to die. I wanted to live, hug

Henry a zillion more times, kiss Gabriel. I wanted to live long enough to make Alonzo pay for what he'd done, and to make sure no one hurt my brother the way Alonzo hurt me right now. I wanted to introduce the sanctimonious ass to the heaven he seemed to aspire to so badly.

"My soul is about as clean as yours, asshole." A heavy blow landed on my stomach like a rock, combining all the pains inside me and around me into one big mass. I would have doubled over if I could have. Instead, I spewed more vomit over myself as the blows kept coming until everything hurt and then nothing hurt anymore.

* * *

Time is a contrary bitch that moves quickly when you want a moment to last and slowly when you want it gone. Like when you're being tortured within an inch of your everlasting life. In the dark, I measured the passage of time depending on the form of my torture. One moment, it was the number of breath-sucking blows that landed in my gut. Just as my mind learned to anticipate the rhythm of the blows, Alonzo's mood shifted. Then, I had to measure time by the burns on my skin, by the strain on my limbs as my body was pulled apart, by the gulps of air between strangling.

I fought to stay awake, afraid if I let myself go I might never come back, afraid of what would happen while I was unaware of what was going on with my body. Somehow, the unknown seemed worse than the Hell I found myself in.

At some point during one of the strangulations, I lost hold on consciousness and traveled through my dreams to the secret garden. Gabriel stood under the tree, watching me, waiting. The whole place seemed duller, as though I were a ghost in my own dream. Yet, I wanted to stay here and never let go. Going through

Hell put a girl's principles in perspective. Gabriel's advice didn't seem so bad now. I should have listened when he told me to kill Alonzo, done all demons a favor. If I ever got out of here, I would listen to a point. I would take care of Henry, whom I loved, then myself. I'd do whatever it took to get the things I needed out of life. Basic things like food, shelter and freedom. Then, after all that, I'd worry about whether I was a monster who could harm others and deal with any guilt I might incur in the search for the basics. Right about now, I wished for that strength and blood lust I'd regretted once before. If I had been a monster from the beginning, I could have hurt Alonzo and prevented all I'd suffered.

Gabriel watched me and I watched him, each of us drawn to the other, but unwilling to move. I searched for the anger I harbored the last time we met. "I was so angry that you hurt me. I thought you'd betrayed me and now...now I have a whole new definition for pain, and I wish you'd pushed harder." My voice cracked, betraying the molten river of emotions seeking to break through my barely composed surface.

Gabriel advanced, enfolding me in his warmth with his arms and his wings, so strong, so constant. I wanted to trust in him absolutely and yet, I couldn't because no one had ever lived up to my expectations. Still, in his arms, in this place, I allowed myself to break apart. Sobs escaped my lips and I let him comfort me as no one had done for the entirety of my life. When I'd exhausted what little reserves I had, little hiccups escaped.

He skimmed a hand down an inch above the small of my back, making an obvious effort to avoid my bruises. He grabbed my waist and moved me so that I sat on his lap, and I bit down on the instinctive wince as my body shifted. I grit my teeth, and he let me go as though I'd burned him with my black and blues. He couldn't figure out where to put his hands. My body was one big bruise. Instead, he carefully sat me on the stone bench and leaned over me, braced his arms on the tree suddenly behind me.

I looked up at him straight in the eye. Something within me shifted as I stared into those glaciers. I wanted him. I wanted his protection, his strength, his brutality. I wasn't about to turn him down. I stood, pushing him back and closing the distance between us.

My hands entwined in his and pulled him against me. He relented, still careful not to press too hard, careful, reverent, and it broke my heart that he tamed himself for me. I kept kissing him and with each kiss, my aches got a little lighter, my bruises a little less prevalent until his arms circled me without pain, and he pulled me against him and possessed my mouth. He poured his soul into me and it healed my wounds as well as the hidden spaces within where I never wanted to look. I gave myself over to him, to his strength, to his help but not his will. I would never yield to another's will again for as long as I lived, and I prayed with all my being that I could keep that promise.

Gabriel pulled away from me. Between more kisses, he said, "We have to get you away from Alonzo."

"How did you know it was Alonzo?"

Gabriel spoke through grit teeth. "I've seen his work before."

I wished I had listened to him before, but it was too late now. "What can I do?"

"Kill him."

I took a deep breath, amazed at how good it felt to just breathe. "Even if I was willing to go there, even if I was able to let go and murder again, I don't have my powers."

His eyes shone with determination. "In a few more minutes, I will finish burning all the drugs from your system. You'll be able to do anything you want."

I closed my eyes. My body was healed, but I could still remember every bruise, every tear, every drop of blood I'd shed at Alonzo's hand. Wasn't I moaning about him being alive? *Would it be so bad to kill him, to rid the world of his evil? Would it be worth the guilt, the stain on my own soul? Maybe.* Yet the wave of anticipation that rose at the thought scared the crap out of me.

Taking a deep breath, my body still adjusting to the fact nothing hurt anymore, I asked, "What other options do I have?"

Gabriel put me down and began to pace around the garden, his wings trailing and moving in obvious agitation. "What the fuck do you think you're going to do? You think you can hurt him and he'll just walk away?" Gabriel advanced on me, his index finger aimed at my chest. "He will never let you go. You are his prey, and he will chase you down until he destroys you or you him."

I swallowed. "There has to be another way."

His gaze as implacable as his words, he said, "There is only one way. Use your power, kill him any way you can."

Maybe I fought him because I wanted to believe there was another way. I didn't want to give in to the part of me that antici-pated killing Alonzo, the part of me that wished I could make him suffer for a good long time before that happened. It wasn't Alonzo I wanted to protect any longer, it was me.

I got ready to tell Gabriel, to argue, but couldn't because something wrenched me from him as he screamed my name. I still called to him and struggled to go back to him through iron restraints when Alonzo's cologne invaded my nostrils, chok-ing me.

A sharp implement ran down my naked torso, no doubt leaving a trail of blood behind. "Who is Gabriel?"

I tried to shake my head in denial, to keep Alonzo from taking this thing that had somehow become sacred to me, my escape from a reality I couldn't face. "He's no one."

The implement parted my flesh, carving an L from the crevice between my breasts to my left hip, no doubt Alonzo's version of body art, violating me in so many levels. My scream echoed around the barren walls of my prison. When my sight returned, I saw glee in his eyes and a shadow of his aura. Just as Gabriel had promised, my sight and my power returned with each passing minute.

"I don't appreciate liars. Try again." I could hear the smile in Alonzo's voice.

I hated him, maybe enough to hurt him the way I hurt Rick and Jessica. Maybe the guilt of sin was better than this. Maybe I should trust Gabriel's judgment. He'd been right so many times and I had been so wrong. I tried to concentrate, to see with my demon vision, but nothing came forth. I was too exhausted, too hurt, or just not the kind of person who could will such a thing to happen. I would have to wait until I had no choice and by the looks of things, it would be soon.

The clang of metal on metal brought relief to me. Whatever knife he'd been holding had been put down. My vision was limited to a narrow sliver of space before me. I couldn't move my head to look beyond the fire and the cement walls of my prison. Alonzo slipped in and out of my field of vision as he moved around, his blond hair plastered to his face, his eyes gleaming, a sick smile on his face. He carried a small container. Then, I heard the sound of sifting rocks and felt burning in my wound as Alonzo rubbed rough pebbles of salt into my wounds.

I screamed one more time, wishing for Gabriel, wishing for my power, wishing for the strength to stop anyone from hurting me ever again. Every piece of guilt, every restraint, everything that ever held me back broke, and my power roared to life. I could see Alonzo through his touch, not just his body, not just what he saw, but everything that he was. I rifled through his memories. I didn't want to see him at church, or with his friends. I did not want to feel sorry when I saw the torture he had long ago endured at the hands of another demon. I didn't want to see him hurting countless others like me, honing the craft of torture, but I did, and each vision fed my rising anger and determination.

The monster inside me fed on all the screams, on the pain, on the tears, and even on his obvious enjoyment of other people's pain. It became a tangible cloud that grew and surrounded him. He tensed as he sensed something was coming for him. That something solidified and it surrounded him. I pulled my consciousness back from his psyche as it entered his ears and his nose and his mouth. I heard him pounding on the ground as he struggled to breathe. His aura turned black with terror and I fed on it. I pulled the long-buried memories of torture he had endured, and I replayed each one for him. I added the memories of my own torture, of what it felt like to have my insides torn, my skin marked, my body pounded. My psychic energy kept him awake through each and every memory, denying him the respite of passing out.

I consumed his screams like the sweetest psychic nectar, and I fed, no longer caring about the cruelty that invaded me, the glee I experienced with every scream of horror. A part of me rejoiced in his pain as another part recoiled.

After his heart stopped, no longer able to take any more, I sagged in satisfied exhaustion. Whatever else was happening, my physical torture was over, and I couldn't be sorry for that.

EIGHTEEN

I thought my torture was over when I heard the steady beat of Alonzo's heart stop. I had killed Alonzo, and in the hours after his death, there was nothing for me to do but think about it. My conscience consumed me faster than the hunger or the thirst or the pain I'd just experienced. I didn't exactly feel bad for killing Alonzo, rather I felt nothing, and that was truly fucked up. What kind of person killed and didn't feel a damn thing about it? My mind whirled and turned, not sure of who or what I was. In those hours, I doubted myself, I doubted my sanity, and I lost touch with my hopes for the future, the things that sustained me. In those hours, I learned pain from the mind can be just as devastating as pain coming from physical wounds. Sometimes, it could be worse.

There came a point where I would have hurt myself to end the despair. I banged my head against the metal in the hopes I'd lose consciousness and maybe see Gabriel. He had a soothing effect on my conscience and my body. He gave me something to hope for, even if I couldn't quite name what that something was.

But my mind refused to cooperate. I was so miserable I couldn't fall asleep. All the banging did was give me a monster headache. The pain grew so intense, I dry heaved, my body so empty I couldn't even throw up properly. I had no idea how much time passed. There was nothing to mark the minutes, hours, or days in this forsaken place.

I learned something else. Hell isn't the pain. Hell is not knowing when the pain will end, if ever.

Eventually, exhaustion did what my will could not, and I ended up in that garden again. Gabriel didn't join me right away. This time, he almost faded in, as if the shadows coalesced to give him form. He wore a black T-shirt and sweat pants, his feet bare, his wings tucked away. His blue eyes focused on me, filled with compassion and longing, mirroring my own.

I sat on the ground, devoid of energy, even in this sanctuary. Gabriel approached me as though I were a beaten dog, making cooing sounds and calling my name. I had no idea what he was saying, but the cadence of his voice made it easier to sink into nothingness, to get away from the events of my recent past.

I settled into the soft grass and lay my head on the ground. I closed my eyes and let the breeze that suddenly sprung around me caress my body, soothe the heat of my wounds and my conscience. Gabriel touched me, pushing away all thoughts that were not about him. I snuggled into him, glad for the moment of respite. I didn't care about my body's protests, he soothed my mind and my soul, and that was more important.

I have no idea how long we stayed like that, long enough for my body to heal the worst of the physical damage, but not long enough to erase the unseen damage. Maybe a lifetime wouldn't be enough.

Gabriel ran his hands down my hair repeatedly. I took comfort in the steady stream of words that didn't make sense to me. Gradually, their meaning became clear. "I think you'll like it at my estate. No one lives within a mile, so your mind can be at peace there, with the pristine white snow and small animals for company. I'll keep you safe and you won't have to do anything...."

His description reminded me more of a soothing mental hospital than an escape. I sprang from his arms and stood on the other side of the garden looking down at his shocked expression.

"What the hell just happened?"

I took deep breaths seeing the enclosed garden and its inhabitant as less than a sanctuary for the first time.

"I don't want to go with you or anyone. Why can't you respect that?"

Gabriel looked away from me when he answered. "Because I want you in my home. I want to see you smile when you see the snow fall. I want to have lunch by the lake, dinner in front of the fireplace, and I cannot accept that you wouldn't want the same. If you experienced it, you would want it."

My wounds were too raw. "That sounds like a new type of prison with binds of spider silk—soft, transparent, but stronger than steel. I want more for myself."

Gabriel's voice remained steady, too steady. Tension defined every contour of his body, his face, kept his hands fisted at his side, his smile frozen in place. "You misunderstand. I am the prisoner here, not you. I am the one who runs from my life, my responsibilities, every time you sleep. I am the one who has given my strength and vitality to a mere slip of a girl barely out of grade school. I am the one whose needs, life, and wants are being dictated by a child. Even now, as we argue, I have every demon at my disposal searching for you. My power, my wealth, my body, my mind is at your service, and you can't hold your tongue long enough to understand what it is I'm offering you."

I swallowed down my retort. He didn't deserve it, but damn it, I deserved a little leeway. My body still lay in a dark cell somewhere, and I couldn't stand the idea that Gabriel would limit my choices just like everyone else in my life. He represented all my hopes and I didn't want to be wrong about him. I approached him with my hands up in a placating gesture. "I'm grateful for everything you've done for me, but try to see things from my side. I'm a slave. I have been used my whole life, and the one thing I want is not something you or anyone else can give me. I want the freedom to determine what happens with my life, my mind, my body. Can you understand that?"

He seemed resigned. "I don't like it."

I smiled. "I don't like the circumstances that brought me to this, so I guess that makes us even."

Gabriel grabbed my neck and pulled me forward. A shot of electricity traveled from his hand through my body, polarizing me, making me arch into him. He pulled me to him and kissed me, a brief meeting of lips over too quickly. "I wish I could say I would give you anything you want, even this. But I'm not sure I have it in me. If I find you first, I'll do everything I can to bind you to me as you have bound me to you."

I pulled out of his embrace and he let me go. "Then I hope it's not you who finds me."

Gabriel's jaw twitched. "You're about to get your wish. Just know that I'll keep searching and when I find Jerry, if Jerry finds you first, I'll kill him for what he's allowed to happen to you."

My heart beat at a fast rhythm. "Jerry is not at fault. Alonzo is. Was."

Skepticism poured out of Gabriel. "He is not an idiot. He knew what could happen, and he allowed it because his precious alliance, his hatred of demons was more important than you. He'll die for that mistake."

I would have kept arguing, but my voice produced no sounds. My body faded from the field as I was wrenched back to reality, and Jerry's concerned face looking down at me.

NINETEEN

Comfort has a funny way of making the memory of pain seem worse than it probably was. Sitting on a big pillow-top mattress, freshly bathed, wearing clean jeans and a T-shirt, it seemed unfathomable to me I had spent three days under Alonzo's less than tender care.

Thanks to my demon abilities, my wounds had healed, leaving nothing but a few scars and a big L on my stomach, the top peeking above the V-neck of my shirt. I absently touched the top of the scar. Despite the anger and worry seething through his aura, Henry tried to make light of it. "How about we kick some GTA ass?"

I didn't even have the energy to admonish him on the language. Instead, I smiled at him, ignoring the memories that haunted me with every breath. When I heard Jerry's distinctive footsteps outside the door, I pulled the covers around me. I didn't want to show him any reminders of my ordeal. I didn't want to remember Jerry covering me up after Alonzo's dungeon or his look of disgust when he'd seen my wounds.

Anger red-rimmed Jerry's eyes and he'd aged in the past week. He moved as if the weight of the world rested on his shoulders, and as the acting head of Alonzo's organization, maybe it did. He ran his hands through his already-mussed hair and worried the button of his rumpled suit. He looked like he hadn't slept in a while.

Jerry sat beside my bed and reached for my hand. I scooted back and away from him until I was up against the back of the bed. He let his hand drop awkwardly. I waited for him to say something kind, something I hoped would help me resist the urge to run screaming out of this house and back into the world where I'd find...other people who pretended to be my friends and betrayed me at the worst possible moment.

Jerry pulled me out of my morbid thoughts when he spoke. "I'm glad you're looking much better. I was so worried about you when you disappeared, and now with Alonzo gone, there is so much to take care of. He left a big gap in our organization."

I raised an eyebrow in disbelief, pulling the covers around me tighter. "I'm sorry if I don't sympathize. After all, that's the same organization responsible for torturing me most of my life."

Henry pursed his lips and took a step toward Jerry. "I think you should leave."

Jerry didn't make a move to leave and Henry started advancing on him. I still wasn't sure of the extent of Henry's power and I had no desire to see it used on Jerry, so I spoke to my brother on Jerry's behalf. "Please stop. I need to talk to Jerry."

Henry studied me, and I feared he saw far more than what I wanted anyone to see, except maybe Gabriel. I smiled, trying to assure him with confidence. His skepticism was written all over his face, but he hugged me and told me to yell his name if I needed him. I believed him, but we both knew I wouldn't yell his name. It wasn't his place to protect me. It was mine to protect him.

Still, a few angry thumps behind the door made it known he

wasn't happy. I heard heavy footsteps double-timing it down the hall, almost like there was more than one person.

I started to get up to talk to him when Jerry put a hand on my arm and it took all my concentration to stop my instinctive cringe. Jerry pulled his hand away from me again and tapped his breast pocket.

"We are providing the best medical care for you, although you don't seem to need it. You're healing fast. Is there anything that would make you more comfortable or less wary of me?"

I wanted to get the hell out of this place, but I knew I'd have a hard time providing for my brother in my current condition, and the next time someone got freaked out by my power, they might call someone even worse than Alonzo, however difficult I found imagining that. Even though it made sense, I still didn't want to be here.

Jerry waited for my response, but I never gave it. He waved his hand in front of my face while exhaling with exaggeration. "You mustn't let your mind wander. It will take you to dark places, make you push away everything you hold dear."

"There is only one thing I hold dear, and he just walked out of this room."

Jerry grimaced. "I suppose I deserved that. I hoped that after what happened with Alonzo we could mend fences a bit. After all, you do owe me."

Fucking unbelievable. "What *exactly* do I owe you and your organization?"

"You owe us for your life. We made you. We clothed you, fed you, took care of you for twenty years. That should count for something."

"You also experimented on me, used my blood for God knows what, and tortured me within an inch of my life."

Jerry grimaced once again. "I'm sorry for that, but I have a solution." He withdrew a semi-clear packet with a syringe from an inner pocket of his jacket and set it on the table next to me, like some sort of gift.

I stared at the medical snake stamped on the envelope and recoiled. "What is that?"

"It's a way out. Something new developed in our laboratories. My gift for you."

The red ink on white paper reminded me of a snake poised for attack. "What's in it?"

"A new life."

I didn't say a word because what the fuck was I going to say? I didn't have enough information and I was really trying to work on the whole resentment toward Jerry thing. It wasn't healthy. I wasn't even sure I wanted to stay here. The world outside sucked and I was more scared than ever that I wouldn't be able to protect Henry, but this place had its own set of dangers. I couldn't trust Jerry. I couldn't trust anyone, come to think of it.

"What do you want?"

"I want what's best for you, and I'm deeply sorry for what Alonzo did to you. I've seen what it does to survivors. The wounds on your body heal fairly quickly, but the event acts like an infection on your mind. It grows and spreads with time and it will destroy you. This"—he tapped the envelope—"is the cure for that."

I stared at the envelope. Whatever lay inside the paper had a price. The problem is I also knew about the infection Jerry referenced, intimately. Memories assaulted me several times an hour, a knife sinking into my skin, a burn on my thigh, and so much more. It was all I could think about.

Jerry grabbed my hand again, attempting to reassure me and failing miserably. "I can wipe your memory of the whole ordeal. I can make sure you never think of it again."

I wanted peace, so badly, but the part of me that had brought me through the torture was stronger than my desire to forget everything. Something in me had broken in the past week, true, but beneath that I'd discovered a far stronger substance. I promised myself I would never be at anyone's mercy ever again. Jerry offered oblivion, he offered that I could go back to the girl who trusted him to take care of me, and shield me from the big bad world, the girl I'd been a few weeks ago. That girl was dead and good riddance. "Thank you, but no."

Jerry seemed stricken, as though I turned down a marriage proposal. His voice threaded with indignation. "How dare you!"

"You asked me a question. I gave you my answer. I lost a lot in the last few days, but I gained one thing I'm not willing to give up. I will never again be the ignorant innocent I was when I walked into this room for the first time."

Jerry's face contorted with disgust. "I could have done this at any moment."

"Why didn't you?"

He smiled, his eyes giving away a deep sadness. "I thought you'd choose to be with me because you liked me. I thought we could be good together, that it could be real. Then, you left." His tone hardened and he fisted his hands. "I asked you to take the drug because I thought after everything you've been through you'd make the right choice. I should have known better."

His anger kindled a reaction in me. I kicked off the covers and sprung in front of Jerry, ready for a fight. "You think you should know better than me? Well, you should have known better than to trust my safety to a fucking psychopath."

He pointed his index finger at me. "He was not a psychopath. He made a mistake in judgment but he wasn't that far off, considering what you did to him. You killed him without cause."

"Without cause? He fucking tortured me for three days."

He snorted. "Yet here you live to scream and enjoy another day of life, and laughing with your brother while he's interred in his grave forever."

I focused on Jerry's eyes, willing him to show his true nature. "If I am so bad, then why help me?"

Jerry's jaw flexe. He smoothed his jacket that already fit him to perfection. "You are important to us...to me."

So that was it. I sought to use him to put a roof over Henry's head. He used me for something unknown. Is this what I really wanted for my life? To use and be used? To be a commodity forever, making trades for that which I held dear? My mind, my sanctuary, was the only thing that hadn't been violated yet, and I couldn't stand the idea of crossing that final barrier.

My gut twisted, my skin itched. Somehow, without knowing it, I had reached a precipice. Jerry offered me something pretty, safe, and devoid of freedom. *Those who trade freedom for safety get neither and deserve neither.* I understood that quote now in the flesh. I marched toward the door and placed my hand on the handle.

Turning it was so easy I wondered why I hadn't done it before.

Jerry put his hand on my shoulder, trying to turn me, but I was stronger than him so I batted him away as one would a leach before it latched on, and kept moving.

"What are you doing?"

"I'm leaving."

"You can't leave."

I stopped and laughed with true delight. "You can't stop me. I'm stronger."

I would grab Henry and leave this place forever, taking nothing but the clothes covering us and we would find a place to live, and I would hurt anyone who came for us. I wouldn't be afraid anymore because anything was better than being a slave and a prisoner, even being a murderer.

I called Henry's name. His name echoed through the hallways of Jerry's mansion, loud enough for a demon half a mile away to hear. I waited, but didn't hear the rat-a-tat of his feet. In fact, I heard nothing. Funny how the absence of sound sent chills through my blood. I turned to Jerry. My power didn't work on him, but I didn't need it to see the guilt written all over his face.

"What have you done?"

"Gained a bargaining chip."

I crushed the doorknob I still held in my hand. It had been so easy to turn, but far more difficult to leave behind. "What happens now?"

Jerry sat on my bed, crossed his legs, master of this house and everything in it, including me. "You choose. Your freedom or your brother's."

"What will you do with him?"

"The same thing I'm about to do to you."

Henry would hate that. He was not meant to be caged, but his freedom wasn't even a choice. I knew that Jerry wouldn't send him out into the world, free to come back for me. I could only save myself, but I couldn't do it. I would rather drown with my brother than leave him behind and alone. There was no choice and Jerry knew it. I remained unmoving as he got up and advanced, as he removed the needle from the packet of plastic surrounding it.

The needle struck and my strength began to drain almost immediately.

Jerry's promise in my ear sent shivers of dread through my body. "I'm sorry for what Alonzo has done. I will make you better, the perfect female blend of demon and human. I will take care of you."

I never wanted to hear another man promise to take care of me. Next time I heard it, I was going to rip something off the man who said it, something precious.

Jerry began speaking. He told me what a good girl I was, and I wanted to believe him. The voice within me that screamed,

"Resist! Run!" got quiet, and all I wanted was to make Jerry happy.

"You are very sick, Ginny. You need to take some medication to keep you healthy. I'm your fiancé, and you love me. I take care of you and you listen to me. You will forget everyone you've met over the past month besides me, and you will forget any pain you have experienced."

Something inside me revolted. I shook my head as my mouth repeated, "I'm sick. I need medication, and I want you to take care of me."

"Forever."

Tears slipped from me as I shook my head.

"You will forget about Alonzo. I'll make sure nothing bad ever happens to you again."

I repeated. "I will forget Alonzo. Nothing bad will ever happen to me again."

That didn't feel so bad. Jerry smiled, and his smile made me feel good because I wanted to make him happy. I would marry him someday, and making him happy was important.

"Forever, Ginny."

I repeated, "Forever Ginny." He seemed exasperated. I didn't like him exasperated.

"You will sleep now and when you wake up, you won't remember this conversation or Alonzo or that you ever wanted to leave. All you'll remember is that you want to make me happy and that if you leave, bad things will happen."

I nodded as I lay in bed, and I slept.

CHAPTER

TWENTY

I looked around at a space much like The Secret Garden of my childhood dreams. I'd gone to a place like this in my mind as a child when the world became unbearable. The white and red of lilies, the sun that always shone, and the tree that always shaded the lone seat underneath it gave me peace then, and it gave me peace now, although I had no idea how I ended up here. The whole place smelled of eucalyptus and flowers, while the wind did its best to soothe my skin, like a thousand fingers caressing me at once.

I walked to that tree, took my time to feel the earth sinking under my feet, enjoying just being here, then running my hands on the stone bench, waiting for something.

That something coalesced from the shade of the tree, tightening into a male form that surrounded me and held me. I wanted more of that warmth, yet I stepped away from it. "Who are you?"

He blinked, seeming first surprised, then suspicious. Storms stirred in the ice blue depths of his eyes as he studied me. "My name is Gabriel."

His voice made me warm all over, it made my body tighten and my shoulders relax. "Do I know you?"

"You knew me once. Are you there, Ginny?"

I smiled, inexplicably content in his presence. "That's a silly question. Of course, I'm right here." He held my hand so gently despite his size and obvious strength. Colors surrounded him I couldn't interpret, but I still sensed deep inside he was sad and furious. His shoulders rippled as though something unknown hid beneath his black t-shirt. "Why are you angry?"

"Someone has stolen something from me today."

I wanted to soothe this stranger, protect him, fix the world for him. I pulled my hand back, not understanding him, not understanding why my mind was muddled and why this man holding my hand and treating me so casually didn't set off alarms in my head. "Can you get it back?"

"I don't know." His voice seemed to break, but I must have imagined that.

"Someone so big and strong has nothing to fear. You'll find a way."

He leaned toward me, stopping a few inches short of hugging me, his arms extended like a protective fence around me, his warmth teasing me. Feathers in gray tipped in purple surrounded us, wondrous and beautiful wings I wanted to touch. "Can I hug you?"

I stepped into him, giving into the temptation of his energy rubbing up against me. His arms surrounded me, his wings created a cocoon around both of us, and I cried.

"Even if I can't get back what's been stolen, I will come for you. No matter who or what I have to step on, I promise you, I will come. I need you to remember something for me."

I merely nodded against his heavy chest, the scent of gunpowder, sage, and male settling my nerves.

"When you wake, type meetmeatthesecretgarden.com into any browser, and I'll find you. By the time you can get to a computer or a terminal or a phone or a tablet or a video game console, I'll be waiting."

"Why not an e-mail address?"

"Too obvious, and you need an e-mail account. If you're running for your life or trying to hide your actions, you'll be found. Almost every device has a browser, you can input the string in seconds and be gone, leaving nothing but an error message onscreen—a search gone bad."

I nodded. I repeated the phrase in my head over and over, but just the thought of using it sent shards of pain through my mind. I closed my eyes and took deep breaths to calm myself down. Gabriel stepped back from me, leaving cold air where his warmth had been. I spread my arms and reached out for him, trying to pull him back but he wouldn't let me. He placed his hands on either side of my face and whispered, "I'm sorry."

Gabriel pushed energy out through his hands and into me. Splintered images, memories of another girl just like me poured through me. I was scared, I was tired, I was powerful and deadly. I killed Rick and Jessica. I fought off a man with a shard of glass. I killed him when he hurt me. I remembered Gabriel and his kiss. I remembered walking away from Jerry and I remembered how Jerry had violated my mind and my will.

When it was over, I sat gasping for air on the grass and Gabriel kneeled before me with sweat beading on his hairline and strain showing around his eyes. I, Ginny Blackwell, his bonded whatever looked at him in wonder. I wanted to kiss the crease between his brows, hold him and never let go. I stood up and gave him a hand to help him up. He took it, his hand warm and strong within my own. "How did you do that?"

His chest heaved as mine did after exercise or pain. I could hear his heartbeats and touched the side of his neck to feel the rapid beating. "Are you okay?"

He nodded, but he seemed pale. "I couldn't let you forget.

You've come so far and I had to do everything to stop them from having you."

"Will I remember when I leave this place?" *Please, God, don't let me forget Gabriel.*

He sighed tiredly and his breath feathered across my face and neck. "I don't know. I think you'll remember while you're with me. When you're away from me, it might take a little longer, a week, a month maybe. If you go to that web address, though, I'll come for you and you'll have all the time in the world."

Rescue sounded so good, but I didn't want to hope again after what happened with Jerry. I didn't want to depend on anyone to rescue me, not even this amazing man. I needed to be stronger and smarter this time. "I have a better idea."

Gabriel stepped away from me, crossed his arms and dug his feet into the ground. "I just gave you every ounce of energy and power I possess to rescue you from your own pigheadedness. If you had called me the moment you escaped, I could have come for you. I would have rescued you, destroyed Jerry and Alonzo. No one would have laid a finger on you."

I placed my fisted hands on my hips. "No one except you. Don't you get it? I don't want to be yours or theirs. I don't want to belong to anyone but myself." I stopped and took a breath when hurt flashed across his features. I didn't want to hurt him.

"So nothing's changed?"

I shook my head. "Everything has changed. I am going to go to that website, but I don't want to sit and wait to be rescued. I don't want to go from Jerry's home to yours."

Gabriel narrowed his eyes at me. "What do you want?"

You're the first person to ask me that. "I don't want to fight you anymore and I'm smart enough to realize I need your help. I am trusting that you will respect that I don't want your world to swallow me. I don't want you to think of me as an extension of you. I want you to respect my decisions even when you don't like them."

Gabriel nodded, a smile lighting up his face, putting a glint in his eyes. "I can respect that." Then he closed those marvelous lips of his and said nothing else.

I shifted from foot to foot. "Now what?"

Gabriel lifted one shoulder in a move that accentuated the lines of his chest and neck. There was a spot where his shoulder met his neck that I wanted to kiss almost as badly as his lips. *Oh, God, his lips.* His gaze and aura heated up to a bright white, a color I had not seen before but that I tasted as pure desire and something else. "What are you thinking?"

He raised an eyebrow and kept looking at me with that sexy smile. "You are mistress of your destiny. That means you have to decide what you want."

I could tell in my soul that he meant every word, as if his soul spoke to mine. "You're really taking this seriously?" He nodded and my breath hitched. I was choosing to bond myself to him this time in friendship, in trust, in partnership and in time maybe more. "Okay, then, I want to destroy the organization that created me, used me and hurt me. I want you to help me spy on them and dismantle them from the inside."

Gabriel didn't laugh at me. He didn't try to dissuade me. He nodded. "If that is truly your wish, I'll help you but I'll need to meet you in person to make sure you remember in the real world and to strengthen the bond between us. You're going to need to learn how to defend yourself, how to use your power and you're going to learn about computers."

I waved my arms over myself. "I'm all yours."

Gabriel's smile had a wicked glint that made me think of us naked in a beach somewhere under the stars. *God, why couldn't I keep my thoughts clean where he was concerned?* He smiled as though he heard me. *"Did* you hear me?"

He nodded. "And may I say there is nothing wrong with your thoughts."

Holy crap. "How? Why?"

"To save your memories and your will, I had to strengthen the bond we share. Some thoughts, particularly thoughts like that, filter through."

Great. "How is it I don't get your thoughts?"

He smiled, as though he pictured undressing me right here and now. "Maybe you are and you simply won't admit it."

The heat of embarrassment crept over my face and spread everywhere else. I concentrated, trying to clear my mind. "Okay. I agree to everything you just said. As soon as I can get to a computer I'll put in the address you gave me. I'm somewhere north of New York, three hours drive Southbound from a little town with a restaurant called Paulino's Brazilian Bar & Grill. When Henry and I escaped, we ran for about an hour from Jerry's estate to get to the interstate."

Gabriel listened to everything I had to say. "I'll start searching based on everything you said. I live in New York City, not very far. When I find you, I'll establish myself in the area and I'll watch you, arrange a meeting."

Gabriel still made no move toward me. I didn't like the physical distance between us so I walked across the space between us and hugged him. I burrowed into his warmth a little deeper and took comfort and strength from him. I stayed there, surrounded by his warmth, repeating his words like a mantra until the garden faded and I resurfaced in a bedroom in Jerry's home. I remembered Gabriel and every moment with him. The two weeks before that were broken scattered memories but I knew one thing--I had to get to a computer and type in an address.

I sneaked out of bed and walked up to the door, stopping to take deep calming breaths. I placed my hand on the handle of the bedroom door, intending to leave and find my brother. The handle was mangled, broken. A memory tried to stir, sending shooting pains through my head. I wanted to leave. I had to get out of here. Jerry would understand. I started to pull, but I couldn't. My wrist ached. The metal of the handle burned my hand, my whole body collapsed in uncontrollable spasms. Nausea sprang through me, and I couldn't, wouldn't step out the door until Jerry came for me.

This wasn't natural. I clutched my throat, trying to steady my breaths, trying to get a handle on myself. I touched the edge of a puckered scar. I raised my T-shirt and followed the scar down my torso and to my stomach, horrified to find my body branded with an L. I searched my mind for any clue as to what had happened, who had done this. I could almost grasp at the edges of a memory, but it slipped from me like a forgotten nightmare. All I remembered was that Jerry had been there.

I crawled to the bed on shaking limbs and pulled myself up onto it. It smelled like eucalyptus, Henry's favorite aroma, and it helped me to calm down. I hugged the pillow and cried until Jerry came for me. He laid a hand on my shoulder and it made me feel branded, dirty, sick. The scent of whiskey and cigars and expensive cologne coming from him made me want to throw up. I scrambled forward, shaking loose his hand.

Jerry didn't ask what was wrong, he brought me tea to drink and two pills to take. I took the pills, then spit them into the tea. I kept it cradled between my hands. "Thank you."

Staring down at my tea, I pretended to sip it. I spilled some of it on the bed, under the covers so that Jerry wouldn't see. It was an instinct coming from a silent part deep inside that I couldn't understand. Still, my hands moved of their own accord to spill the tea. I didn't swallow the medicine or the tea, and my stomach turned at the idea of Jerry's touch.

I focused on the video game console in Henry's room, the one with a browser to connect gamers across the world. Henry had been so excited to show me while we huddled in his room waiting for him to heal. I tried to remember what it was from, but it slipped from me. All I remembered was the time spent in his room playing video games, a good broken memory in a sea of bad ones, something to hold onto. "Can I go to Henry's room?"

Jerry started to say no, but I put on my sweetest smile and asked, "Please. I just feel better with him." I fingered the top of the scar peeking through my top and watched his face twist in guilt.

Letting out a loud sigh, Jerry relented. "Okay. But please don't leave his room until I come for you."

The compulsion of Jerry's new command washed over me, but I didn't care. There was a browser in that room and I trusted down to my soul that Gabriel would come for me and together, we would crush Jerry's organization. That was my goal now. I had forgotten many things, but I remembered that. I also remembered that I loved Henry, that Gabriel and I were partners. I wasn't alone anymore.

CHAPTER
TWENTY-ONE

A week after I had woken up in my room with the taste of drugs in my mouth and broken memories swimming around my head, I sat in Jerry's garden. Despite my invitation, Henry remained in his room playing games. He had spent the last week staring at the screen, pushing buttons. He rarely looked up, rarely ate and almost never talked to me anymore. Jerry had hurt Henry the day he drugged me and I didn't know how to help my brother. If I could just pull my memories together, maybe I could help him.

I stomped around a bit, considered going for a run inside the boundaries of the estate to burn off some of my frustration. Ever since Jerry had drugged me, he didn't really think I would escape and he was right. The thought of running away from this place gave me a headache. If I actually tried to do it, it would get worse until I couldn't function.

Still, Jerry was a careful man. A watcher sat on a balcony on the second floor, sipping from a mug and concentrating on her tablet. A small camera whirred beside me.

The grounds were prettier and larger, the warden nicer, but this was still a prison. The only difference was that I wasn't exactly the prisoner my warden expected anymore. I was the secret agent here to expose all their secrets and shut the place down.

The temperature hovered just above freezing. The sun shone, making the white patches of unmelted snow gleam in the afternoon light. I sensed a change in the air, almost like an electric charge calling me to the line of trees. I stepped aside stomping on the camera beside me, creating a convenient blank path for me to travel through.

The watcher above me seemed preoccupied with her tablet and I took advantage of her lapse to run toward that charge as fast as my body would allow, which was pretty fast. I looked around the trees, looking for the source of that energy. The little red flags marking the perimeter of Jerry's estate were still about a hundred yards farther back so my headache was bearable. I turned left, moving farther away from the electric whirring of cameras and closer to the smell of coffee and sugar and male. Exactly the scent of Gabriel.

I reached an open space in the trees, far enough that I couldn't be seen from Jerry's garden, now maybe fifty yards from the little red flags. I sensed Gabriel on my right, behind a large pine. "They'll be looking for me."

The ground crunched as he stepped around a pile of snow. "I took care of your watcher. We have a few minutes."

I held my breath as I watched him in the flesh. He looked the same as he had in the secret garden, ice blue eyes with a wicked glint to them, a smile that made me want to spend every afternoon in his arms, an intensity that made me think he would protect me until the end of the world. I just stood there like an idiot unable to come up with a single intelligent thing to say.

He smiled as he approached me, lithe like a predatory cat, his muscles contracting in beautiful symphony. He stopped in front of me. I stared up into his eyes, close enough to see the pinpricks of black shrink.

"I want to kiss you, but I won't."

I closed my mouth, which had inadvertently popped open at the sight of him. *Pull yourself together.* I stepped up to him and kissed *him*. Electricity flowed between us, made little charges of pleasure and energy go off in my head. The world rearranged itself and I remembered all about Gabriel, how he'd taught me to fight, how he'd held me, how he'd kissed me and I wanted more of him. I wrapped my arms around his neck and pulled our bodies tighter together. I slipped my tongue through his lips to taste him. *God, he tasted better than chocolate.*

He must have heard that thought because he chuckled and pulled back a bit, kissing my lips repeatedly, then my chin and finally drawing back. He caressed my face and I turned into it. "That was... unexpectedly amazing."

I laughed, warm tingles of pleasure still making round-trips around my body. "Yes, it was." I cleared my throat, remembering Gabriel's intensity, remembering his promises to dismember Jerry. "So, are you still on board with this plan for me to you know..."

"Destroy the enemy of the demons by placing yourself in further danger even though you are young, untrained and recently tortured." His voice was dry and disapproving, but he smiled which took the sting away.

"Yeah, that's exactly right. Are you still going to respect my choice or are you going to back out, start destroying people and things?" I held my breath, waiting for his answer, hoping I had been right to trust him.

Gabriel's hand kept caressing me while he looked me in the eye. "I will honor my word to you always, even when I don't like it. You control where we go from here."

I got the feeling he was talking about more than my plans to spy on H.A.G., but now was not the time to go down that route.

"Okay, partner. One more thing. If this doesn't work out, I need you to get Henry out. I don't know what they've done to him, but he won't leave his room."

Gabriel nodded. "You have my word."

I bit my lip, reluctant to admit this next part. "I have no idea what I'm doing, but I figure the first step is to get closer to Jerry, get him to trust me and this little trip to the woods won't help in that regard. Any advice?"

Gabriel laughed. "It's been a long time since I was a spy, but all I can say is follow your instincts."

My instincts kind of sucked. Right now, they screamed at me to figure out what had happened to Henry and fix him, then repeatedly crush Jerry against the nearest wall. I guess we would figure this out as we went along. "So, when do I see you again?"

He smiled and started backing away. I listened and realized that doors were opening and closing back at the mansion. My watcher had sounded the alarm. Gabriel smiled reluctantly. "My compulsion on your watcher to focus on her tablet didn't last long enough. I have to go."

I raised my hand as if to stop him but he stepped out of my reach. "Wait, you can do that?" He nodded. "And you didn't answer my question. When will I see you again?"

"Tonight, in your dreams."

He left as quickly as he had come. I headed back toward the house toward the voice of the Watcher looking for me and Jerry, ready to wreck all kinds of havoc in his life and in H.A.G.'s existence, confident that for once I wasn't alone. Maybe, if I were very lucky, I would never have to be alone again.

Acknowledgments

A huge thank you to my readers. As an independent author, reviews are what get my book in front of readers so if you took the time to write one, thanks for sharing your experience with others. I really appreciate it.

It takes a village to raise a child or a book. I could not have written this book without the people in my life and without the professionals who worked with me, taught me and held my hand from start to finish.

My husband is first and foremost because he puts up with me, and because he always makes sure I know what love feels like and what it's like to be able to depend on another human being. I have to thank my daughters for understanding when mommy has late nights and my mother for showing up at the worst and best possible moments to give me a break. She has given my daughters and me her time and her love and I'm grateful for both.

I thank the RWA for giving me support, knowledge, insights and for giving me the opportunity to meet so many writers that selflessly help others to succeed. I want to thank Bella Andre for telling me to cancel my pitches and just publish the damned book. I want to thank Jean Brashear for telling me what's important. I want to thank Kerry Vail, my editor, for her insights and for giving me an excuse to eat cheesecake at Junior's in NYC at ten o'clock in the morning.

This novel is my first published work, but I've been writing since I was a teenager and my dad sat beside me at the kitchen table to teach me how to polish a poem he had written. I still have the finished product memorized and I never forgot the lessons from that time. In honor of my dad, Leonardo Costa, and his poem about the struggle between head and heart, I'll paste the content here (in the original Spanish):

El querer yo no quererte
A fundido mi razon
Y cabeza y corazon
Ya no van en harmonia
Y se crece mi agonia
Y se acaba mi paciencia.
Ni los brujos ni la sciencia
Han podido con mi mal
Mas que amor es un calvario,
Mas que un libro, un recertario.
Juras, misas, penitencias
Que sacudan mi consciencia,
Que clavo saca otro clavo
Y cabeza y corazon van de amo,
Yo de esclavo
Si usted sabe de amores,
Desenreda corazones,
Por su santo y devocion,
Quiero ser un hombre sano.
Presteme una oracion,
Y venga, deme una mano

By: Leonardo Costa

ALSO BY MARGARITA MATOS

Book 2 of the PsyDemons Series is coming out on October 1st 2026. Ginny has a lot more challenges ahead and she'll have to decide what she's made of. I hope to see you again in October.

* * *